THE BOOK OF
GRIMOIRES

"Lecouteux is a genius. I have been gratefully following his research—which provides information I have never found in other locations—for years. As someone who has seen no small amount of grimoires, I can attest to the practical as well as scholarly nature of this book. Whether you are hunting for healing charms or just trying to find out more about the history of grimoires, this work will not disappoint you. Lecouteux's brilliant observations are the icing on the cake for this amalgamation of various works, outlining workable incantations and valuable lost techniques. I was particularly pleased to find a list of Solomon's demons with their diseases and remedies within the pages. This book is a serious contribution to occult work and a joy to read."

MAJA D'AOUST, WHITE WITCH OF L.A., ASTROLOGER, COUNSELOR,
AND COAUTHOR OF *THE SECRETS SOURCE*

THE BOOK OF
GRIMOIRES

THE SECRET GRAMMAR
OF MAGIC

CLAUDE LECOUTEUX

TRANSLATED BY JON E. GRAHAM

Inner Traditions
Rochester, Vermont • Toronto, Canada

Inner Traditions
One Park Street
Rochester, Vermont 05767
www.InnerTraditions.com

Text stock is SFI certified

Originally published in French under the title *Le Livre des Grimoires* by Éditions
    Imago
First U.S. edition published in 2013 by Inner Traditions

Library of Congress Cataloging-in-Publication Data

Livre des grimoires. English.
  The book of grimoires : the secret grammar of magic / [collected and commented on
by] Claude Lecouteux.
    pages cm
  ISBN 978-1-62055-187-5 (pbk.) — ISBN 978-1-62055-188-2 (e-book)
 1. Magic—France—History—To 1500. 2. Occultism—France—History—To 1500.
3. Witchcraft—France—History—To 1500. 4. Amulets—France—History—To
1500. I. Lecouteux, Claude. II. Title.
  BF1582.L5813 2013
  133.4'309440902—dc23

                                                                    2013016045

Printed and bound in the United States by Lake Book Manufacturing, Inc.
The text stock is SFI certified. The Sustainable Forestry Initiative® program promotes
sustainable forest management.

10 9 8 7 6 5 4 3 2 1

Text design and layout by Brian Boynton
This book was typeset in Garamond Premier Pro with Adobe Calson and Myriad Pro
as display typefaces

Inner Traditions wishes to express its appreciation for assistance given by the
government of France through the National Book Office of the Ministère de la
Culture in the preparation of this translation.

Nous tenons à exprimer nos plus vifs remerciements au gouvernement de la France
et au Ministère de la Culture, Centre National du Livre, pour leur concours dans la
préparation de la traduction de cet ouvrage.

CONTENTS

Acknowledgments   vii

Introduction: The Six Kinds of Magic   1

Part One
ON THE MAGIC OF THE MIDDLE AGES

1	Names and Signatures	36
2	The Magical Characters of the Planets	53
3	Demons and Illnesses	57
4	Magical Healing	63
5	Remedies Taken from the Human Body	95
6	Love Magic	99
7	The Protection of Humans, Livestock, and Property	107
8	Magic Rings	127
9	Magic Operations	137
10	The Magic of Images	165
11	Orisons	177
12	Magic Alphabets	181

Part Two

FROM SCHOLARLY MAGIC TO FOLK MAGIC

13   The *Romanus-Büchlein*   191

14   The Doctor of the Poor   209

15   Extracts from Various Grimoires   217

Notes   230

Bibliography   248

Index   257

ACKNOWLEDGMENTS

This book could never have been completed without the help of my friends and colleagues, who provided many documents and assisted in determining the meaning of the texts. I would like to thank Diane Tridoux (Bibliothèque nationale de France), Ronald Grambo (Kongsvinger), Dieter Harmening (Wurzburg), Herfried Vögel (Munich), Guy Saunier (Paris-Sorbonne), Emmanuelle Karagiannis-Moser (Montpellier), and Florence Bayard (Caen). Finally, thanks to his computer skills, the help of my son Benoît pulled me out of a jam on more than one occasion!

THE SIX KINDS OF MAGIC

Magia sapientiam sonat *(Magic speaks wisdom)*

PICATRIX LATINUS

There are certain words that fire the imagination because they evoke a disturbing yet fascinating world. "Grimoire" is one such word. It quickly conjures up mental images of the sorcerers and magicians of a bygone age, of Kabbalistic symbols, and of strange midnight activities in a cemetery, at a crossroads, or in the recesses of a secret chamber. One can easily picture an individual hovering over a massive tome positioned on a lectern and filled with mysterious glyphs.

These clichéd images have been popularized through films and novels, although they probably bear little resemblance to the reality of our remote ancestors. Even comic books make use of certain aspects of traditional magic,[1] so it is worthwhile to go back to the original sources in order to discover what was really going on. This book has no other ambition than to provide examples of what the ancient grimoires looked like, which should allow everyone to form their own opinions about their contents.

Grimoires deal with magic, but this latter term has become synonymous with stage magic, and today even the most pedestrian sleight-of-hand artists call themselves "magicians." Thus, the sense of the word has become quite vague and distorted, so it will be helpful to see just what it once meant.

MAGIC

"Magic" is a word related to the Latin *magia,* which was borrowed from Greek *mageia.* The word ultimately derives from the Indo-European root *magh-,* meaning "to have power, to be able." *Magus* (plural *magi*), which originally designated the member of a priest class, then took on the meaning of dream diviner. The working of "good magic" was ascribed to a magician, that of "evil magic" to a sorcerer. In distinguishing between those who are "good" and "evil" practitioners of magic, we use "mages" for the former category, as is the case in Bible translations—the three kings that come to Bethlehem to pay homage to Christ are magi, sages, scientists. Thus, first and foremost, magic is the science of the divine powers of nature. It is thus described as the practical utilization of these powers in certain operations, such as divination, and finally it came to signify charms and deceptive illusions.

Magic has many facets. To gain a proper sense of this fact, we may take Paracelsus (1493–1541) as our guide; since defining the categories of magic was one of his chief concerns.[2] He lists six different kinds of magic in his *Philosophia sagax:*

The first kind is the interpretation of the natural signs in the sky and is called *insignis magica.* It includes the interpretation of the stars that are unnatural and herald certain events.

The second kind teaches about the shaping and transformation of bodies: this is *magia transfigurativa.* This magic permits, for example, the transmutation of one metal into another.

The third kind teaches how to form and pronounce words or letters: carved, written, or drawn signs that hold the power to do with words what the physician achieves with his remedies. This is the *magia caracterialis.*

The fourth kind teaches the carving of astral constellations on gemstones so they provide protection; these stones also make it possible to become invisible and hold many other powers. This is the magic called *gamaheos.*

The fifth kind is the art of crafting powerful images that possess the same or increased powers as simple herbal remedies. The name for this kind of magic is *altera in alteram*. It permits the sorcerer to paralyze, blind, or make individuals impotent, among other things.

The sixth kind is the art of making yourself heard and understood at great distances—for example, all the way to heaven—of traveling more quickly than naturally possible, and of achieving in the blink of an eye what normally takes days to accomplish. This is the *ars cabalistica*.

Collectively, Paracelsus adds, these various types of magic are referred to as the "arts of wisdom" (*artes sapientiae*). For him, magic is a natural thing and the object of study. Even the necromancer (*nigromanticus*) is not considered a minion of Satan, and his art is divided into five types. The first type involves the spirits of the departed and is called "knowledge of the dead." The second type forces these dead spirits to act and is known as "nocturnal torture," while the third type involves recognition of their astral birth and is called "living meteor." The fourth type, the "necromantic enclosure," permits the practitioner to physically influence the body—to remove something, or to introduce something inside it. The fifth type consists of covering a visible body with an invisible one and its name is "necromantic blinding."[3]

THE GRIMOIRES AND THEIR ANCESTORS

The word "grimoire" is a distortion of *grammaria*, "grammar." It originally designated a book written in Latin, but it quickly took on the meaning of a book of magic. It appeared as a mixture of various recipes both for healing certain ills as well as for conjuring or invoking demons, obtaining advantages, manufacturing talismans and amulets, sortilege, and so forth.

Magical treatises existed long before the appearance of the word "grimoire," which as a generic term came to designate a wide range of works that shared the common feature of being writings that had been anathematized by the Church. To get a glimpse of this, we need only consider a few medieval authors who compiled lists of these manuals between the thirteenth and sixteenth centuries. Their nomenclatures are interesting because they clearly show that the essential features of Western magic come from the Mediterranean world, which was itself subject to even more remote influences, such as those from India. Thanks to the authors cited, some of whom have been identified, we can see that a line directly connects Babylon to Greece, then the Arab world, and finally Western Europe.

The first of the magicians was Albertus Magnus (1206–1280), assuming that *The Mirror of Astronomy* was actually written by him. This treatise mentions the "abominable images of Toz Graecus, Gremath of Babylon, Belenus, and Hermes"—images of the planets that are invoked by addressing, for example, the fifty-four angels that accompany the moon in its course. He speaks of "characters," by which he means magic signs and symbols, and the "detestable names found in the books of Solomon on the four rings and on the nine-branched candelabrum" or in his *Almandal*.[4] In Albertus's opinion, Raziel's *Book of Institutions*—I should note, incidentally, that Raziel is an angel![5]—is full of necromantic figures. Toz Graecus has left a treatise on the *Four Stations of the Worship of Venus,* a *Book of the Four Mirrors* of the same planet, and another book containing images of it. In terms of quantity, Hermes has the lion's share of books attributed to him, and only Solomon offers him any serious competition for this honor.

The other books cited by Albertus include, for example, *The Book of Charms, The Book of the Moon,* and *The Book of the Images of Mercury,* "in which there are several treatises," one on letters, another on seals, and a final one on images. All of these works discuss astral magic and their contents include recipes for creating planetary, decanic, and zodiacal talismans and amulets, as well as remedies connected with the configuration of the heavens, the names of the angels and demons of the celestial bodies, and the stations of the moon, along with their secret symbols.

The philosopher Roger Bacon (1214–1294), who was famed for his *Mirror of Alchemy* and his *Letter on the Secret Workings of Art and Nature and the Vanity of Magic* (works that subsequently earned him a reputation as a magician), wrote the following in a letter to William of Paris:

Albertus Magnus was considered a magician. The Secret of Secrets *is attributed to him.*

Hermes Trismegistus, the father of magic.

Our duties should be to have a care of such Books, as are fraught with Charms, Figures, Orizons, Conjurations, Sacrifices or the like, because they are purely magical. For instance, the Book *De Officis Spirituum, liber de morte animae, liber de arte notoria* with infinite others.

We should note that the second of these books has another title, *The Treasure of Necromancy,* and that Jean-Baptiste mentioned the *Notorious Art* in 1679 as demonstrating how, by this art, the demon:

promises the acquisition of certain sciences by easy infusion, provided certain fasts are practiced, certain prayers are recited, certain figures adored & and certain ridiculous ceremonies are observed. Those who profess this art swear that Solomon is its author and that it was by this means he acquired in one night the great wisdom that made him famous around the world, & that he included its precepts and method in a small Book that they take as their guide and model.[6]

The most thorough of all the medieval authors was Johannes Trithemius (1462–1516), the famous German abbot of Sponheim, a Benedictine Abbey located between Bad Kreuznach and Mainz.[7] He provided a list of eighty-nine titles, which in his day represented a veritable library. In it we find the authors cited by Albertus Magnus and others such as Zeherit the Chaldean, Zahel, Messala, Roger Bacon (!), and Pietro d'Abano.

Trithemius gives us his assessment of these books, all of which he read. *The Book of the Four Kings* is "pestiferous" and "one dares attribute these cursed works to Saint Cyprien." Saint Cyprien's lasting fame rests upon the fact that he was a great magician before repenting. Trithemius cites *The Treasure of the Spirits,* by a certain Rupert, which is also known as the *Treatise of Necromancy* because it teaches how to compel the obedience of evil spirits. *The Lucidary of Necromancy* by Pietro d'Abano (thirteenth century) "contains nothing healthy"; *The Secret of the Philosophers* "is perfidious and stupid"; *The Bond of the Spirits* "contains numerous orisons and conjurations with which vain men and lost spirits can link themselves"; *The Book of Charms,* by a certain Thomas, "promises great wonders and tells of rings fabricated in accordance with the thirty-eight houses of the moon, their letters, and vain fumigations"; Balenitz wrote a *Book on the Inclusion of Spirits in the Rings of the Seven Planets.* We might conclude by mentioning two handsomely titled volumes, Albedach's *Book of Spells* and Algabor's *Book of Spells.*

Two works that receive a much more thorough consideration than the rest are the *Picatrix* and the *Kyranides.* "The *Picatrix,*" Trithemius says:

*Johannes Trithemius,
Abbot of Sponheim and
a great magician.*

is a very large volume consisting of four books . . . it was translated from Arabic into Latin in 1256. It contains many frivolous, superstitious, and diabolical things. . . . It provides orisons for the spirits of the planets, as well as images and rings with numerous and varied letters.

In 1456, Jean Hartleib, the personal physician of Albrecht III, Duke of Bavaria, evaluated this book as follows:

> There is yet another very remarkable book on the necromantic art that begins this way: "To the glory of God and the very glorious Virgin Mary." Its title is *Picatrix* and it is the most complete book that I have ever seen on this art. . . . It is larger than three psalters.

Rabelais also echoes the celebrity of this book when he informs us that Panurge studied in Toledo with "the reverend Father of the devil Piccatris, doctor of the diabolical faculty."

This work has survived up to the present day in the form of seventeen complete Latin manuscripts. The *Picatrix* is presented as a compilation of books on magic and astrology from India, Persia, the Middle East, and Greece (*corpus hermeticum*). Its author reveals his purpose in the first chapter of the first book:

> The secret I wish to describe in this book can only be acquired after the necessary knowledge has been obtained; whosoever wishes it must study the sciences deeply because the secret can only be entrusted to a sage who observes the order of the science.

The author remains unknown and the Arabic version of the text was attributed to the pseudo-Magriti. Trithemius noted earlier that it owed a great deal to Greek astrology. Furthermore, the compiler often cites his sources and among them we find Hermes, Aristotle, Plato, and Crito. In short, the *Picatrix latinus* is the source from which the Renaissance esotericists drew their knowledge.

The book enjoyed considerable success, as is evident from its various translations into French,* Italian, German, and Hebrew, but it should be stressed that the treatises it contained were passed down independently, in their own separate lines of transmission. The history of the Ghent manuscript offers an example of one such transmission.

During the destruction of a fireplace in an old mental asylum in Ghent, Belgium, which dated from the sixteenth century, a chest was discovered in the wall. It contained the manuscript[8] and the tools of a sorcerer-astrologer. Although badly damaged by humidity—which made the top of the folios illegible—we still have a good sense of its contents. The manuscript includes *The Treatise on Images* by Thebit ben Corat (Thabit ibn Qurra; 835–900)[9] and another on the same subject by the pseudo-Ptolemy.[10] There is also *The Book of the Seals of the Twelve Signs of the Zodiac,* mistakenly attributed to Arnaud de Villeneuve (ca. 1240–1311),[11] which specifies that the seals should be carved on metal and accompanied by magic spells and prayers. It further includes *The Book of the Seals of the Planets* by a certain Balenis, who is undoubtedly identical to Baleemius or Balaminus (= Jirgis al-'Amid, author of an identically titled work with the subtitle *The Images of the Seven Planets*),[12] as well as *The Seals of the Planets*[13] by Behencatri, who may be one and the same person as the Behencacin cited by Trithemius.[14] But this extraor-

---

*A translation of the first book and the beginning of the second book into French are preserved in three eighteenth-century manuscripts.

dinary compilation contains even more: *The Book of the Rings of the Seven Planets* by a certain Bayelis; *The Figures of the Seven Planets by the Number* by Geber of Seville (= Gabir ibn Hayyan, a twelfth-century Arab astronomer); *The Composition of Images According to the Twelve Hours of the Day and Night* by Hermes; and finally, *The Crafting of Rings According to the Houses of the Moon,* an apocryphal text whose author is not Pietro d'Abano despite what the manuscript claims.

Arnaud de Villeneuve, a famous alchemist to whom treatises on magic were attributed.

The *Book of the Kyranides* similarly falls under the category of magic and contains four books that teach how to craft remedies and talismans.[15] Its astrological orientation is less pronounced than in the *Picatrix* and its magic is alphabetical.

According to the theory of emanations, the planets disperse their influence throughout nature. By collecting together the elements that absorb the influence—in other words, by reconnecting the links of a "sympathetic chain," which include, for example, a planet, a stone, a metal, a plant, a bird, a quadruped, and a fish—an effect can be obtained that far surpasses the natural virtue of each individual element. The choice of the elements is based on the initial letter of each one. The oldest example is a Latin manuscript dating from 1272. It is a translation made in Constantinople in 1169 from a now-lost Greek original. A comparison of it with later Greek manuscripts that have come down to us reveals significant distortions of the tradition, but such is the general rule for magic texts: these are "open texts" that are in constant flux

Mederante Auxilio Redemptoris Supremi,

KIRANI KIRANIDES,

Et ad eas

RHYAKINI KORONIDES.

Qvorum ille

In Qvaternario tàm Librorum, qvàm Ele-
mentari, è totidem Lingvis,

*Primò de GEMMIS XXIV. HERBIS XXIV. AVI-
BUS XXIV. ac PISCIBUS XXIV. qvadrifariàm semper,
& ferè mixtim ad Tetrapharmacum consti-
tuendum agit ;*

*Inde Libro II: de Animalibus XL. Lib. III. de Avibus XLIV.
sigillatim; & Lib. IV. de LXXIV. Piscibus iterùm,
Eorumq, viribus medicamentosis:*

Hic verò studio pariter qvadrifido

*Mf. post semi - millenarium annorum ex immemensà
vetustissimo primùm edidit, 2. Notis interspersis subjunctisq;
illustravit, 3. Præfatione Isagogicà ornavit;
& 4. deniq, Indicibus auxit.*

The Book of the Kyranides, Frankfurt, 1638.

according to the whims of compilers, translators, and copyists. The influence of the *Kyranides* can be seen in the *Quadripartitus* of Hermes and in many lapidaries.

Similar treatises likewise gave birth to the grimoires that began to be printed in the sixteenth century and which enjoyed a remarkable vitality right from the start. The Catholic Church put these books on the Index of forbidden works, and censorship forced printers to provide fanci-

ful indications about the place and date of publication. The oldest book mentioned in this regard is the *Thesaurus necromantiae* by Honorious, from before 1376. Starting in the sixteenth century, numerous grimoires were printed, the most notable of which are the *Enchiridion Leonis papae serenissimo imperatori Carolo Magno* (Rome, 1525), which Pope Leo gave to Charlemagne; the *Grimoire of Pope Honorius* with a collection of the rarest secrets, printed in Rome in 1670; the *Grimorium verum* or *The Veritable Keys of Solomon,* allegedly published in Memphis by Alibek the Egyptian in 1517; *De magia Veterum* by Arbatel, published in Basel in 1575; and the *Clavis maioris sapientiae* by Artefius published in Paris in 1609. The titles of such works can bring to mind the horror-fantasy author H. P. Lovecraft, who is constantly reminding his readers of the *Necronomicon* by a certain "mad Arab." Lastly I should mention *The Mirror of Natural Astrology or The Pastime of Youth,*[16] which Nicolas Oudot published in Troyes in 1711.

In the category of grimoires we should also include all the collections of medical prescriptions intended for the general public: appealing to the supernatural, whether pagan or Christian, these chapbooks offer some strange recipes. I should mention here *Le Bastiment des receptes,* printed in Lyon by Jacques Bouchet in 1544, then by Jacques Lion in 1693, in Troyes in 1699, and republished continuously until 1824! There is also *The Doctor of the Poor* (which is reprinted in chapter

14 as an example of such texts) and *Natural Magic, or an Entertaining Miscellany containing Marvelous Secrets and Enjoyable Tricks* (Troyes, 1722, 1738).

Today in France, the most famous grimoires are the *Grand Albert* and the *Little Albert,* which can still be found in esoteric bookstores. The first known edition of the *Little Albert,* whose actual title is *The Secret of the Secrets of Nature,* dates from 1706; it was reprinted by Jacques-Antoine Garnier (Troyes) in 1723 and reprinted in countless popular editions.[17] Republished over long stretches of time, some grimoires have been collected into anthologies with tantalizing titles like the following:

The Veritable Red Dragon, in Which Is Examined the Art of Commanding Infernal, Aerial, and Earthly Spirits, Summoning the Dead to Appear, Reading the Stars, Uncovering Treasures, Underground Springs, etc., plus the Black Hen; expanded edition

with the *Secrets of Queen Cleopatra, Secrets for Becoming Invisible, Secrets of Artephius,* and so forth, with the mark of Astaroth on the 1522 edition.

In 1854, Victor Joly estimated the number of volumes distributed annually among the French and Belgian farming populace at four hundred thousand, and he cites a list of the following books:

The Admirable Secrets of Albertus Magnus; The Future Unveiled; The Red Dragon appended with *The Black Hen; The Elements of Chiromancy; Enchiridion Leonis papae; The Grimoire of Pope Honorius; Red Magic; The Magic Works of Henri Cornelius Agrippa* appended with *The Secret of the Queen of the Furry Flies; The Lesser Treatise on the Divinatory Wand; The Marvelous Secrets of the Little Albert; The Old Man of the Pyramid's Treasury, The True Lesser Keys of Solomon* appended with *The Great Cabala known as the Green Butterfly; True Black Magic; The Complete Manual of Demonomania; Phylacteries or Proctectives Against Diseases; Curses and Enchantments; Prescience; The Great Etteila.*

Joly notes that these books were called "the evil books" and that families often owned a "black notebook" (*neur live*), a collection of benevolent and malevolent spells and incantations.[18]

In Germany, *The Little Book of Roman* (*Romanus-Büchlein*),* the *Spiritual Shield* (*Geistliches Schild*), and the *VI and VII Books of Moses* enjoyed huge popularity with the latter continuously available for purchase.† A Freiburg publishing house released *The Egyptian Secrets* (*Egyptische Geheimnisse*), falsely attributed to Albertus Magnus, and *The Heroic Secret Treasury* (*Geheimnisvoller Heldenschatz*) by Staricius.[19] In France and Germany, *The Lesser Key of Solomon* (Latin: *Clavicula Salomonis Regis*; French: *La Clavicule de Salomon*) was always one of the primary reference works, and it is amusing to note that the majority of the profane understood "clavicule" in an anatomical sense, whereas the Latin *clavicula* refers to a "small key."

Some grimoires achieved truly legendary status, such as *The Agrippa,* which took its name from the renowned Henry Cornelius Agrippa von Nettesheim. It was claimed that this book could not be gotten rid of either by fire or water, or by selling it—in which case its owner would die in a state of damnation. The book was allegedly the size of a man and had to be chained to the main beam of the house, and it had to beaten if one wished to master it. There are other grimoires offered for sale today, but typically these just rehash material that has already been published and is often distorted. Their authors, who hide behind exotic pseudonyms, confer an air of mystery upon the texts by asserting that they were found chained up in the cellars of a monastery and had been written either in blood or phosphorous and sealed with the imprint of a human skull. Another example resembles a pocket Bible with a black cover and red pages.[20]

---

*[The title is sometimes translated as *The Little Book of the Roma,* which is likely a misnomer since the book contains spells for protection against gypsies. —*Trans.*]

†It has even been translated into French and can be found in Parisian bookstores.

The old grimoires appeared in one of two forms. The first was a small format (duodecimo) of twenty to fifty pages, a true pocket book intended for consultation when the sorcerer or magician was called by someone requesting his services. The other format was that of a large folio, a monumental book for consultation and study in the home. This latter type was never printed and is only found in manuscript form in library collections. It is much more lavish than any of the sort that can be obtained from book dealers and antiquarians.

A large number of manuscripts offer extraordinary information, but it is necessary to track them down,* as well as be able to read and transcribe them, which is no small matter considering that the texts are by nature obscure, encrypted, crammed with symbols and letters, spells, and Kabbalistic words whose meaning has yet to be deciphered. An example of one such word is ANANIZAPTA. This is the acrostic of

---

*They are hidden away in the medical and astrological holdings of libraries like the Laurentian in Florence, or the libraries of Ghent, Erfurt, Prague, and the Vatican.

the spell *Antidotum Nazareni Auferat Necem Intoxicationis Sanctificet Alimenta Poculaque Trinitas Amen*. To create the magic word, the initial letters of each word were taken from this spell, which means "Antidote of the Nazarene who delivers us from death by poison; may the Trinity bless food and drink! Amen."

The symbols that we find in grimoires include crosses, both simple and enclosed, as well as those of Saint Andrew or Lorraine; stars of David; depictions of the planets; and the signs of the zodiac. These are fairly straightforward, but since the symbols change according to the manuscripts and the copyists did not always grasp what was in front of their eyes, the variants are innumerable and often dreadfully obscure. Moreover, magicians used secret writings to retain their monopoly on this science known as the "notorious art" (*Ars notaria*), of which necromancy is but one branch. The influence of Christianity, which attempted unsuccessfully to superimpose itself over much more pagan elements, appears in the use of God and the saints. Biblical quotes are legion. The beginning of the Gospel of John has been a magical conjuration for almost two thousand years. According to the inquisitors Jacob (or James) Sprenger and Heinrich Kramer, it was worn around the neck as an amulet and used in healing practices: "Write from the Gospel of John: 'In the beginning . . .' hang it around the neck of the patient, and in this way he will await from God the grace of health"[21] Despite such Christian borrowings, the Church continued to condemn these spells, which it labeled "superstitions," at its councils and synods.

Because magic compelled the intervention of supernatural forces in the form of angels or demons, it was absolutely imperative to know their names if you wanted to order them to do something for you. It was also important to know their symbol or signature, mainly for drawing the magic circle. It so happens that a different angel and demon exist for every hour of the day and night, and they are also different for each day of the week, which gives us a total of 168 angels and 168 demons! To this must also be added the angels of the cardinal points—five to the east, six to the west, six to the north, and six to the south—and those of the seasons. All, or nearly all, of them have exotic names that hinder any easy memorization, hence the common appearance of long lists, which acted as a kind of mnemonic aid. This same is the case for God, whose true name is concealed among others, most often a total of seventy-two. Here, magicians use numbers to discover it.

Magic requires a long apprenticeship, and this is also why the iconography frequently depicts the features of the magician as those of an elderly man. Mastery of the "notorious art" came at the cost of long years of study. And even when this knowledge has been gained, it is still necessary to follow its prescriptions to the letter. These concern time and place, because the configuration of the heavenly bodies plays a primordial role; they concern the officiating individual, who should, for example, be chaste, clean, clad in certain garments, and have gone to a specific place with certain objects. Any changes whatsoever to the transmitted spell of a ritual amounts to annulling its power. It was even said that the simple fact of revealing a spell to a noninitiate would render it ineffectual. In his treatise on *Occult Philosophy* (III, 1), Henry Cornelius Agrippa writes:

> Every magic experiment abhors the public, seeks to be concealed, is strengthened by silence but destroyed by declaration, and its complete effect does not come about because all its advantages have been lost by exposing it to babblers and nonbelievers.

For a long time, the language of the grimoires was Latin—a disjointed Latin without syntax or consistent spelling, a macaronic Latin with a mixture of heavily distorted Greek and Hebrew words. It was often incomprehensible due to the simple fact that what truly mattered was obviously the melody of the incantations. This is why alliteration and assonance form the foundation for many spells like this one: "Ante † Superante † Superante te †††" The crosses that we find in the incantations and other orisons indicate the moments at which the individual performing the spell should make the sign of the cross.

MAGIC SPELLS

When looking at grimoires, talismans, or amulets, the hardest thing to grasp is their meaning, because very often their creators encrypted their text or engraving by using obscure expressions (which we cannot be certain the original creators even understood). The profane observer is thus confronted with a succession of Latin, Greek, or Hebrew letters, often mixed together, and with "barbaric" (so described in the Middle Ages) and unknown names. These signs are called *caracteres* (characters) in Latin. We then come across countless enumerations of the names of deities, angels, and demons, or descriptive terms that serve as names, interspersed with crosses or other symbols. In Christianized charms, the cross indicates that the person reciting the spell should make the sign of the cross, which was both a means of protecting himself and demonstrating his reverence toward the powers being invoked. It should never be forgotten that it is dangerous to mobilize occult forces because, if the rituals are not strictly followed, the mage runs the risk of being torn to pieces by what he summoned. Moreover, the encrypting of important elements was intended to prevent the divulgation of the secret and its use to just anyone. The knowledge was reserved for experts—whether they called themselves seers, mages, sorcerers, or even priests! Indeed, as curious as it may seem, many clerics devoted themselves to magic, especially meteorological magic, and a certain Agobard, Bishop of Lyon, fulminated against those who dared use it. There is one long-overlooked but telling clue that is instructive in this regard: the texts forbidding these practices were written in Latin and could not, therefore, have been aimed at the common people. Only those who knew how to read could use the charms and conjurations, which, in the past, considerably limited the number of individuals concerned. For further proof, one need only glance at the large collections of Christian charms collected by Adolph Franz[22] and Elmar Bartsch. These texts have nothing Christian about them, except for the words used and their denomination. They are called "benedictions" and "conjurations." Sometimes they are even actual prayers.

The majority of the magical formulas that have come down to us

The pact signed with the demon by Urbain Grandier, which was entered into evidence at his trial in Loudon in 1634. The text is written backward in Latin: a mirror must be used to read it.

consists of heavily Christianized charms—a marvelous example of the syncretism between paganism and Christianity. Men never repudiated the learning of bygone eras—quite the contrary! As it had already allegedly been proven effective, it was carefully and even piously preserved, but since two precautions are always better than one, elements of the true faith were superimposed over the ancient ones. The structure of the charms did not change; the terminology simply evolved. In this way Jesus and the saints became neighbors with the deities and demons of paganism.

What we are dealing with here is, in fact, a veritable magic of words and language. The magic atmosphere is created not only by secret words but by their rhythm as well. Alliteration, homophony, palindromes, and acronyms serve to heighten the mystery. In accordance with the tradition, it was important not to change anything lest the spell be rendered ineffective. This is what makes the reading of these grimoires so difficult: in the Middle Ages these manuscripts were written in an abbreviated and terribly flawed Latin, crammed with terms from the common vernacular that had been summarily Latinized. Thus it is hardly surprising that we find serious distortions and omissions in a single spell at the various stages of its transmission. This is of no real importance, though, since the use of the spells is based on an act of faith. I think I can also safely state that the users were unaware of these distortions, for they possessed nothing by way of comparison that would have revealed to them how this name or that sign was incorrect.

SORCERERS AND MAGICIANS

A distinction has always been made between white magic, that is to say, beneficial and permissible magic, and black magic, which was quickly equated with necromancy and sorcery. Among the ancient Romans, the Law of the Twelve Tables condemned those who engaged in evil spells. In the Middle Ages, the Christian Church continuously fulminated its anathemas against those it called "Sorcerers, Evil Wizards, Storm-raisers" and many other names, whom they regarded as heretics, idolaters, and minions of Satan. A distinction must be drawn, however, between sorcerers and magicians.

The sorcerer was primarily a healer, a lifter of ills, a secret caregiver, who was called a *remégeux** in the French countryside, whereas the magician was often a scholar who knew how to read and write, knew certain sciences, practiced divination, calculated nativities (horoscopes), interpreted dreams with the help of books, and manufactured amulets and talismans, employing those means which a benevolent nature places at our disposal. This natural magic (*magia naturalis*) was connected with physics; the name *Physica* recurs repeatedly in connection with magic books, and this tendency has survived up to the present day in rural areas where grimoires are frequently called *Phigica*. Over the course of time, this distinction between natural magic and sorcery blurred but did not vanish entirely, as the story of Doctor Faustus at the end of the sixteenth century shows.

Grimoires were generally a product of scholarly milieus. From the Middle Ages to the Renaissance, this involved an erudite tradition that perpetuated itself through the channel of medical and astronomical manuscripts, and which gradually spread to other levels, mainly through the intervention of priests (who were the real country wizards). This assertion should not come as a shock or surprise: it is based on a gigantic corpus of testimonies, one of the oldest of which is by Bishop Agobard of Lyon (779–840). The synod of Laodicea (343–381) required "the members of the high and low clergy to not be magicians, enchanters, or horoscope makers, or astrologers, and that they refrain from making what are called amulets that are shackles upon their own soul."[23] We have numerous accounts from the early Middle Ages castigating priests who practice magic. Isidore of Seville speaks of it, and Pope Gregory the Great mentions the punishment of Sicilian clerics condemned for these deeds.[24] The Archdeacon Paschalis, an opposition candidate to Pope Sergius (697–701) was suspended from his duties for using healing charms.[25] In 1387, a manuscript tells us that "monks and clerics prepare amulets and write magic words (*caracteres*) on communion wafers, apple quarters, debt certificates, and phylacteries."[26] The provincial council of Rouen, held in 1445, condemned those who summon demons and "if

---

*Today we would say *rebouteux*, "bonesetter."

they are ecclesiastics, they are removed from their positions and then placed in perpetual imprisonment."[27] So it is clear that these magic spells and charms were used by members of the religious community. In the famous grimoire *The Agrippa,* it states:

> Originally, only priests owned the *aggripas.* Each had his own copy. On the day following their ordination, they would find it on their night table when they awoke, without knowing where it came from or who had brought it. During the great revolution, many churchmen emigrated. Some of their *agrippas* fell into the hands of common clerics who, during their time in school, had learned the art of using them. They handed them down to their descendants. This explains the presence of this strange book at certain farms.[28]

To understand grimoires, we need to specifically identify the sphere in which these ill-reputed individuals worked. To do so, I have chosen the testimony of Jean Bodin, who lived during the sixteenth century and was a witch hunter.[29]

Sorcerers "pretend to be doctors," he said. "They profess to heal illnesses, dispel charms, and request first of all of the person they wish to heal that he firmly believes they will cure him." This is why "one will request the power to heal toothache; another will request the power to heal quartan fever or other illnesses; or they will slay people or cause them to die; or they will make other abominable sacrifices."[30] They "brighten the moon, darken the sun, and raise the tempest," which is one of the recurring accusations for more than a millennium. They "toil with strange means that would be incredible had they not been seen placing their images at the crossroads, at the graves of their fathers, and beneath doors." Bodin mentions the case of a witch who "made people crippled and misshapen, in a strange way, and who caused men, beasts, and fruits to die,"[31] and he adds that these women bewitch men and prevent women from conceiving. These things "are only done in the darkness and in deserted places and by quasi-incredible means," he continues. This smacks of superstition to Jean-Baptiste Thiers, and he gives us a brief overview of what he means.

There are ridiculous and extravagant remedies, Fernel says, & what I call superstitious, because the minds of men have been feeble enough to allow themselves to be long infatuated with their superstitions. These are remedies about which no one can say where the virtue with which they are attributed comes from. Here are some examples. Heal the falling sickness by saying, or carrying on your person these verses "*Gaspar fert myrrham,*" & so on. Relieve toothache by touching these teeth during Mass & by saying, "*Os non comminueris ex eo*"; heal scrofula & restore the uvula when it is dislocated by means of stones brought back by Aëce; cause vomiting to cease by observing certain ceremonies & by saying certain words, albeit in the absence of the patient, since knowledge of the latter's name alone will suffice. To stop blood flow from whatever part of the body it is spilling by merely touching that part & by saying certain words, which some assure are these: "*De latere ejus exivit sanguis & aqua . . .*"[32]

It is worthwhile to compare this overview with what Montaigne said in his *Essays* (II, 37), when indulging in a sharp criticism of doctors with extravagant remedies:

The very choice of most of their drugs is neither mysterious nor divine; the left foot of a turtle, the urine of a lizard, the dung of an elephant, the liver of a mole, blood drawn from beneath the right wing of a white pigeon; and for us colic sufferers . . . pulverized rat turds, and other such antics that look more like a magician's enchantment than solid science. I leave aside the odd number of their pills, the orientation toward certain days and festivals of the year, and the distinction of the hours for harvesting the herbs of their ingredients.[33]

In fact, "it is necessary for the faith of the patient to be filled by good hope and expectation of their effect and operation."

What did sorcerers make use of? Bodin remains discreet on this point and, on more than one occasion, expressly refuses to tell all he knows so there is no risk of it being put to evil use. He does say that these folk "read the grimoire at night between Friday and Saturday, or on Saturday morning before sunrise." Dark works must be done in darkness!

Sorcerers use "barbaric and incomprehensible words," because "these have more magical power than those that can be understood," but it is clearly the work of the demon insofar as "the devil in every language deceives men by means of Greek, Latin, barbaric, and unknown words." Moreover and just like the theologians of the Middle Ages, Bodin clearly stresses this point: "All the remedies of words, letters, bindings, and other things are the snares of Satan."[34] Sorcerers are all the more dangerous because they employ elements of Christianity. Their recipes "are full of beautiful orisons, psalms, the name of Jesus Christ all the time, as well as the Trinity, the cross at every word, holy water, the words of the canon at the mass . . . hosts."[35]

Occasionally, Bodin allows us a glimpse into their activities, for example:

> They write *Omnis spiritus laudet Dominum* on four tablets of white parchment and hang them on the four walls of the house. And for other wicked acts about which I will not write a word, they say the one hundred eighth psalm.[36]

The reader should not be surprised, then, to find all these elements—or what we might call ingredients—mentioned by this famous demonologist in the extracts from the grimoires collected in the present volume.

I should briefly describe what "virgin parchment" is. In a sixteenth-century manuscript of *The Key of Solomon,* it is said to be the skin of an animal that died before reaching the age of reproduction, or even that of a stillborn animal. As for "virgin wax," which is frequently mentioned in the prescriptions, this is wax made for the first time by bees and which has never been used. Furthermore, the parchment and wax should be enchanted.[37]

In summary, sorcerers are "conjurers, poisoners, exorcists, imposters, mathematicians, and evil wizards"—all names that can be found in Jean Bodin's writing.[38]

SIMILIA SIMILIBUS

Similia Similibus curantur ("like cures like") is the expression used by the medicine of antiquity to describe the laws of sympathy that govern the entire cosmos and which are revealed in numerous magical healing practices. If the links of a sympathetic chain are joined together, the patient's chances of healing are substantially increased. According to this way of thinking, a yellow stone heals jaundice, a red one cures bleeding, and so forth.

Since magic and sorcery share the principal goal of healing or preservation of human beings—this is what emerges from the number of charms and practices passed down by the manuscripts—I should say a word about illnesses. In the distant past, illnesses were regarded as entities, as supernatural beings that attacked human beings out of spite. The ancient Greek hermetic text the *Poimandres* (XVI, 12) basically states that demons are innumerable and are organized in accordance with the stars. They are the cause of all disorders on earth. Disease is a disorder and healing is the reestablishment of order. In order to fight the demons of disease and banish their harmful effects, it is necessary to resort to supernatural means, and this is where magic comes in. This explains why so many spells are conjurations and exorcisms, and why so many recipes are crammed with extracts from the Scriptures, the canon of the Mass, and so forth. Such Christian aspects are rarely untainted by a certain amount of paganism, however, and what we have before us is an extraordinary mixture of pagan and Christian elements. People were seeking to marshall all of the forces of good fortune on their side, and God and his saints were thereby combined with the planetary gods or demons of the zodiac. The fact that Jesus Christ and the saints turn up again and again is no accident, since illnesses were considered to be demons (or the emanations of demons) and sometimes divine punishment for a sin as well. Christ was considered to be a doctor (*iatros* in Greek), as Matthew 4:23 relates, and especially as the celestial physician (*medicus coelestis*),[39] which clearly emerges from a fourteenth-century magic spell: "The devil binds, the angel unbinds, Christ cures" († *diabolus ligat* † *angelus solvit* † *Christus sanat* †).[40] Another charm states that "Christ, who spilt his blood for us, heals." And the pseudo-Paracelsus is of the same opinion: "Nothing should be executed or hoped without the aid and succor of the very Father of medicine, Jesus Christ, the true and only doctor."[41] Similarly, we often come across the expression "May God Almighty the Father heal you!"[42]

The sympathetic chain also plays a role in what we might call situations of reference. Here the therapist takes a proven fact from the Bible that has a direct parallel with the illness he wishes to cure. When Jesus entered the river Jordan, the water ceased flowing; therefore, by remembering that incident, a hemorrhage can be arrested. To heal a burn, appeal will be made to the memory of Saint Laurent or the three children in the furnace: by the grace of God they were spared by the flames, thus the same will be the case for this or that person.[43] The names of the saints that pop up at various points in charms and orisons all have their reasons for being there: an episode from their life or their martyrdom serves as a reference for the magical healing.

NAMES, SIGNS, AND SIGNATURES

A fundamental rule of magic is that the names of numinous and supernatural beings must be at the magician's disposal so they can be summoned and compelled to appear and act. Without the names, everything will be in vain. In the case of God, the problem is how to learn his true name, which will provide a kind of hold over him. It is impossible because the Holy Scriptures assign him a huge number of titles. The exegetes, and later the magicians, stopped counting at seventy-two; they deemed that the true name, the most potent one, would be found among them. People also resorted to the entire alphabet, for it was believed to necessarily contain God's name.[44] In Islam, we might note, Allah has ninety-nine names.

When it concerns angels or demons, the task is more arduous. Indeed, each element of the cosmos possesses at least one malevolent and one benevolent aspect. It is therefore necessary to discover the names of the angels and demons of the planets, the constellations, the signs of the zodiac and their degrees, and the days and the hours. As one can readily imagine, this adds up to a substantial number. Henry Cornelius Agrippa says in this regard:

> The celestial bodies have their souls. An excellent mage can divert many approaching ills due to the arrangement of the stars by foreseeing them and carrying phylacteries against their occurrence. Spirits govern the signs, the trines, the decans, the quinaries, the degrees, and the stars. Twelve demons preside over the XII signs of the zodiac, XXXVI others over the decuria, LXXII over the quinaries of the sky, over the languages of men, IV others over the trines and over the elements, and seven governors of the world by the seven planets.

These "unknown, barbaric, strange names" always alarmed the medieval Church, which viewed them as a threat: the obscurity of the names made it difficult to know whether or not one was concluding a tacit pact with a demon by making use of them, and therefore it was better to abstain from requesting their service!

The practice of magic required a considerable amount of other knowledge as well. Each angel and each demon possessed its own signature, its own symbol, but such signatures were not necessarily unique and each angel or demon could have several. Furthermore, the number of signatures seems to have multiplied over the course of time, with distinctions being made between those to be applied to pentacles and those used for rings or their seals. The signatures are regularly called *caracteres,* about which Agrippa writes: "The characters are nothing other than certain letters and obscure writings that prevent the profane from employing and reading the sacred names of the gods and spirits."[45] The pseudo-Paracelsus says about the matter:

> They too—the signs, characters, and letters—have their strength and efficacy. If the nature and distinctive essence of metals, the influence and power of Heaven and the Planets, the meaning and arrangement of the characters, signs, and letters, harmonize and simultaneously correspond with the observation of the days, time, and hours—what then, in Heaven's name, could prevent a sign or

seal manufactured this way from possessing its force and ability to work?[46]

As a result of influence from the Mediterranean world, and more specifically the Middle East, numerology became a further important aspect of magic. Thus, there is a number that corresponds to every astral or heavenly body, and which is used in the crafting of defensive amulets and healing phylacteries. In the sixteenth century, Henry Cornelius Agrippa explained how to do this:

> The Hebrews were given ten divine principals that, through ten numerations called sephiroths, took action on all other creatures: the nine orders of angels, the choir of the blessed souls, planets, and men, and everything receives its strength and virtue from them.

He also provides the explanation for the number squares that appear again and again in grimoires:

> The Kabbalists have another kind of character. They divide the XXVII Hebrew letters into three classes, each consisting of nine letters. The first includes the marks of the simple numbers and the intellectual things in the nine orders of angels; the second, the marks of the dozens and the celestial things, in the nine orbs of the heavens; the third contains the four remaining letters, the marks of the centenaries and the lower things. They divide these three classes into nine chambers, the first of which consists of three units, that is, the intellectual, celestial, and elemental; the second is made up of the dyads; the third, the triads; and so forth. These chambers are formed by the intersection of four parallel lines that are cut at a right angle.

There are yet more difficulties that await those who wish to read these texts, for sorcerers and magicians used codes and ciphers that remain indecipherable even today. As Staricius noted in the seventeenth century, "he who wishes to know the secrets must know how to keep

Tables de Mars

en compte, **en caractères hébraïques.**

11	24	7	20	3
4	12	25	8	16
17	5	13	21	9
10	18	1	14	22
23	6	19	2	15

נ	כ	ז	כא	יא
ז	חח	כה	תד	ד
טי	כא	יה	ה	יז
כ	יד	א	חי	י
הי	ז	יט	ו	סו

Signes ou Caractères

de Mars,   **de l'Intelligence de Mars,**   **du Daimon de Mars.**

Tables du Soleil

en compte, **en caractères hébraïques.**

6	32	3	34	35	1
7	11	27	28	8	30
19	14	16	15	23	24
18	20	22	21	17	13
25	29	10	9	26	12
36	5	33	4	2	31

א	הל	לה	ג	לב	ו
ל	יא	כז	כח	ח	ו
כד	כג	יה	די	יה	יט
יח	כ	כב	כא	יז	יג
כה	כט	י	ט	כו	יב
אל	ה	לג	ד	ב	לא

Signes ou Caractères

du Soleil,   **de l'Intelligence du Soleil,**   **du Daimon du Soleil.**

 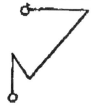 

Livre II.   20.

Henry Cornelius Agrippa, Philosophia occulta II, *22.*
Sacred tables of the planets.

them secret, so as to avoid giving bread to dogs and casting pearls before swine" (*qui vult secreta scire, secreta secrete sciat custodire, nec panem det canibus, nec margaritas projicias ante porcos*).

Henry Cornelius Agrippa

THE MAGIC OF IMAGES

Images are primarily used in the crafting of talismans and amulets, or otherwise in the case of a figurine called a *voult* (from the Latin *vultus* meaning "visage"), which is used as a support for a long-distance curse. We have learned this way that witches "placed wax figures . . . beneath the altar cloth, then hid them beneath the sill of the house so that passing through it would bewitch the one for whom the things had been placed."[47] A man whose wife was the victim of an evil curse found "a wax figure the length of a palm (hand)" beneath the threshold of his house, "whose sides were pierced through by two needles going from right to left and vice versa, right at the place his wife felt stabbing pains."[48] Magicians carved or cast images inscribed with their intended effect; this was put on the back when it was harmful, and on the stomach when it was beneficial. On the front of the image it was necessary to indicate the name of the species or individual designated by the image and place on its chest the name of the sign or decan of its ascendant and dominant houses, as well as the characters and names of the angels. These images are ineffectual, however, if they are not vivified in a way that allows a supernatural, angelic, or demonic force to enter them.

Other images that turn up very often in the ancient grimoires are entirely astrological in nature;[49] these are called "seals." Hundreds exist that relate to the planets, decans, constellations, and signs of the zodiac. They are also known as "Solomonic images," since Solomon is remembered as one of the most famous magicians because God had given him power over demons. The stories of *The Thousand and One Nights* are full of djinn escaping from jars where Solomon had imprisoned them, or cities built at the orders of this king. Images are also used in the manufacture of rings and other magical objects, and Agrippa has this to say about them:

> The means of making these rings is to take an herb that is subject to a fortunate star when this star is dominant in a good relationship with the moon, and to make the ring from an appropriate metal, and to put a small stone inside with the subject herb or root, and to not fail to make fumigations when putting inscriptions, images, and characters on it.[50]

The *Picatrix* (thirteenth century) indicates, for its part, that it is "the fumigations that give images their strength and draw spirits to them" (I, 2).

To protect or cure a person, images also serve to make seals that can be worn on the person like amulets and phylacteries, which the Church has always considered idolatrous. To the author known as the pseudo-Paracelsus, though, it is simply way to make use of means that Nature places at our disposal:

> Characters, words, and seals themselves possess a secret strength that is in no wise contrary to nature and has no link whatsoever with superstition! Furthermore, it should not appear extraordinarily impossible to you that medicine can offer relief to man not by means of absorption but by being worn around the neck in the manner and custom of a seal.[51]

THE BOOK OF GRIMOIRES

For greater clarity, I have organized the material under various headings, while essentially retaining the most representative pieces of evidence of an immense corpus. For any given example, we have, on average, fifty other attestations. I have intentionally not included texts concerning divination and astrology, as these were spread in specialized booklets that are not grimoires.

This book takes the approach of a guided tour. Since we are dealing with an extremely hermetic domain, access to which presupposes highly varied kinds of knowledge, there are commentaries (or guides) that accompany the headings when there is a risk the texts may not be understood. With respect to the magical instructions themselves, the commentary appears beforehand if it is intended to clarify the text or afterward when the spell needs to be read first. In these latter cases, the commentaries answer the questions raised by the spell.

I have translated the texts to the best of my ability,* but they are sometimes dreadfully obscure from a philological standpoint because the syntax follows no rules and both verbs and nouns are missing here or there. The Kabbalistic expressions have been left intact because, in accordance with good magic, a spell or recipe must be passed on faithfully lest it lose its efficacy!

In the second half of the book, I will provide some examples of the enduring nature of the tradition.

It will be noted in the prescriptions that N (= *nomen*) indicates where the name of the person must be inserted. We sometimes find NN (*nomen nominandum*), which means the same thing. Crosses indicate when the person casting spell must make the sign of the cross.

To avoid any misunderstanding on the part of my readers, I should further note that the purpose of this book is to provide a historical account. It is not aimed at New Age circles or some sect of practitioners. This needs to be stated when working with any more

---

*The majority of them has been translated from medieval Latin, the rest from older dialects of German, English, and Dutch.

or less esoteric material, in order to avoid situations in which the author is suddenly treated as a believer—or worse, someone seeking to create emulators. A historian who studies earlier beliefs does not identify with his subject; an essential distance from it must be maintained, otherwise there is no scientific objectivity. Thus, I hope the reader will take the ancient documents I have assembled here for what they are.

Rembrandt, The Magician, *ca. 1652.*

PART ONE

On the Magic of the Middle Ages

1

NAMES
AND SIGNATURES

A fundamental rule of magic is that it makes available the names of numinous (divine) beings and supernatural beings for the purpose of summoning them to come forth and take action. In Greece, the gods were given the title of *Polyonomos* (those "known by many names"), and in Rome, Macrobius informs us that the petition made by the believer included a formula assuring he had made good use of all the addressed deity's names.[1]

"Thou shalt not take the name of the Lord thy God in vain," the Holy Scriptures tell us,[2] and this idea crops up continuously throughout the Bible. Without the names, everything is vain. And in God's case, how is one to know his true name? It is impossible, because the Holy Scriptures assign him with many. The number was halted at seventy-two, as it was assumed that the true name—the most powerful one—would be found within that group. In Islam, Allah has ninety-nine most beautiful names (*al-asmâ' al-husna*) and Muhammad has more than two hundred.[3] A contemporary author, Amin Maalouf, based his novel *Balthasar's Odyssey* on the theme of the secret name of God, and he places the following words in the mouth of one of his characters:

Quotes from the prophet . . . confirm that there is clearly a supreme
name that need only be uttered aloud to dispel any kind of danger,
and obtain from Heaven any favor. Noah knew it, it is said, and
this is how he was able to save himself and his family from the
Flood.[4]

In the magical prescriptions, the divine names are a blend of
Greek, Hebrew, and Latin, and they gather together a large number
of adjectives attached to the names of God or of Jesus. Moreover,
the two most powerful words are *Tetragrammaton* and *AGLA.*
Tetragrammaton refers to the four Hebrew letters, YHWH, that
make up the name Yahweh. AGLA is an acrostic formed from four
Hebrew words taken from a Jewish prayer that form a phrase—*aieth
gadol leolam Adonai,* or *Atlah gabor leolam Adonay,*[5] "Thou shalt rule
forever, Lord."

The list of divine names varies from one manuscript to the next.
The lists are often found gathered together as is the case in the *Sachet
accoucheur,* a medieval talisman found in the Massif Central area of
France in the twentieth century, which is composed of images and
text for the purpose of facilitating the labor of birth. The *Sachet* contains several lists that are reproduced below—undoubtedly because our
ancestors believed that each list had its own power and by adding them
together the power of this talisman would be increased.

We should note, incidentally, that this method of operating did not
die out with the advent of the Renaissance. Pope Leo's *Enchiridion* contains several lists with the headings for the columns given as follows:

Here are the seventy-two names of Our Lord; whoever carries them
on their person shall have no fear of any ill or danger.

These are the name of the Savior Jesus Christ: whoever speaks
them once with devotion, and carries them on a voyage, whether on
land or sea, will be spared from all manner of dangers and perils,
and shall be saved.

Here are the names of the Blessed Virgin Mary.

CHRISTIAN NAMES

1 ◈ HERE ARE THE LXXII SACRED NAMES[6]

All the following names are taken from the Holy Scriptures, with some errors. Sothes is Sother, "savior" in Greek; pantogrammaton *is* Tetragrammaton, *the four letters forming the name of Yahweh;* Paroclitus *is the* Paraclete, *which literally means "the Invoked";* Principium and finis, *as well as* Alpha and Omega, *come from the Apocalypse (1:8; 1:17);* vita, via, veritas *from the Gospel of John (14: 6); and so forth.[7] The accumulation of names provides one with almost full assurance that their requests will be granted. The Bible says: "they will cast out demons in my name" (Mark 16:17), as well as "even the demons submit to us in your name" (Luke 10:17), and "faith in the name of God heals" (Acts 3:16).*

Agyos. Sothes. Mosias. Sabaoth. Emanuel. Adonay. Atanatos. theos. pantogramaton. yrus. rion. Eley. hon. ysion. salvator ["savior"]. Alpha and w. primogenitus. principium. finis. vita. via. veritas. sapientia. sirtus. Paroclitus. ego sum. qui sum. qui est mediator. angnus. ovis. vitulus. aries. leo. serpens. vermis. os. verbum. ymago. gloria. sol. luxs. splendor. panis. fons. vitis. flor. janua. lapis. petra anglis. Spiritus. pastor. sacerdos. propheta. sanctus immortalis. rex. Christus. Jhesu. pater filius. spiritus. sanctus. omnipotens. misericors. caritas. eternus. creator. redemtor. primus and Novisimus. unitas. sumum.

These are the LXXII names of Christ. He who † car † ries † them † on his † person † shall dread no charm if they are written in accordance with the good hour and the good day.

2 ◈ HERE ARE THE NOBLE NAMES OF CHRIST[8]

No one should read them without first having fasted for three days.

†.†. abla † abla † abla †. Jhesus. oc. ul. Pe. F. r. ps. Jura noves. † ontes. † agra †. avalcentom. † ovid. † eloy † niesrom †. Ylie. † alla †. A † v † paule. B. †. reaif † jova. Tetragramaton. † primus et novissimus † inicium et finis Ihesus † vita. A eo. Erueray urcaomi.

3 ◈ HERE ARE THE NAMES OF GOD IN HEBREW[9]

In this list, the Hebrew names are partially glossed. For example, codar *is translated exactly as* potens, *"powerful" (Arabic* kader*);* abba *as "father," and so forth.*

Inicium ful deus abba pater fib filius then spiritus sanctus Rubb trinitas codus unitas Theluch Ton unus Hyluch trinus verth dominus Rachim milator onelech rex onohith continues codar potens haly conscius Iyothe. Fear the Lord. Deign, by these holy names that are yours, to free me, your servant N. † of all evils, Lord, father, Jesus Christ, by these letters R. O. A. V A G X Q Grammata Thrachotin S Palleo Zobola sa Rex on thiothr. Father, son, holy ghost, help me. Amen.

4 ◈ HERE BEGIN THE NAMES OF GOD IN HEBREW, GREEK, AND LATIN[10]

On † Deus alpha et ω † benedic me domine deus meus † tetragramaton † hel † hischiros † hieritos † Jhesu fortis † heloe † thos † sabahot † celyon † sotir † binamon † nesimen † adonay † hely † hesererie † sadar † venas † anet † fenahton † sabaoth † tibi comendo spiritum meum et animam meam et corpus meum † pantur † aleth † ia † flos † herenes † alabesonem † neilloc † paco † dalaphet † aia † grat † appo † aele † region † abac † abraca † angnus † vox † vitulus † serpens † aries † leo † vermius † virtus † salus † pax † lux † lex † rex † fortitudo † manus † potential † sanctus Deus † fortis † immortalis † henrainarati † boberi † falax proanabonac † geron † tinesi † fanti † purgata † doc † aia † gle † galioth † thit † mem † batbar † acay † eluro † belbeon † adorna † Segetre † monthecor † bacor † barut † cami † cambusileto † guido † melismaron † alquadar † abra † bis † athamus † transb. † manuchata † dd † dd. † segoge † mangla laus † factor benedicisionem tuam super me famulum tuum illo largire † Domine Deus † hemanuel † spititus † hon † usion † arathon † heloy † studia † custodictis adjuva me trimus omnipotens deus libera me ab omnibus crem. Deus hemanuel tibi est nomen et omnipotens pater propreius sis mihi pecator amen.

5 ◆ HERE ARE THE NAMES OF THE XXIII PATRIARCHS[11]

They will aid in every place those who invoke them in good faith, and carry them on their person.

† yarebidera balea mariea chorel. Sereb. Hyba. Abya onthe.

Banney. Clinor. Jhesus. Seichemmy ececihiel. Samuhel.

Afesorcherin. Chobia. Theos. Benjamin anacibi. Marin sanctus Deus.

Sanctus fortis. Sanctus et immortalis.

Take pity on your servant so that I may serve you in every place, Lord my God. Amen.

The names of the Trinity according to the Sachet accoucheur.

DEMONS AND SPIRITS

The number of demons, often called "spirits" by magicians, is quite simply tremendous, and it would require a hefty tome to list them all. They are literally swarming over the earth and through the air, and they are assigned to every hour of every day and night of the week. Fortunately, their power is always limited because angels, representing the power of Good, oppose them. The battle between the principles they embody is that of order against chaos.

Here are two texts that are quite representative of earlier beliefs. Did I say earlier beliefs? Considering some of the books available for purchase at the beginning of the twenty-first century, such views may not have died out at all! The first text we shall look at falls under the heading of Solomonic divination and prophecy, and provides a list—far from exhaustive—that will give us a good idea about the number of angels and demons. Someone seeking good and fearing evil will invoke the angel of the day and the hour, conjure him by ritual methods and expressions, and implore him to neutralize the demon of that same time. A person seeking to work evil will address the corresponding demon. Solomon's *Hygromancy* is accompanied by evocatory prayers to the planetary gods, and is of particular interest because it yields the secret names that allow the divine powers to be subjugated to one's will. They are the names of each planet's angel and its demon.

Where demons are concerned, the name alone is insufficient. It is also necessary to know their signature, that is, their symbol, which in later centuries was called their "mark." It is this signature that must be inscribed within the magic circle when performing the conjuration, along with the name of the demon and other graphic designs. This is where our second text comes in, as it gives us a long list of names accompanied by each spirit's mark. This text is of a unique sort and fully deserves to be lifted out of its centuries-long obscurity. It opens with Belzebuth—to each lord, his honor!—followed by the demons of the four cardinal points (Amaymon, Paimon, Egin, and Oriens),[12] followed by better-known figures like Lucifer and Astaroth, the gods of paganism like Mahomet, Amon, Belial, and Apollin (that is, Apollo or Apollyon, the name of the Angel of the Bottomless Pit in the Apocalypse [Revelation 9:11]), and other less famous individuals.

Lastly, I will cite an extract from the *Picatrix,* the greatest magic manual of the Middle Ages, in which we find an excellent example of the power of names and signatures.

6 ◈ The *Hygromancy* of Solomon[13]

	SUNDAY			MONDAY	
Hour	Angel	Demon	Hour	Angel	Demon
1	Michael	Assmodai	1	Gabriel	Mamonas
2	Arphanaël	Ornai	2	Pharsaphaël	Skoliôn
3	Perouel	Perrad	3	Pindoël	Thetidôph
4	Iorael	Siledôn	4	Kopiël	Arban
5	Piël	Sitros	5	Kelekiël	Azan
6	Iochoth	Sephar	6	Tariël	Menachth
7	Pel	Maniër	7	Meniël	Skamidinos
8	Ioran	Ossimié	8	Ezekiël	Stirphan
9	Kataël	Pnix	9	Ioël	Giram
10	Vidouël	Gerat	10	Sinaël	Menaktinos
11	Hedinël	Nessta	11	Menaël	Makaktinos
12	Sanaël	Peliôr	12	Rochaël	Mexiphôn
13	Opsiël	Istos	13	Aresiël	Outolôch
14	Terael	Hapios	14	Trapedoël	Nuktidôn
15	Audiël	Negmos	15	Akinatiel	Ouistos
16	Nalouël	Arax	16	Organiël	Kasierôph
17	Oekiël	Nestriaph	17	Romatiël	Kessiépopos
18	Perinël	Askinos	18	Selpidôn	Androphai
19	Iarél	Kinopigos	19	Ouitôm	Nioech
20	Athouel	Araps	20	Metabiël	Entauros
21	Thananiël	Tartarouël	21	Akvael	Syritor Phlinaphe
22	Vradel	Melmeth	22	Eikoniël	Kyknit
23	Klinos	Methridanou	23	Genekiël	Kenops
24	Ion	Phrodainos	24	Krotiël	Sarkidôn

	TUESDAY			WEDNESDAY	
Hour	Angel	Demon	Hour	Angel	Demon
1	Samouël	Kakistôn	1	Ouriël	Loutzipher
2	Ishmaél	Lithridôn	2	Arakaël	Goukoumôr
3	Phrereël	Maïloth	3	Miemphiël	Eispniryx
4	Eudél	Sarapidié	4	Trosiël	Midoket
5	Piktoël	Kerinoudalos	5	Chartissiël	Ntadadiph
6	Okaël	Klinotios	6	Sphykinoël	Skintoger
7	Gnathaël	Tyrrutor	7	Oulodias	Skamidinos
8	Perganiël	Plelatan	8	Kalvagiël	Karatan
9	Gestiël	Sythos	9	Skitamiël	Miag
10	Legmiél	Osthridié	10	Tiroël	Gatzar
11	Nachoël	Omimot	11	Miël	Pnidor
12	Oknam	Aprox	12	Charakiël	Toivlas
13	Gorphil	Skoén	13	Ydroël	Taxipôn
14	Patiël	Prophaï	14	Sidrel	Ophitan
15	Partan	Akhlitôl	15	Paratiël	Avlychos
16	Saltiël	Ornan	16	Mourouël	Malakis
17	Abaël	Khalmôth	17	Kourtaël	Vlemgich
18	Stragiel	Askinos	18	Koupeël	Cheirôn
19	Opadouël	Touddeden	19	Peraniël	Hephippas
20	Marniël	Teplura	20	Santaël	Orkistaph
21	Methiël	Niran	21	Katziél	Loginaph
22	Stiroël	Rakirô	22	Louriél	Pharâs
23	Ismatiël	Irgotié	23	Saltaël	Roktat
24	Trizioël	Gegaôr	24	Gabtél	Opnax

THURSDAY			FRIDAY		
Hour	Angel	Demon	Hour	Angel	Demon
1	Raphael	Meltiphrôn	1	Agathouël	Gouliôn
2	Perniphel	Ochlos	2	Nidouël	Vizik (Bizek)
3	Kisphaël	Ouëros	3	Amphiloël	Zorzorath
4	Kaliël	Thaphôt	4	Kanikél	Raphiôph
5	Glôstas	Tzippat	5	Seliniel	Ermag
6	Mnimeël	Amôr	6	Karkanpher	Kerinoudalos
7	Chalriël	Orphor	7	Aniel	Tavaltalis
8	Skiaël	Outaët	8	Mouriël	Thapnix
9	Missoël	Ergotas	9	Tophatiël	Eliasém
10	Dalvôth	Azouvoul	10	Skirtouël	Amih
11	Chartoël	Aplëx	11	Armôël	Galgidon
12	Kiphar	Sogôs	12	Otraël	Ephirit
13	Sitioël	Asmôdas	13	Talkidonios	Straget
14	Vokiel	Ouôch	14	Roudiël	Anthiros
15	Senoël	Nikokep	15	Thikiel	Pizitos
16	Oriator	Kopinos	16	Glykidôn	Aprix
17	Chymeriel	Kaëté	17	Psalmatios	Niphôn
18	Orphniël	Lastôr	18	Stauphnël	Otrichos
19	Kidouel	Epïi	19	Deaukôn	Himeri
20	Goth	Organ	20	Asphodël	Mely
21	Phisnael	Nierér	21	Petilôl	Kapnithel
22	Karaaël	Oualiélos	22	Gorgiel	Tachman
23	Kôndar	Galielôr	23	Vataaniël	Oukissem
24	Kispôl	Houkon	24	Poliôn	Ouniphrër

SATURDAY

Hour	Angel	Demon
1	Savapiel	Klitadôr
2	Salôël	Heirim
3	Vesaël	Spindôr
4	Avaël	Keriak
5	Gielmôn	Nikem
6	Retaël	Môriël
7	Pelaphiël	Synigeirôm
8	Samôëssan	Aphios
9	Pletanix	Thorios
10	Marmichaël	Stelpha
11	Niecharinx	Kypos
12	Arkiel	Skar
13	Geaviël	Tëhar
14	Pitriel	Akrok
15	Golgoël	Argitan
16	Sanipiël	Atomeos
17	Velaraël	Gnötas
18	Opissel	Merkou
19	Ophchinël	Enaritar
20	Patriël	Niouchan
21	Ianiël	Amphou
22	Kondienël	Mankôs
23	Ouxounouel	Moigrôën
24	Thanaël	Nisgriph

Reboam,* I engrave there a method for knowing exactly what needs be known at any price at the moment when you wish to do your will. First say the prayer to the planet, to the one present at that moment, then conjure the angel and the servant, that is the demon.

Prayer to Cronos (Saturn)

God eternal, independent power that organizes all for our salvation, grant us your grace so that I may submit this planet to my will. Planet Cronos, I conjure your path, your air, your descent, your heavens, your brilliance, and your energy, by the names that follow: Gassial, Agounsaël, Atasser, Veltoniël, Mentzatzia, so that you may give me your grace and energy and power at the hour when you hold sway.[14]

Prayer to Zeus (Jupiter)

Lord God, all-powerful father, creator of things visible and invisible, king of the rulers and the governor of the governors, grant us the strength of your grace so that Zeus submit to us, for all is possible Lord. Zeus, I conjure your wisdom, your knowledge, your healing energy, your heavenly course on which you walk, by these names here: Anôph, Orsita, Onivegi, Atziniel, Ankanitï, Tyneos, Genier, Kaniptza, so that you pour your grace over me in this task I am achieving.

Prayer to Ares (Mars)

Terrible god, inexpressible god, invisible god that has not been seen nor can be seen by any human being, god who has caused the abysses to shudder when they saw him and who reduced the living to the status of the dead, grant us your grace so that we may subjugate the planet Ares. Ares of fire, I conjure the god who created intelligible substances and the entire army of fire; I conjure your energies, your course, and your brilliance by these names here: Outat, Nouët, Chorëzë, Tinaë, Dachli, Ambira, Noliem, Siet, Ardichaël, Tzanas, Plesym, so that you may give me your grace for the task I am performing.

---

*Roboam (Latinized version of Rehoboam) is the son of Solomon and the information in many grimoires is intended for him.

7 ◇ SIGNATURES OF THE SPIRITS[15]

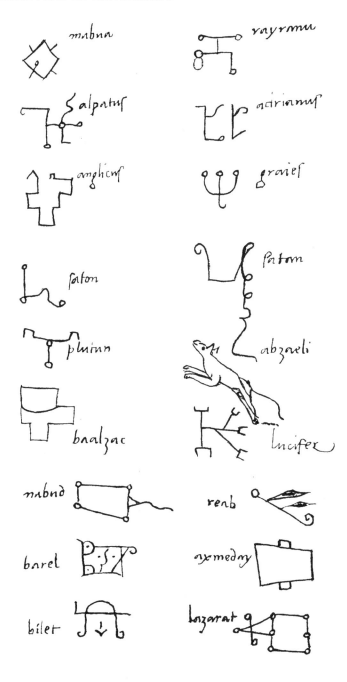

mabna

rayrmu

alpatuf

acirianuf

anghcuf

graief

fafon

fatom

pluinn

abzaeli

baalzac

lncifer

mabnd

renb

barel

axmedny

bilet

bazarat

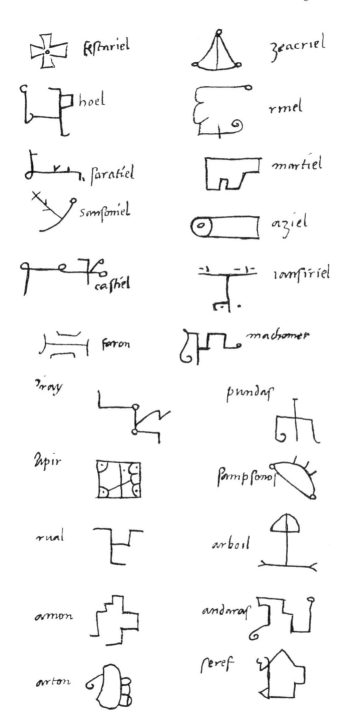

festnriel

zeacriel

hoel

rmel

faratiel

martiel

samfomiel

aziel

cafhel

iamfiriel

faron

machomet

?ray

pundaf

?apir

famp fonof

rual

arboil

amon

andaraf

arton

feref

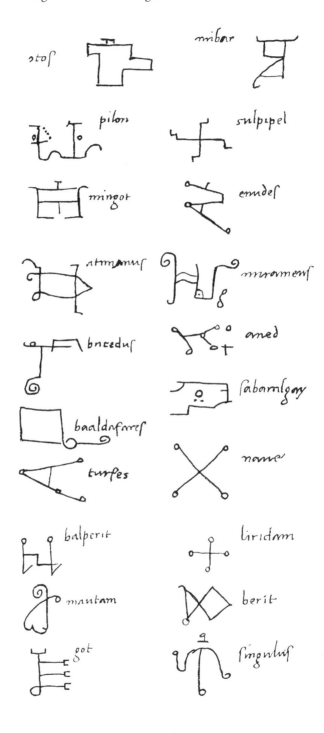

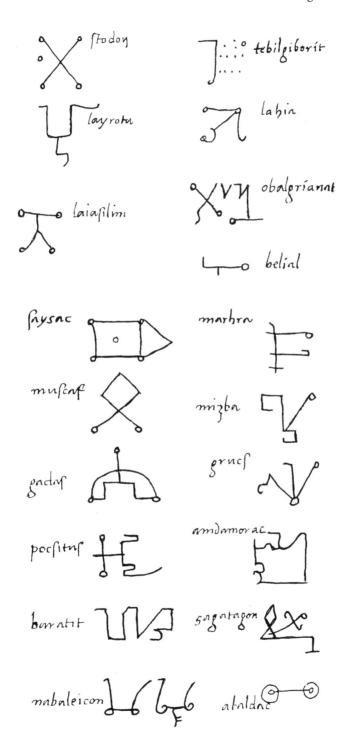

8 ◈ On the Use of the Names[16]

Someone who came from the land of the Blacks, and who worked and experimented on what we have spoken earlier as well as these sciences, wrote a name on a small strip of brass and carried this on his person. When a scorpion stung someone, he washed this brass strip in water for the injured person to drink and immediately the pain went away and he was healed.

It was also said that when he did not have this strip of brass, he wrote these names on a small clean cup where he could inscribe them in their entirety, with chalk or an ink like that of the crocus or other similar things that could be drunk. He washed it in the water that he then gave to the patient to drink, and the pain stopped immediately.

If I was not fearful of being a chatterbox, I would tell of the wonders he performed with these names because the individuals to whom he gave them as a drink are so numerous that it would be impossible to name them all in a short time. But as I have experimented with these names, I have decided to let you learn them in my book. They are

zaare zaare zaare zaare zaare fegem

zohorim borayn nesfis albune fedraza

affetite taututa tanym zabahat aylatriayn

haurane rahannie ayn latumine queue

acatyery nimieri quibari yehuyha

nuyyim latrityn hamtauery vueryn

cahuene cenhe beyne ✡

All these names should be written on exactly seven lines and the seal of Solomon should be placed at the head of the seventh line.*

There are some who say that they must be written on the first day of Jupiter during the month of May, but I have seen them written on the day as it pleased others. Take care not to be wrong in the names, in the shapes, and in the figures so that you make no errors. I have seen a sage who wrote bohorim *nohorim,* with an *n,* but I recorded this name with a *b.* I tell you all this so you may discover the secrets of this science.

---

*Since the text is of Arab origin, it reads from right to left. Thus the pentacle of Solomon (the Star of David) is located at what is the start of the seventh line.

2

THE MAGICAL CHARACTERS OF THE PLANETS

As was apparent with Solomon's *Hygromancy,* the heavenly bodies play a very important role in magic because their power can be infused in objects that can then be used as phylacteries, amulets, and talismans. To do this, it is necessary to engrave the secret symbols of a planet on a metal or stone that it governs. This is followed by fumigations of the support material while reciting certain conjurations or prayers. At the end of the working, the strength of the planet will have been transferred into the object and it will possess its powers; for example, to fight certain health complaints or oppose some evil spell.

The first example (which appears on page 54, top) is taken from a fifteenth-century astrological manuscript and reproduces the common magical characters of the seven planets, whereas the second (on page 55), which I have taken from *The Variety of Things,* by the Milanese physician Gerolamo Cardano,[1] distinguishes three types of symbols in terms of their use: those that are written on parchment, those that are carved on rings, and those that are used as seals. As a general rule, the characters are engraved on the setting of a ring that is then sealed with virgin wax, some of which is given to the individual who wishes to share the protection the ring grants the wearer.

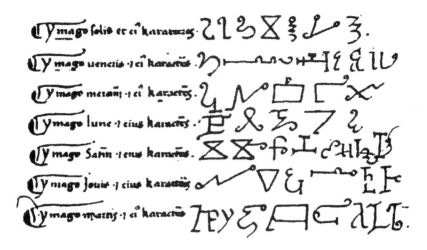

Images of the planets and their secret symbols (characters)

Seal of Taurus (zodiac sign) used as a talisman. Ghent, University Library, ms 1012A, sixteenth century.

¶ Primùm, Characteres igitur Planetarum sic scribit:

Sol

Luna

Mars

Mercurius

Iupiter

Venus

Saturnus.

Annulos uerò sic:

Sol

Luna

Mars

Mercurius

Iupiter

Venus

Saturnus.

Sigilla autem sic:

Sol

Luna

Mars

Mercurius

Iupiter

Venus

Saturnus.

Characters of the planets for various uses: parchment (top), rings (middle), seals (bottom)

LES SECRETS

MERVEILLEUX

DE LA MAGIE NATURELLE

DU

PETIT ALBERT

Tirés de l'ouvrage latin intitulé :

ALBERTI PARVI LUCII

Libellus de mirabilibus naturæ Arcanis

Et d'autres écrivains philosophes

ENRICHIS DE FIGURES MYSTÉRIEUSES, D'ASTROLOGIE, PHYSIONOMIE, ETC., ETC.

Nouvelle édition corrigée et augmentée

A LYON

Chez les Héritiers de BERINGOS fratres

A l'Enseigne d'Agrippa.

M. DCCC. LXVIII.

The Little Albert Grimoire

3

DEMONS AND ILLNESSES

In the time of pagan antiquity, the illnesses that afflicted man and beast were believed to come from a multitude of visible or invisible demons that haunt all the four elements and the entire cosmos. During the Middle Ages, these demons were incorporated into dwarves and elves, and, in the Germanic languages, for example, there are numerous health complaints with striking names coined from the words for "dwarf" (*dverg, zwerg,* etc.) or "elf" (*ælf, alf,* etc.). This is how lumbago became known as "elfshot"[1] and so forth.

Christians believed that illness was an attack mounted by the devil or else incurred as punishment for sins or transgressions. In this event, the intervention of God and his saints is called upon and they are mobilized to serve as an obstacle to the attacks of the one who is simply called the Enemy.

One text, *The Testament of Solomon,* which likely dates from the third or fourth century CE, gives us an excellent overview of the proliferation of demons and their specialties, but that is not the only reason it is of interest.[2] In fact, it clearly indicates how to destroy the power of these demons and what will send them fleeing. Every harmful principle is opposed by a good principle, generally in the form of an angel.

The position of the *Testament* brings to mind a passage from the legend that tells how Solomon obtained his power over the djinn.

When God placed the djinn in service to Solomon, Gabriel cried out, "O djinn and shayatin answer, by the permission of God, the call of his prophet Solomon, son of David!" The djinn and shayatin came out from their caverns, mountains, hills, valleys, deserts, and thickets, repeating: "At your command!" The angels drove them out in front, like a shepherd his flock, until they had all been gathered together—humble and tame—before Solomon. On this day they formed the 420 divisions. They stood before Solomon, who gazed long upon their amazing faces and shapes. They were white, black, yellow, pink, and multi-colored, and looked like horses, mules, wild beasts, with muzzles, tails, hooves, and horns. Solomon went down on his knees before God and said: "My God, make me strong and formidable enough so that I may be able to look upon them!" Gabriel then told him: "God has given you strength over them: arise!" He stood up with the ring on his finger, then the djinn and shayatin fell to their knees, lifted their heads and said: "O son of David, we have gathered together before you and the command had been given us to obey you."[3]

9 ◆ THE TESTAMENT OF SOLOMON[4]

I commanded that another demon appear before me. The thirty-six elements* came to me, their heads like those of misshapen dogs. Among them, some had the appearance of a man, a bull, or had a face of a wild beast, serpent, sphinx, or bird. On seeing them, I, Solomon, asked them: "Who are you, you others?" They answered in unison: "We are the thirty-six elements, the Masters of Darkness of this Age of the World. You cannot, O king, cause us harm or imprison us. However, as God has given you power over all the spirits of the air, earth, and hell, we come before you like the other spirits."

I, Solomon, called a spirit to me and spoke to him: "You, who are you?" and he answered: "I am the first face of the circle of the zodiac: my name is Rhyax. I cause men headaches and cause their temples to pound. When I hear 'Michael, imprison Rhyax!' I flee into the clouds."

---

*There are, in fact, thirty-six decans.

The second said: "My name is Barsaphael. I cause the aches on one side of the head of men who sleep during my hour. When I hear, 'Gabriel, imprison Barsaphael!' I escape immediately toward the heights."

The third said: "My name is Artosael. I cause sharp pains in the eyes. But if I hear 'Uriel, imprison Artosael!' I flee into the clouds."

The fourth said: "I am called Horopel and I send boils, inflammations of the throat muscles, and abscesses. Once I hear 'Raphael, imprison Horopel!' I fly away toward the heights."

The fifth said: "My name is Kairoxanondalon. I clog ears. When I hear 'Ourouel, imprison Kairoxanondalon!' I flee into the air."

The sixth said: "I call myself Sphendonael. I cause parytidas [?] and the illnesses that grab the limbs from behind. If I hear 'Sabael, imprison Sphendonael!' I flee aloft."

The seventh said: "I call myself Sphandor. I weaken the strength of the shoulders, detach the ligaments of the hands, and paralyze the limbs. If I hear 'Arael, imprison Sphandor!' I also flee into the clouds immediately."

The eighth said: "My name is Bebbel. I seek to twist the hearts and spines of men. If I hear 'Karael, imprison Bebbel!' I flee immediately into the air."

The ninth said: "Kourtael is my name. I send intestinal ruptures. If I hear 'Jaoth, imprison Kourtael!' I flee immediately into the clouds."

The tenth said: "I am Metathiax and I cause kidney pains. If I hear 'Adonael, imprison Metathiax!' I fly into the air immediately."

The eleventh said: "I am called Katanikotael, I send quarrels and disputes into the home. If you wish to restore peace there, inscribe on seven laurel leaves these names that will disarm me: 'Angel, Eae, Sabaoth, imprison Katanikotael!' The leaves must be folded and the house sprinkled with holy water, and I will vanish at once."

The twelfth said: "My name is Saphtorael. I send discord into men and rejoice each time I cause them irritation. If one writes 'Jae, Jeoo, son of Sabaoth' and wears these names at one's throat, I disappear immediately."

The thirteenth said: "I am Phobothel. I relax the tendons. If I hear 'Adonai!' I flee at once."

The fourteenth said: "I am called Lerooel. I bring cold, shivering, and stomachaches. If I hear 'Jaz, get out of here! Cause no hot fever because Solomon is more powerful than the eleven patriarchs!' I leave immediately."

The fifteenth said: "My name is Soubetti. I send the shivers of fever and numbness. If I hear 'Rhizoel, imprison Soubetti!' I flee immediately into the clouds."

The sixteenth said: "I am called Katrax. I inflict men with incurable attacks of heat. Whoever wishes to be healed must crush coriander and anoint his lips with it while saying: 'By Dan, I conjure you! Get out of this image of God!' and I will vanish at once."

The seventeenth said: "My name is Jeropa. I sit on the bellies of men and cause cramps when they bathe. If I encounter a man on my path, I will strike him at once. He who says three times in the patient's right ear 'Jouda, Zizabon,' compels me to go away."

The eighteenth said: "I am Modebel. I part man from woman. If one writes the names of the eight patriarchs and places them on the sill of the door, I vanish immediately."

The nineteenth said: "I am called Mardero. I bring incurable shivering from fever, but I will flee immediately from the house in which my name is written."

The twentieth said: "My name is Rhyx Nathotho. I plant myself on the knees of men. If one writes 'Phounebiel' on a leaf, I disappear without delay."

The twenty-first said: "I am Rhyx Alath. I bring asthma to small children. If one writes 'Rarideris' and clenches it in one's fist, I disappear immediately."

The twenty-second said: "I am named Rhyx Audameooth. I send cardiac diseases. If one writes 'Rhaiouooth,' I vanish immediately."

The twenty-third said: "I am called Rhyx Manthado, and I cause renal pains. I vanish at once if one writes 'Jaooth, Ouriel.'"

The twenty-fourth said: "My name is Rhys Aktonme. I cause stitches in the side. If one writes on the wood of a vehicle that has failed to reach its destination 'this belongs to Marmaroth of the airs,' I will flee at once."

The twenty-fifth said: "I am Rhyx Antreth. I send fevers and convulsions into the entrails. I disappear at once if I hear 'Arare, Arare.'"

The twenty-sixth said: "I am called Thyx the Enautha. I steal the senses and change hearts. If one writes 'Kalazael', I vanish immediately."

The twenty-seventh said: "I am named Rhyx Axesbyth, I cause chest pains and hemorrhoids in men. If I am conjured into the wine the patient is given to drink, I disappear immediately."

The twenty-eight said: "My name is Rhyx Hapax. I prevent people from sleeping. If one writes 'Kok phnedismos' and attaches these words to one's temples, I vanish immediately."

The twenty-ninth said: "I am Rhyx Anoster. I send uterine cramps and painful swellings. If one grates three laurel leaves into virgin oil and uses it as an ointment while saying: 'I command you to go down to Marmaraoth's home,' I vanish immediately."

The thirtieth said: "My name is Rhyx Physikoreth. I cause long illnesses. If a grain of salt is dropped in oil and it is then used to anoint the patient while saying: 'Cherubim, Seraphim, help him!' I will immediately disappear."

The thirty-first said: "I am called Rhyx Aleureth. If someone swallows a fishbone, I will vanish at once if a bone of this same fish is placed on the patient's chest."

The thirty-second said: "I am Rhyx Ichthyon. I soften the tendons. If I hear 'Adonai, malthe,' I vanish at once."

The thirty-third said: "I am called Rhyx Achooneooth. I cause pains to the throat and tonsils. If one writes 'Leikourgos, grappiforme, disappear!' on ivy leaves, I will be sent fleeing."

The thirty-fourth said: "My name is Rhyx Autoth. I instigate envy and quarreling amongst friends. I am vanquished by the *a* and the *b* if they are written down."

The thirty-fifth said: "I am Rhyx Phthteneooth. I bewitch the entire man. An engraved eye renders me harmless."

The thirty-sixth said: "I am called Rhyx Mianeth. I am the enemy of the body. I empty houses and cause the disappearance of the flesh. If one writes *melpo, ardad, anaath* in the vestibule of the house, I will flee from that place."

When I, Solomon, heard all of this, I praised God of heaven and earth and commanded the spirits to carry water. And I prayed to God so that the thirty-six demons who bind mankind might enter the temple of the Lord.

4

MAGICAL HEALING

Any remedy, even a magical one, is doomed to failure if destiny has decided that the patient will pass away. The name encompassing the individual's being—which is expressed by the saying *nomen est omen,* "the name is a portent"—is fateful: it carries and reflects a destiny. In the Middle Ages, therefore, we find a kind of prediagnosis that relies on the mantic understanding of letters and numbers. The reproduction below of the diagram from a manuscript clearly indicates the kinds of tools used by the healer. In order for the procedure to be more easily understood, I sought out the explanations provided by another manuscript, the text of which follows.

10 ◇ To Know if a Patient Will Be Cured[1]

Take the name of the patient and add up the number of the letters using the following table, then count the days starting from the phase of the moon when the man was afflicted.

1	2	3	4	5	6	7	8	9	10	12	13	14	15	16	17	18	19	20	21	22	23	24	25	26	27
a	b	c	d	E	f	g	h	I	j	k	l	m	n	o	p	Q	r	s	t	u	v	w	x	y	z

Sol ☉	Luna ☽	Mars ♂	Mercurius ☿	Jupiter ♃	Venus ♀	Saturnus ♄
15	14	20	20	11	15	14

Sol	14	☉
luna	18	☾
Mars	20	♂
Mercurig	20	☿
Jupiter	11	♃
Venus	14	♀
Saturn	18	♄

If the number of the patient's name is higher, he will live; if that of the moon prevails, he will die. Here is the calculation table:

One and one: the small prevails	Four and four: the larger prevails
One and two: ij prevails	Four and v: v prevails
One and iij: iij prevails	Four and vj: iiij prevails
One and iiij: iiij prevails	Four and vij: vij prevails
One and v: v prevails	Four and viij: iiij prevails
One and vj: vj prevails	Four and ix: ix prevails
One and vij: vij prevails	
One and viij: viij prevails	Five and v: the smaller prevails
One and ix: ix prevails	Five and vj: vj prevails
	Five and vij: v prevails
Two and ij: the large prevails	Five and viij: viij prevails
Two and iij: iij prevails	Five and ix: ix prevails
Two and iiij: iiij prevails	
Two and v: v prevails	Six and vj: the larger prevails
Two and vj: ij prevails	Six and vij: vij prevails
Two and vij: vij prevails	Six and viij: vj prevails
Two and viij: ij prevails	Six and ix: ix prevails
Two and ix: x prevails	
	Seven and vij: the smaller prevails
Three and iij: the larger prevails	Seven and viij: viij prevails
Three and iiij: iiij prevails	Seven and ix: vij prevails
Three and v: iij prevails	
Three and vj: vj prevails	Eight and viij: the larger prevails
Three and vij: iij prevails	Eight and ix: viij prevails
Three and viij: viij prevails	
Three and ix: iij prevails	Nine and ix: the smaller prevails

11 ◈ For Pains of the Head[2]

Like Abracadabra, Ararita is derived from what we could call a regressive healing diagram: with the subtraction of each letter, the illness diminishes. The advantage of the text below is that it provides us with the description of the accompanying ritual, which is composed of gestures and words.

Ararita	When you enter the presence of the patient or he comes
Ararit	toward you, take a new knife and make a cross
Arar	on his forehead while saying: *Jhesus Christus* hung from the cross,
Ara	said *Consummatum est,* and this was at the end of all his suffering
Ar	and his passion. May leave and disappear in this way, all
A	pain from the head of the patient.

These words must be spoken while signing the cross on the forehead without letting them be heard. After that, with the same knife, cut the words written above—*consummatum est.* After that, using the same knife, then make another cross on the forehead and say the same words appearing above: *Jhesus Christus* and so forth. Next, while the patient recites seven Our Fathers [i.e., the Lord's Prayer], you shall cut the characters of the first line in a cross, with the same knife and while saying *Jhesus Christus* and so forth, over each the above-mentioned words as they are cut.

When this first line is finished, take up the same knife again and make a cross on the patient's forehead while saying *Jhesus Christus* and so forth as before, while the patient recites six Our Fathers, as there are six letters in the second line. While he is reciting them, cut each of these characters in a cross while speaking the same words: *Jhesus Christus* and so forth.

You shall continue to make the patient say as many Our Fathers as there are letters in the word, the number of times is reduced as they are reduced, until you reach the end, continuously making a cross on the patient's brow and cutting the letters with a cross as you did at the beginning. Cut into a cross each letter of the first line while saying *Jhesus Christus* and so forth, each time.

12 ◈ Against Headaches[3]

A charm is based on the theme of an encounter that has been quite fruit-
ful and remains representational of the heavily Christianized charms.[4] A
situation is depicted in which an individual who is suffering is healed by a
blessing, which in this instance comes from the Virgin. These benedictions
can also come from Jesus or a saint.

Our Lord was standing at the door of the church; Mary, his mother, passed by and asked him: "Dear, sweet Lord, why are you so afflicted today?" He answered: "Very dear mother, I have no other choice as my poor head is ailing so badly it has robbed me of my senses. Who would have believed it?" "I will help you because you have told me about it. What will you give me if I cure you with a blessing?" "I will give you heaven and earth to feel better," he responded. She blessed him with her hand and his pain rapidly vanished.

13 ◈ Against the Plague[5]

The following phylactery, which should be carved on a strip of silver, draws its apotropaic powers from the addition of God's names to those of two angels and to the sacred table of a planet. Henry Cornelius Agrippa tells us these tables "are endowed with several great virtues of celestial things insofar as they represent this divine reason or form of the celestial numbers."

†	† ELOHIM † ELOHI †			†
† ADONAI †	4	14	15	1	† ZEBAOTH †
	9	7	6	12	
	5	11	10	8	
	16	2	3	13	
	† ROGYEL † IOSPHIEL †			

Carry this figure on your person and you shall be protected!

The sum of the numbers of the table above is thirty-four in whatever direction they are added together, even diagonally. The number obtained this way is that of the planet Jupiter. Each number represents a "spirit," for example: 4 = Ab, 9 = Hod; 5 = He; 6 = Vau. Furthermore, He and Vau form part of the sacred name Yahweh. It is said that if this table is etched onto a silver blade, it will confer riches, love, peace, and honor, but if it is carved on coral, it will prevent evil spells. An identical square of numbers can be seen in Albrecht Dürer's engraving *Melencolia I*. The Hebrew *Elohim,* plural of *eloah,* "god," designates the true god when used with a verb in the singular form. Rogyel is undoubtedly the angel Ragiel, and Josephiel is another angel.

14 ◆ FOR THOSE SUFFERING FROM LIVER COMPLAINTS OR FROM FRENZY[6]

The following therapy shows us how to link together a sympathetic chain in order to obtain the maximum effect. This text is connected to the Kyranides *treatise mentioned in the introduction; it employs alphabetical magic, for in the Latin original, the crow is called Borositis, the stone, Berillis, the crab Bissa, and the savine plant, Brathy.*

Take the beryl stone, engrave upon it a crow with a crab beneath its claws"; set said stone in a gold or silver ring, with a little savine or a piece of a crow's heart beneath it. All of this must be nobly sealed in at the hour when the face of Jupiter is ruling. Bear this ring on your person wherever you wish and know that it possesses these virtues: it heals all those who are mad, frenetic, and hepatic; gives joy and jubilations; procures great love in marriage; and gives he who wears it good fortune and wealth.

15 ◆ FOR A LUNATIC[7]

The two accounts that follow—and I will cite yet more—are the work of an unknown author who in all modesty signs his texts "Jesus"! To the best of my knowledge, his small treatise, which uses the psalms of David combined with magic characters, has never been cited before now. In the Middle Ages, lunatics were considered to be persons persecuted by demons, and exorcisms were used to heal them. The psalm cited from the Bible is addressed to the storm god and opens with these words: "Ascribe to God, O sons . . ."

Afferte Domino filii. Recite this psalm in the patient's ear when he is in the grip of epilepsy. It will restore him. Also write it with these characters, cense them with musk and thyme, and bury them at the corners of the house. A great blessing shall fall upon it.

16 ◆ For a Long Illness[8]
Exaltabo te Domine quoniam. If someone is sick every day, read this psalm seven times over clean water and wash the patient with it. Read it once again, seven times, over oil, and write these characters ⟨characters⟩ and cense them with musk, dilute them with the above-mentioned oil, and anoint the patient with it.

17 ◆ Phylactery[9]
Here is an amulet, but you should be aware that the swan in fact represents the constellation Cygnus, about which Henry Cornelius Agrippa says: "The Swan [Cygnus] heals paralysis and quartan fever" (Occult Philosophy II, 37).

If ever you find a stone upon which a swan is carved and you bear it on your person, never shall you have quartan fever or paralysis.

18 ◆ Against the Bite of a Rabid Dog or Wolf[10]
The magic of the prescription stems from the alliterations provided by the chain of incomprehensible words, which gives them the character of a monotonous chant. We have seen earlier how it is necessary to anoint with oil or drink water in which these characters have been diluted. Here we learn that magical remedies can be drawn on a foodstuff then ingested.

Write these characters on bread and give it to the patient to eat:
　　† ditem † priscom † dryxom † pi isco † brisum † sic Greco remani
　　In the name of the Father, the Son, and the Holy Ghost.

19 ◈ Charm for Fistulas, Boils, and Wounds[11]

Take a piece of lead and have it pounded until it is as thin as a leaf and can be folded, then with a knife draw five crosses in this shape on it:

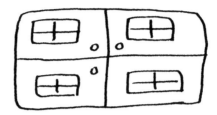

While doing this, recite five Our Fathers in honor of the five wounds of Our Lord Jesus Christ. And when you do the three holes, two on the left and one on the right, say three Our Fathers in honor of the holy trinity and the three nails that crucified Our Lord Jesus Christ. Next, recite an Our Father in honor of the passion before saying this charm:

> I conjure you, N., to heal the fistula, boil, or wound in the name of the five wounds suffered by Our Lord Jesus Christ, in the name of the Holy Trinity and the three nails that crucified Our Lord Jesus Christ, in the name of the holy passion, without risk of suffering.

Then place the lead sheet on the afflicted area with the cross facing it, and make sure that this lead is washed every three days and put back on the afflicted area. Take pains to avoid letting this lead touch the ground while you are enchanting it, and while you are reciting the charm, bless it.

20 ◈ Against Nosebleeds[12]

In the following charm, max nax pax *is an alliterative magical expression that is extremely widespread under various forms,[13] the most venerable of which is* Hax pax max. *In the sixteenth century, this was expanded into* Hax pax max deux adimax. *It was written out fully or in abbreviated form on a note, a piece of bread, a host, or the quarter of an apple. The spell works against hemorrhages, rabies, fevers, and toothache. During the restoration of the Saint George Basilica in Prague, a parchment strip requesting the cure of a case of trench fever for a certain Dobrozlava was found under the plaster of an alcove. The prayer ended with: "May* Pax † nax vax *be the remedy for this servant of God. Amen."*

If someone is losing blood through their nostrils, say these three names three times: max † nax † pax †.

21 ◈ To Stop Blood Loss[14]

The two following charms direct an appeal to the Virgin Mary and have an extremely ancient structure as they can be found much earlier in sixth-century medical treatises. The second charm derives from an assemblage of two different expressions that exist independently of one another.

Agla forms part of the three secret names of God (Agla, On, Tetragramaton); according to legend they were revealed to Lot and allowed him to save his family. They can be found everywhere: in prayers and conjurations, and on pentacles.[15]

> The true lady is seated on her bench.
> Her true child is seated on her lap.
> True is the lady, true is the child.
> True vein stanches your blood.

Say this three times and recite three Our Fathers.

22 ◈ To Staunch Blood Flow[16]

To stop the blood flowing out of the nostrils or whichever vein it is pouring from, write these letters on the patient's forehead with his own blood and speak this charm:

† a † g † l † a

> Our Lady was seated on a bench and held her dear son on her lap?
> True mother, true child, true vein, hold your blood! In the name of
> Jesus I command you to not let one more drop emerge henceforth.

The patient should say three Our Fathers and three Ave Marias [Hail Marys] with the person who speaks this charm. It should be recited three times. Never should it fail.

23 ◆ To Halt Bleeding[17]

In this Old English prescription, the magic spell uses heavily distorted Celtic words. Some have been identified,[18] but most make no sense. It is also thought that the graphic design +++ could be ogam, the ancient Irish script, and represent the letter Fearn, which stands for alder; ⋈ could be the rune /d/.

If a man or horse is bleeding, write this on him:
> + Ægryn. Thon. Struth. Fola argrenn. Struth. On. Tria. Enn. Piath. Hathu. Morfana. Onhæl + ara. Carn. Leou. Groth. Weorn. +++. ffil. Crondi. p ⋈. Mro. Cron. Ærcrio. Ermio. Œr. Leno

and the blood flow will cease.

24 ◆ Against a Hemorrhage[19]

The letters of the spell should be the initials of words forming a prayer or conjuration addressed to a saint. The name Serenisa is unknown; on the other hand, however, Saint Bernice[20]/Veronica steps in on a regular basis to staunch blood flow, so we must assume that her name here has been deformed. In the Gospels of Matthew (9:20–22), Mark (5:25–34), and Luke (8:43–48), Jesus healed a woman who had suffered from a discharge of blood for many years. This woman was given the name of Veronica, who therefore became a reference and a means of healing.

Write these characters on virgin parchment and attach them around the neck of the person who is losing blood:
> S. q. r. tz. Os. T. q. e. t. o. a. c. ge. E. h. x. sancta. Serenisa.

25 ◆ For Staunching Blood Flow[21]

Exaltate Deo. Write these characters *[top of page 73]* on olive-tree leaves, cense them with mastic, and place them over the kidneys of the patient and read this psalm over him. His blood will cease flowing out.

26 ◈ Against the Heavy Bleeding of Women[22]
Miserere mej Domine quoniam. If a woman is hemorrhaging blood, take
a cup of wine and recite this psalm over it seven times, then make her
drink it. The blood discharge will stop immediately.

27 ◈ To Ensure Good Sleep[23]
Comparison of the text below with others in the same vein reveals that
EXMAEL is a distortion of Ishmael, the name of the son of Abraham and
Hagar, as well as the fact that our version is incomplete. This name should
be written on a laurel leaf. In the fourteenth century in the British Isles,
this leaf would be placed beneath the patient's head without his knowing,
and he would be given lettuce to eat and poppy juice to drink, a powerful
somniferous substance.

Write EXMAEL EXMAEL, then place it on the head without the person knowing (while saying): "I implore you, by the angel Michael, to
make this man sleep."

28 ◈ For a Patient Who Cannot Sleep[24]
Ad te levavi Domine animam meam. If a patient cannot sleep, write out
this psalm and place it upon his head. He will sleep.

29 ◈ Another Charm[25]
On virgin parchment write the following words and place it beneath
the pillow of the bed while saying: "In the name of the Father, the Son,
and the Holy Ghost. Amen."

Arox axax Aportaxa

30 ◈ To Sleep[26]
Here is a fine example of the recourse to analogy: by carrying on your
person the name of the Seven Sleepers, you will no longer suffer from

insomnia! Popularized by Pope Gregory the Great (and referred to by Gregory of Tours),[27] *the legend tells of seven individuals who were perse-cuted under the reign of Emperor Decius; they took refuge in a cave near Ephesus, where they slept for several centuries before reawakening in a world that had become Christian. The first seven names of the saints,*[28] *which are clearly interpolated in this prescription, have no connection with sleep. They are here to reinforce the power of the names of the Sleepers.*

May he who cannot sleep bear these names upon his person:

† Eugenius † Stephanus † Prochasius † Caudiscius † Dionisius † Chericius † e Quiracius † Malcus † Maximianus † Martinus † Dionisius † Constantinus † Johannes † Seraphion.

31 ◈ FOR CHILDREN WHO CANNOT SLEEP[29]

Dominus deus noster. If a child is crying very much and cannot sleep, write this psalm out entirely and tie it to the child's arm.

32 ◈ FOR A WEEPING CHILD[30]

Deus Deus meus ad te de luce vigilo. Write this psalm out entirely and tie it to the child's arm: it will cease to cry.

33 ◈ AGAINST WORMS[31]

Here are three variations of Job's Charm.[32] *The magic spell of the first makes no sense and comparison of several versions simply gives us a glimpse of the distortions to which magic words were subject. In a manuscript from Heidelberg, the spell reads:* Job † trayson magulus † Job tridanson † gruba † zerobantes †, *and in another, from Copenhagen, we find:* pergama perga † pergamata † abraham † alume † zorobantur † magula † malagula † Job † magula † malagula. *A Norwegian grimoire from around 1520 offers the following:* job idrasson † job zarobabatos † job tha nobratos.[33] *It is easy to see that it would be futile to try to translate any of these mysterious words.*

Three worms were devouring Saint Job; one white, the second black, the third red. Milord, Saint Job, all the worms are dead. Dead are the worms.

Job grax son macula †
Job guilia †
Job sorakamijs Job trahu †
Gon anacula †
Connubia macula gula †
Job sarobant †

In the name of the Father alaia agla † and of the Son Messiah † and of the Holy Ghost † sorrchistin † Amen.

34 ◈ Charm Against Gout[34]
This variant of Job's Charm *is applied to gout because there is an illness called "falling gout," which appears to be confused here with the "falling illness" (epilepsy). The charm follows a regressive numerical pattern like the one we already saw by Marcellus of Bordeaux[35] and which—demonstrating the marvelous nature of these traditions—is still used in the twenty-first century. The phrase "Christ is born" and so forth, is one of the most frequently occurring Christian spells.*

In the name of the Father, the Son, and the Holy Ghost. Amen. Job had worms. How many did he have? He had ix. From ix he had viii, from viii to vii, from vii to vi, from vi to v, from v to iv, from iv to iii, from iii to ii, from ii to I, from I to 0. True as God healed Job, heal this man or woman of this impairment, of or fistula, or of gout. In the name of the Father and the Son, Christ is born, Christ is dead, Christ is resurrected. I am A and Ω, the first and the newest, the beginning and the end of the world, I am life and peace † In the name of the Father, the Son, and the Holy Ghost.

35 ◈ Against Worms
In the name of the Father, the Son, and the Holy Ghost. Amen.
Kaijda † Kaijda † densaria † panaria † gomson † efrison † abachasis †
gerobancon † sanctificatione † Job.
By the Father, I banish you!

36 ◈ Charms of Saint Apolline[36]

*The construction of the following charm represents a "classic" form. The first part, which is called a "little story" (*historiola*), recalls what happened to Saint Apolline and the reason she should be invoked. The magic words are simply names and epithets for God. This saint is still called upon in the present day, but the magic spell has vanished from the contemporary charms.[37] Alpha and Omega is a phrase taken from the Apocalypse of Saint John (21:6) and meaning "the beginning and the end," in other words, the Whole. We see this repeated with the Latin words at the end of the spell,* principium *and* finis.

The teeth were torn from the mouth of the virgin Saint Apolline because of her love for Christ. She obtained a promise from Our Lord the Christ that whoever bore her name on their person would suffer no toothache.

† alpha † omega † primus † et novissimus † principium et finis protect me from toothache, Thou who created all from the original nothingness.

37 ◈ Charm for the Teeth[38]

I, N, am suffering, and for the love of God request a medicine. As true that God suffered on the holy cross to redeem sinners from death and give them life, likewise heal this Christian of toothache, if God so please.

38 ◈ Saint Susanna's Charm[39]

During the Middle Ages, Saint Susanna, among other things, was the patron saint for people afflicted by smallpox, so it was normal for people to turn to her for healing them of this disease. Some charms explicitly state that Jesus healed her of this disease.[40] The number of references to the New Testament are noticeable.

Here is the charm that the angel Gabriel brought to Saint Susanna on behalf of Our Lord to heal Christians of worms, fistulas, pustules, abscesses, cankers, and all kinds of gout.

First chant a mass to the Holy Ghost in the morning in the patient's presence, then recite this charm for him!

In the name of the Father, the Son, and the Holy Ghost.
Amen.

As true as God is, so it is true that when he speaks, he
speaks well,

So is it true that when he acts, he does good,

So is it true that he became flesh from the holy maiden,

So is it true that he was put on the holy cross,

So is it true that he suffered five wounds to redeem all
sinners from death,

So is it true that he was stretched upon the holy cross,

So is it true that he was hung between two thieves,

So is it true that a spear pierced his right side,

So is it true that his head was crowned with thorns,

So is it true that nails were stuck into his hands and feet,

So is it true that he rested in his tomb,

So is it true that he resurrected from the dead on the third day,

So is it true that he went into Hell,

So is it true that he broke the doors of Hell,

So is it true that he bound the Evil One,

So is it true that the saints led,

So is it true that he ascended into Heaven,

So is it true that he sits at the right hand of his Father,

So is it true that the day of jubilation will come,

So is it true that every man will see him in flesh and
blood at the age of thirty,

So is it true that Our Lord will judge everyone as he
wishes,

So is it true that it is true and true it will be,

So is it true that God, Father, Son, and Holy Ghost,
true king who is simple, gentle, kind, humble, and
full of pity and mercy for this anguished saint for
whom you suffered on the Holy Cross, heal N. of
this illness.

Tell the patient to avoid eating any kind of meat. Recite this charm
in secret.

39 ◆ To Heal the Sick[41]

The prescriptions beginning here include a consecration of water so that it will become charged by a supernatural presence, then a rite of circumscription: by sprinkling the perimeter of the house, a frontier is established that forms an obstacle to illness-bearing demons. The whole is reinforced by an even more magical (and very old) procedure that works on corners. As we now know, corners were sacred and household spirits lived in them.[42]

Dilligam Domino invictus mea. If the patients are inside any kind of house, take a new pot and fill it with water, then read this psalm over it seven times, after which sprinkle that water while walking around the house including in the corners. Write these characters and bury them at the corners: the patients will be cured.

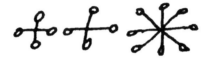

40 ◆ For Repelling Bad Moods[43]

Here is a good example of investing a fluid with magic power by means of characters. By diluting the magic signs, the oil incorporates their virtues.

Quare fremuerunt gentes. If a person is unable to rid himself of his bad humors, read this psalm three times up to *hodie genui te* over a good oil and coat the patient with it: he will heal. Write these characters on a clean, new tile and wash the characters with this oil, then coat your face with it and you will be warmly received by the princes.

41 ◆ AGAINST THE FALLING SICKNESS[44]

Epilepsy, which was known as the "falling sickness," "grand mal," or the "sacred disease," was particularly dreaded as it was initially viewed as a punishment sent by supernatural forces, and then by God, for a misdeed or sin. There are a huge number of prescriptions, which come in a wide variety. Here is a representative sample.

Write these letters on a copper ring and wear it on the index finger of your right hand; you will not fall. Take the ring and pour three drops of holy water through it onto the afflicted person. Here are the letters:

a. g. j. a. b. j. C. A. e. s. q. s. l'.

42 ◆ ANOTHER VERSION[45]

The names of the Three Kings (Matthew 2:1, 2, 9*) were used for all kinds of purposes because their bearers were magi.[46] Divine names like Messias, Sother, Emmanuel, Athanatos, Alpha, and Omega were sometimes added. They were used as an amulet. The most common expression is the one copied here that says: "Gaspard brought myrhh, Melchior incense, and Balthazar gold." It was used just like this by Pope John XXII (1276–1277).

Gaspar fert mirra, turris Melchior, Balthazar aurum.

Whoever carries these names on his person with piety shall never succumb to the falling sickness.

43 ◆ ANOTHER VERSION[47]

While the mass of the Holy Ghost is being performed, make seven candles from virgin wax, write Sunday on the first, Monday on the second, Tuesday on the third, Wednesday on the fourth, Thursday on the fifth, Friday on the sixth, and Saturday on the seventh, then light them so they burn until the end of the mass. Arrange for the patient

---

*Caspar or Jaspar means the "White"; Melchior, the "King of Light"; and Balthazar, the "Master of the Treasures."

to take one of these candles and whatever day is indicated, he shall on that day fast on bread and water until the end of his life, or his father and mother will fast for him until he is of an age to do it himself.

See to it that the patient is well washed and that he sees what has been written. He should drink water from the priest's third ablution during the mass. If he follows these instructions, he will be cured.

44 ◊ AGAINST THE SACRED DISEASE[48]
Here is another kind of amulet that is followed immediately by a remedy, although the author neglected to say when and how it should be taken. The names of Christ are not identifiable; they are clearly divided into two groups, the first marked by an alliteration in /t/ and separated from the second—whose alliteration is /s/—by the word Borcay, which must represent a high point. It has a certain rhythm.

† .v. † .e † .b † d. † z. S. gor † xg. † eu † xc

Write these characters on a virgin parchment and carry them on your person every day.

Write these names of Christ on the plant called Bitter Veronica:

Tinira. Tyri † Borcay. † Sicalos. † sirosio † salique † linarbas

45 ◊ AGAINST EPILEPSY[49]
ANANIZAPTA is an acrostic, which according to a sixteenth-century author means "May the antidote of the Nazarene (Jesus) prevail over death by poison! May the Trinity sanctify food and drink! Amen." Another reading has been suggested by someone claiming the words represented by their initials are Greek, which would give us: "May the bitterness of the Nazarene's death remove from us the verdict of eternal damnation, by the power of the Father, for a harsher persecution." The term is also regularly used as an amulet against the plague.[50]

† Ananizapta †

Speak this word in the patient's right ear while flexing the knees. There is no doubt that he will come to.

46 ◇ To Heal the Falling Sickness[51]

The two magic circles below are phylacteries to be carried on one's person. The first makes an appeal to the characters and to the names of God— Adonay, Sabaoth,* Tetragra Maton, Yschiros, on, alpha, and o(mega).[52] Two names are unknown: heunoya and Kadosh. The second circle is entirely in code and we do not have the means to decipher it.

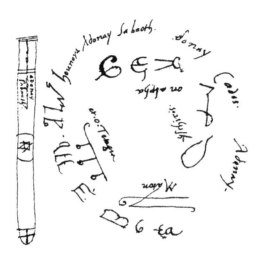

47 ◇ Against the Falling Sickness[53]†

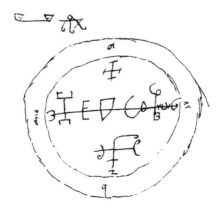

---

*Sabaoth (Hebrew): "of the armies"; epithet applied to Yahweh, the celestial armies being the stars.

†This figure must be drawn on the patient's body.

48 ◆ AGAINST FEVER[54]

Write these words* on a piece of barley bread for a man with a fever, and make him eat it.

VI captos. Saduces.

49 ◆ FOR FEVERS[55]

This magic spell comes from the same domain as ABRACADABRA[56] and is divided up into two series marked with the three stars of David or Solomon's pentacle. It should be kept in mind that "a Pentangle also, as with the vertue of the number five hath a very great command over evil spirits, so by its lineature, by which it hath within five obtuse angles, and without five acutes, five double triangles by which it is surrounded," says Henry Cornelius Agrippa (Occult Philosophy, II, 23).

Plenesmo. Abrocala ✡ Abra ✡ Abraca ✡ Abracalaps ✡ Abralaps ✡
    Abracalas ✡✡✡ Abracalaps ✡ Abrocalaps ✡ Abraca ✡ Abracala ✡
Abra. F.G.
    Naqui nostros castatunta mihi Jhesus Christus bris quod dedit bris quod tulitz bris quod Christus ursim in nomine Domini. May the Lord be with you, the forfeit 𝒰 𝒰 Father, Son, and Holy Ghost.
    He who carries this note on his person, fevers will flee from him, and if he is stricken, the fever will immediately go down.

50 ◆ AGAINST TRENCH FEVER[57]

Here is what became Abracadabra. In the following text, the expression appears as a variation with a quite perceptible regressive pattern,[58] This is no longer the case with the charm that follows it, in which the regression is interrupted and gives way to "Christian magic" with "saint" repeated three times in Latin, and once in Greek.

Write a short note and hang it from his neck:
    † aladabra † ladabra † adabra † dabra † abra † ra † a † abraca and add the person's name to it.

---

*The invocation is a blend of Latin and, undoubtedly, Catalan.

51 ◈ AGAINST FEVERS[59]

In the name of the Father, Son, and Holy Ghost. Amen.

† Abracha † abrac laus † agyos † sanctus † sanctus † sanctus strong
and immortal take pity on your servant N.

Say the Lord's Prayer and have these words taken to the patient.

52 ◈ ANOTHER VERSION[60]

*Here we have an alliterative phrase intended to be worn as an amulet.
Another manuscript offers:*[61] ire vre are wire Christus filanx artifex, *in
order to protect from trench fever, and a final one suggests:* † Christus
† rex † yre † artifex † ranx † yriorum. *The comparison of the writing
indicates that* xre *is the abbreviation of Christ,* arafax *is the deforma-
tion of* artifex *(artisan) and that* filiax *stands for* filius *(son), and* arex *is
something like* o rex *(O king).*[62] *For another use of this spell, see charm
no. 56.*

Carry this note on your person! In the name of the Father, the Son, and
the Holy Ghost. Amen.

† ire † arax † xre † rauex † filiax † arafax † N

53 ◈ ANOTHER VARIANT[63]

Write on a debt note the words below as indicated and tie the debt note
to the right hand of the patient, who should say three Our Fathers, the
Salutation of the Glorious Virgin, and the Credo with the most extreme
devotion. He should fast keeping his stomach empty for three days. On
the third day, remove the debt note and burn it, then cast its ashes into
running water.

††† hympnus † artus † arus † tremens † eloy † ventus † affricat †
angelus † nunciat † Christe † liberet † amen †††

54 ◈ AGAINST FEVERS[64]

In the name of the Father and the Son and the Holy Ghost. Amen. Saint
Peter was lying in front of the gate of Jerusalem. Jesus came and asked
him:

"What do you have Peter?" and Peter answered the Lord: "I am full of fever."

The Lord touched him and he was healed. Whoever writes down or carries on his person these words will not be feverish. † fiat † fiat † fiat

55 ◆ A Charm Against Fevers[65]

Here we come across the same notion we saw earlier in The Hygromancy of Solomon, *but here the spirits of the diseases are demons and they are seven in number. In the early Middle Ages, there were nine, fifteen, or forty-nine kinds of fever and it was only toward the year 1000 that tradition settled on seven as in the* Charm of the Three Angels.[66] *This type of charm is found in many different countries of the Medieval West, however the names of the sisters always vary and are sometimes encrypted.*[67]

I banish you, fevers, who are seven sisters! The first is named Elia, the second Sicilia, the third Vellea, the fourth Suffocalia, the fifth Commonia, the sixth Genia, and the seventh Eena. I banish you, fever, and you, vile visible and invisible spirits whatever your nature may be and from whatever land you hail! By the Father, the son, and so on!

56 ◆ Charm Against Trench Fever[68]

In the name of the Father, the Son, and the Holy Ghost. Amen.

† Ire arex † xre † rauex † filiax † arafax †

57 ◆ Another Charm[69]

The amulet described here contains divine names and most importantly the magic square (Sator-rotas), which is used in many different contexts. For a more detailed explanation, see charm no. 66.

Write:

Jhesu † eloy † eloy † elyon † adonay † sabaoth † messias † patior †
Wear this around your neck!

N. sicut anglero .v. ca in se ho . i . ni . v. sator tenet opera rotas
Christi

May he be delivered from fever with these words! Amen.

58 ◊ ANOTHER VERSION[70]

The use of eggs in magic is quite common. Here we have a spell for trans-
ferring the fever onto eggs by means of phrases reinforced by masses. At the
end of each phrase, an egg is burned so that the fever is gradually reduced.

Take four eggs and write the following on each of them starting with
the first. In the name of the Father, the Son, and the Holy Ghost.
Amen.

Bassor † masson † agar † quem † ysa res † hytq † Ad matanor †
groner † hosa

In the name of the Father, the Son, and the Holy Ghost. Amen.
Next, have four Masses said and burn each egg.

59 ◊ AGAINST HEMORRHAGE[71]

It is rare to run across any expression of reservations or doubt by the users
of magic prescriptions. The verification offered here is well attested in sev-
eral manuscripts (see the illustration below and charm no. 257).[72]

P . x . b . prag . cp . ex . I . min . y . 3 . rd . y . N

Write out these characters and attach them to the neck or place
them on the chest. If you do not believe in their power, carve them on
the hilt of a knife and stab a pig with it: the animal will not bleed.

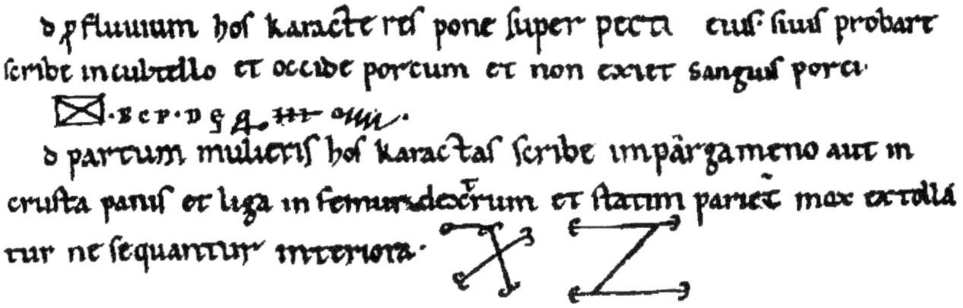

60 ◆ Against Eye Problems

Here is a phylactery from the Sachet accoucheur. *The Latin inscription reads "Wear this image on your person against the ills befalling the eyes," and its defensive power is contained in the central figure.*

61 ◆ Against the Falling Gout[73]

† Appacion †† Apria † Appremont et qua settanua †
Hang this short passage around your neck!

62 ◆ Against Canker Sores[74]

This conjuration targeting canker sores seeks to leave no stone unturned: by listing all the different kinds of cankers, the spell is guaranteed to be effective against them (see also charm no. 71). Furthermore, the agents of power are mobilized by invoking the planetary bodies and other elements such as Masses, steeples, and God and his saints. The evocation of the River Jordan is out of place in this charm because it normally comes into play to stop bleeding.[75] Its presence is justified, however, if we consider the fact that a purulent canker sore is envisioned here.

Canker, I banish you, whatever kind you may be, so that you may leave this Christian, and depart from his marrow, his bones, his blood, and his flesh!

Leave, brown canker! Leave red canker, bright canker, damp canker, burning canker! Canker, I conjure you by the sun and the River Jordan! I conjure you by the wind that blows, the mass that is sung, the steeples that ring, and by all the saints God has in his heavenly kingdom and upon the earth, so that you may depart from this Christian and no longer afflict him anymore in his marrow, or in his flesh, or in his blood. Don't stay any longer! When God sets his right foot into the Jordan, the water draws away from his sacred flesh and his holy blood. May the canker do the same, and resist no more in the marrow, or in the flesh, or in the blood, or in the bones! In the name of the Father, the Son, and the Holy Ghost. Amen.

63 ◈ For a Birth[76]

K . m . g . c . t . o . a . q . p . p . q . j

Read these letters over the right side of the woman in labor and she will give birth without pain.

64 ◈ Against Sterility in Women[77]

Exultate iuxti in Domino. If a woman is barren, write this psalm with these characters, fumigate them with incense, attach them to her right arm, and when she sleeps with her husband she will conceive.

65 ◈ For a Speedy Birth[78]

Celi enarant gloriam Dei. If a woman is in labor and unable to give birth, write this psalm up to *exultabit ut gigas ad currendam viam* on a new, square pot, shake it briskly three times, then place it beneath her right foot: she will give birth immediately.

Also write this psalm on a glass blade with these characters, fumigate them with aloe wood, wash them with dew, and make her drink it; also read this psalm over oil and anoint her belly with it.

66 ◈ Place This Figure on a Woman in Labor and She Will Give Birth[79]

The following amulet is interesting because it contains, in its second part, the famous magic square whose existence was first vouched for in 70 CE It was found in a Christian church at Pompei.[80] It is believed to be based on the four letters of the Paternoster [Lord's Prayer] to which an A and an O have been added. The words should be written in a column forming a square that can be read from top to bottom, from bottom to top, from right to left, and from left to right. It will be noted that the letters TENET form a cross occupying the center of the square.

This formula has inspired a myriad of interpretations, none of which seem truly convincing, for example: "The laborer Srepo carefully guides his plow," or even: "The worker holds the wheels, the sower the plow," and many other similar translations that ignore the context in which this spell is used. No one until now has realized that this magic square is nothing more nor less than the name of God. To demonstrate this, one need only substitute the letters with the numbers corresponding to their position in the alphabet, and then add the two figures that result:

S	A	T	O	R		19	1	20	15	18	= 73	7+3= 10
A	R	E	P	O		1	18	5	16	15	= 55	5+5 = 10
T	E	N	E	T		20	5	14	5	20	= 64	6+4 = 10
O	P	E	R	A		15	16	5	18	1	= 55	5+5 = 10
R	O	T	A	S		18	15	20	1	19	= 73	7+3 = 10
					=	73	55	64	55	73		

In every direction, the sum of the two resulting numbers is 10. The zero does not count, like today when proof is shown by none, that is to say the One, the Unique God. In addition, the fact that TENET forms a cross in the center of the square should dispel any lingering doubts about the basis of the square.

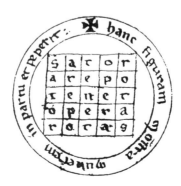

67 ◇ FOR A WOMAN IN LABOR[81]

The following document includes a sequence of phrases that we have seen used for other situations. There is first the key phrase of the charm of Saint Elizabeth; then the magic square explicated above; then the reminder of Christ's omnipotence, with the story of Lazarus who he summoned back from the grave (John 11:43) which has been placed in tandem with the child to be born. Lastly there are the secret names of God (Agla, etc.) reinforcing the incantation. The genealogical reminders of famous people whose births were problem-free anchors the present act of giving birth within a protective framework: since it went this way for the individuals cited, it will go the same for the woman upon whom this short passage is placed. The John referred to is John the Baptist (cf. Luke 1:24). The set of formulations (blrurcion, etc.) just before the end of the charm remains indecipherable. By recalling a series of quasi-mythic birth episodes, the charm places the present situation within a context that will be beneficial: all went well in that earlier mythic time, it will do the same here and now. The closing phrase opens with the triumphant title of Christ (Jesus of Nazareth, King of the Jews), who is quite often simply referred to as INRI.

Attach this brief text around the waist:

† in † name † of the Father † and of the Son † and of the Holy Ghost † amen, and by the virtue of God, may they offer me remedy!

Holy † Mary † birthed † the Christ † Saint † Anne † birthed † Mary † Saint † Elizabeth † birthed † John † Saint † Cecile † birthed † Remy †

sator † arepo † tenet † opera † rotas †

Christ † vanquishes † Christ † reigns † Christ † commands † Christ † calls you † to the world † rejoices in you † the law † desires † you † Christ † spoke † to Lazarus † come out † God of vengeance † lord † vengeful god † free your servant N † the right hand of the lord makes virtue.

† a † g † l † a † alpha † and o †

Anne † birthed † Mary † Elizabeth † the precursor † Mary † the Lord † our † Jesus † Christ † without pain or affliction. O child, come out living or dead, come out because Christ calls you to the light.

† agios † agios † agios †

Christ † vanquishes † Christ † reigns † Christ † commands † sanctus † sanctus † sanctus † lord † god † allmighty † you who are and will be † and who has come. Amen.

Blrurcion † blrutun † blutanno † bluttiono †

Jhesus † nazarenus † rex † judeorum † fili † dei † miserere † mei † etc.

68 ◇ For a Pregnant Woman[82]

Dixit iniustus. If a woman is pregnant, write this psalm upon the hood of her garment, attach it to her right arm, and the fruit of her belly will be preserved until its birth.

69 ◇ Against False Labor[83]

Expectans expectavi Dominum. If a woman rejects her fruit, write this psalm with these characters and attach it to her right arm: she shall keep her child.

70 ◇ To Keep One's Child[84]

As in charm no. 59, a verification is suggested and a parallel established between a fruit tree and a woman, which is interesting because there is a belief according to which the souls of children waiting to be born can be found in trees.

If a woman is unable to keep her child to term, write this psalm: *Beatus vir qui non abiit,* up to: *folium eius non defluet,* on a virgin parchment or phylactery with these characters, cense it with mastic, attach it to her right arm, and she shall not reject her child. As an experiment, do this on a tree that aborts its fruits. Write the characters below *[top of page 91]* on a new tile with a new iron stylus, then place it on the roots of the tree.

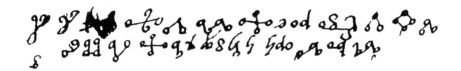

71 ◆ AGAINST THE BITES OF SERPENTS
AND ALL VENOMOUS BEASTS[85]

Ask for clear water and say over it three times: In the name of the Father, the Son, and the Holy Ghost. Amen. Then three Our Fathers in the name of the Father, the Son, and the Holy Ghost. Then say these names:

Poro poro poro pota zaba zaro zarai

By the paraclete Mariai. In the name of the Father, the Son, and the Holy Ghost. Amen. Give [the water] to the one who bears this message, be he man or beast, he shall be cured. This is a proven fact.

72 ◆ AGAINST HORSE WORMS[86]

Gentle Job was sitting upon a dunghill. He called the holy Christ: "Lord, the worms are biting me fiercely." "Job, I shall bring you succor. Since you have told me that the worms are white, black, red, or yellow, or however they are made, here now they have all been slain. I command it by the holy death of Jesus Christ! May the worms die, those which are in this white, black, or red horse!"

73 ◆ TO HEAL A HORSE THAT IS OUT OF STEP[87]

The cure is carried out here by creating a parallel with an ancient, paradigmatic situation, but it is hard to see any real connection between a horse whose back hoof bangs into that of the front leg when it trots and the spilling of Christ's blood. The Lord's side pierced by a spear smacks of the Charm of Longinus,[88] the name given in the Acts of Paul[89] (an apocryphal scripture) to the anonymous soldier in the Gospel of John (19:34) who verified whether Christ was truly dead this way.[90]

Three Fridays in a row before dawn, go to the stable when the horse is resting on its bedding. Place your right hand on its buttocks and say:

"Jesus Christ was wounded on the right side, from which spilled the sacred water and the sacred blood. Horse, whether you are white, gray, or black, this shall heal you. In the name of God. Amen."

74 ◇ For a Horse Sprain[91]

The spell below has a long tradition, but was gradually altered over time. In the seventeenth century, one said, "Ante, patante, suparante in nomine Patris," and so forth; in the twentieth century, "Ante, superante superante te."[92]

Write this on a piece of parchment and hang it on the foot. It will get better.

† zinupt † anta † peranta † anta †

75 ◇ For a Horse with a Nail in Its Hoof[93]

According to the Gospel of John (19:38–42), Nicodemus helped Joseph of Arimathea take Christ down from the cross.[94] Because he was the one who removed the nails from Our Lord, he is called upon every time a man or animal is hurt by a nail. His story provides the referential situation.

Pull the nail out while saying the following words:

Nicodemus pulled the nails from the hands and feet of Our Lord Jesus Christ. Because these words are true, may this iron come free of his flesh, his foot, or his bone. In the name of the Father, the Son, and the Holy Ghost. Amen.

76 ◇ Against the Bite of a Rabid Dog[95]

This should be written on bread that will be given to the patient and animals bitten by a rabid dog to eat.

† erpa † agalerpa † erpa † galerpa † diptoni † bristoni † bersis † rami †

77 ◇ Against Fevers

The amulet at the top of page 93 bears the following inscription: "Carry this image on your person against fevers, whatever kind they may be." In the four branches of the cross, we can recognize one of the secret names of God, AGLA, which supplies him all his power.

78 ◈ Against Lightning

This is one of the talismanic designs from the Sachet accoucheur. *The inscription recommends it be carried on one's person as protection against the lightning that strikes and consumes.*

79 ◈ Against a Violent Death

The inscription of this circle indicates what this design is good for: "Whatever the day on which you see this image, you shall not have your throat slit."

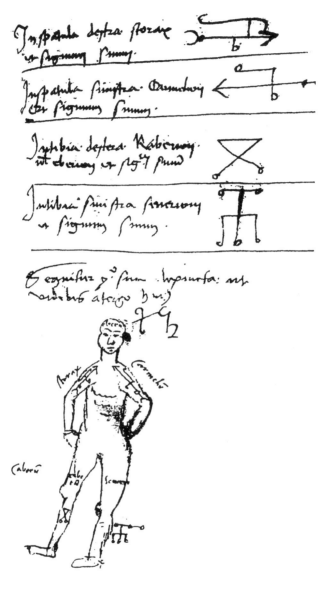

The use of figurines, called "voults," or of images in evil spells or healing magic was very widespread and still exists in Europe as as in other parts of the world. In the above illustration we can see that the ailments are treated by means of an image. The word storax has been written over the right shoulder with its corresponding occult sign; another name, which I have been unable to decipher, is written over the left shoulder; and something similar was done over both legs.

5

REMEDIES TAKEN FROM THE HUMAN BODY[1]

Magic and sorcery have always relied upon a vast array of ingredients. For example, witches were rumored to use the fat of small children to make their ointments, and it was also said that they went to cemeteries to procure what they needed. The iconography often depicts them seated in front of a cauldron from which ominous vapors are rising. But white magic also makes use of elements from the human body in remedies. The *Picatrix* (thirteenth century), the most complete manual of magic in the Middle Ages, has bequeathed us a long list of everything that can be taken from the body. Here is the main section.

80 ◈ THE MANY USES OF BODY PARTS

There are many other marvels performed by virtue of the human body. I say that the brain of man helps those who are losing their memory if they eat it.

Reduced to ash and drunk with syrup of spring squill for a period of nine days, the skull will heal epileptics.

No evil eye or pernicious tongue can harm someone who carries on his person a human eye joined to that of a wolf.

Burned, crushed, and blended with laudanum, hair will heat the brain.

The saliva of a fasting man heals itching if the affected areas are moistened with it often.

The tongue of a woman helps those who wish to perform tricks and cast spells.

If someone wishes to steal or carry something away, he should carry on his person the tongue of a man and the tongue of a kite.

Earwax blended with opium causes long sleep.

Drinking the fluid from the head of a man that has been mixed with brain heals the insane.

The nails of the hand and feet cut with a red copper knife, when the Moon rises with Jupiter, and burned when it joins with the Sun; give this powder to drink to someone whom you wish to love you, or cast it over his or her clothing.

To prevent early leprosy or scabies, a kind of leprosy, from developing, give the patient the powdered foreskin of a burnt man to swallow, and it will not spread.

Male urine will burn all spots on which it is placed. If someone has scabies, he should wash himself with it and he will be healed immediately.

Human excrement dried in the sun, crushed and thrown on gold mixed with iron, will attack the iron and purify the gold.

Those who suffer from acute fever shall be healed if they wash themselves with the fluid of human blood.

Make a purse of a man's heart, fill it with the blood of three other men, and burn it while summoning demons: they will respond.

Menstrual blood administered to someone causes leprosy and someone who has it on his person while bathing shall soon die.

Dried human testicles that have been pulverized and eaten with incense, mastic, cinnamon, and clove will rejuvenate the man and give him good color, it is true.

The umbilical cord wrapped in red silk cloth with the tongue of a fig tree frog will bestow honor on its bearer from his lord and other people.

Take the entire head of a man who has recently died, place it in a large pot with eight drams of fresh poppy, human blood, and sesame oil until it is entirely covered. Seal the pot as tightly as you can with clay and place it on a gentle charcoal fire and leave it there for a full twenty-four hours. Next, remove it from the fire and let it cool; cover your face and filter the whole thing. This resembles a liquid oil that you will set aside. It is said that this oil contains marvelous virtues: if you light a lamp with it, or smear it on something, or give it to someone to eat, you shall see whatever you wish.

Sil y a supçon quil y ait quelque charmeur ou —
noueur d'eguillette en l'assemblée. Les espoux et l'espouse
estans a la porte de l'eglise auant que les mariez le
curé dira.

Combien que de droict tous sorciers et sorcieres, charmeurs
et charmeresses soient excommuniez de l'auctorité de monseigneur
M. nostre euesque et pasteur: nous denonçons pour certain
à faict ceux ou celles qui par charme ou noud d'eguillette
ou aultrement pretendent empescher par consommation de
mariage entre les deux personnes qui sont icy presentes
et leur enioignons de partir de ceste compaignie leur —
deffendans l'assistance a la solemnité du mariage qui se fera
en l'eglise et les enioins en la puissance de Dieu, pour
estre puniz en leur corps affin que pour penitence et
amendement de dix liures ... fois payé en toute ...
pour seigneurs. Apres cela le curé fera dire a l'espoux et
à l'espouse les motz qui s'ensuiuent.

Abrenuntio tibi satana et coniungor tibi xpe.: et les fera
signer au front du signe de la croix disans: In nomine
patris et filij et spiritussancti amen.

Oraison ...

Dulcissime Deus ... omnium et fons ...
postulatas ... mille ... angelum
...rum, Thobia ... (N)
... N custodiat ab omnibus ...
... infestationibus. Et sicut ...
... Thobiam ...
... Domine ... sanctissimi
... Cyprian ... omnium ...
... in famulum tuum (N) et ...
... ... Domine ...

6

LOVE MAGIC

One of the most prominent areas of medieval magic concerns feelings, especially those of love. The romances from this time provide only a vague picture of this magic, and fairies, witches, and other enchantresses are female physicians: they craft potions, the most famous of these being the one drunk by Tristan and Isolde that sealed their fate. There are numerous recipes for love magic in the grimoires that rely on magical signs, sometimes written with one's own blood (charm no. 85) or that of an animal (charm no. 92); sometimes by burning the cloth on which they were written (charm no. 87), as the combustion allegedly inflamed the targeted individual with love; sometimes by calling upon astral magic (charm no. 87); sometimes by relying on talismans that one carries personally or places in the targeted individual's house. Of course, one can always turn to spells that are even more powerful because they are unintelligible— and if one wishes to do such work in good conscience, one uses psalms!

81 ◈ For Love[1]

Dominj est terra et plenitudo eius. Write this psalm with musk, saffron, and rosewater, until *introibit rex glorie;* add these characters and carry it all with you.

82 ◆ Four Love Charms[2]*

Write these letters on an apple with a stylus or a new quill, in a way that they cannot be seen, then give the apple to whoever you desire to eat.

83 ◆

Write these characters and carry them on your right arm. You will be beloved by men and women.

84 ◆

Draw these characters on a piece of virgin parchment and carry them on your person.

85 ◆

On the first waxing moon, on the day of Venus, and while facing to the east with a piece of virgin parchment that you have prepared, prick your ring finger on the right hand and write with your blood the signs below together with the name of the one you love [and] with that of her mother. You shall conceal the parchment without her knowing.

---

*The last charm is in medieval Italian.

86 ◆ FOR LOVE

Write on a piece of paper the characters for the planets Jupiter, Venus, and the Dragon's Tail, with their seals and the name of the person whose love you desire. Place it in front of a virgin wax candle on the day and the hour of Venus with the moon waxing in the sign of Sagittarius. Light the candle before going to bed while naming the two planets mentioned above and the sign of the zodiac.

87 ◆ ANOTHER CHARM[3]

If you want a beloved person to come to you, draw the following design on a piece of new linen on the day and hour of Venus, when the second decan of Taurus is rising and Venus is there. Burn the end of the cloth while naming the individual; he or she will come running!

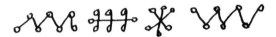

88 ◆ TO BE ESTEEMED[4]

If you wish the esteem of someone, write these characters on a piece of virgin parchment with his or her name and carry it on your person every day.

Oggo † et B.l.o.p.n. GG † è X̲.n.G.t.o.l. †

89 ◆ TO BE BELOVED[5]

If you want to be loved by all, write these characters* on a piece of virgin parchment and carry it on your person, every day and everywhere.

z. b. a. c. i. d. n. † X † ro: ooooo—oooo—ooooo—

---

*The three final signs after the colon represent an asterisk in the manuscripts of the Middle Ages.

90 ◆ So Your Enemy Will Love You

If you want your enemy to love you greatly and hold you in high honor, write these characters with his name on a virgin parchment and carry them on your person everywhere.

yh. D. h⁹. d. N. z. i. U. ton. B. h. a. b. x. n. o. †

91 ◆ To Obtain the Love of a Woman[6]

Take gazelle marrow and mutton dung, two drams of each, blend them together, and add camphor and the brain of a hare to them, two drams of each. Place it all in an iron vessel that you will place over the fire until all its contents have liquefied. Add crushed camphor to it. When everything is well mixed together, remove it from the fire. Then make an image from new wax, that is, wax that has never been used, while thinking of the one you desire.

Make a hole in the mouth of this image down to the belly and pour in the above-mentioned liquid remedy while saying: *Dahyeliz, Hanimidiz, Naffayz, Dabraylez.* Next, place two drams of white sugar in its mouth. Take a silver needle, stick it in the chest of the image until it reemerges beneath the shoulder blade. And when you stick the needle in, say: *Hedurez, Tameruz, Hetaytoz, Femurez.*

Once this has been done, wrap the image in a white cloth, and place over it another silk cloth that is white in color, which you shall attach with a silk thread. Tightly clasp all this to your own chest, and attach two hairs to it in which you shall make seven knots. And you will say these words over each of them: *Hayranuz, Hedefiuz, Faytamurez, Arminez.*

Next, place the image inside a small earthen vase that you shall seal up with emery. Make a hole in the house where this woman lives or where she spends her time, bury the image inside it with its head up, and seal the hole back up. Then take incense and galbanum, two drams of each, and cast them into the fire. While the smoke is rising from it, you will say, "*Beheymerez, Aumaliz, Menemeyduz, Caynaurez,* turn the mind of this woman, N, and her desire toward this man! By the power of the above-named spirits and by the power and the force of the spirits *Beheydraz, Metlurez, Auleyuz, Nanitaynuz!*"

Once this is done, return home. Know, indeed, that all the spirits will turn the thoughts and desires of the woman, for whom this operation has been carried out, toward this man for whom it has been performed. She shall not be able to rest, nor sleep, nor do anything whatsoever until she obeys the man for whom this has been done. And this woman shall be guided to the home of the buried image by the above-named forces.

92 ◆ To Bring a Husband's Heart Back to His Wife[7]

Exaudi Deu deprecationem. If you wish the heart of a man to return to his wife, write this psalm and these characters with the blood of a white rooster and bind them to the woman's arm. He will come back to her.

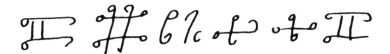

93 ◆ For Love and Friendship[8]

Leyequin, Leyelgane, Leyequir, Leyequerich, Leyeric, Leyerus, Leyexeris.

Write these names on a sleeve, which you shall then burn. Once it has been consumed, read the above names and they will inspire love and friendship.

94 ◆ If You Want a Young Woman to Love You[9]

Take an apple and write these words on it: griel statuel elael, and give the apple to her to eat.

95 ◆ To Make a Woman Lift Her Skirts[10]

On a piece of virgin parchment, write these names
　　　† labon † dolon † acus Lucifer † lucis † luctans
beneath the light of the door, and when crossing through it, she will lift her skirts.

96 ◆ To Have a Dear Girlfriend[11]

Speak these three words into her ear:

> Sancitan Sanamiel samafoelis.

97 ◆ For Love[12]

You will make two images, one of silver and the other of tin, on which you will carve these seven names of love:

> Amonacilyn melchacihym taanalin farteilin horaitilin
> afraicilin bodracilin

Then you will attach the images together and bury them in the house where these two people live; they will love each other for eternity.

98 ◆ Magic Pentacle for Love[13]

This kind of pentacle was carried on the person or hidden in the home of the desired individual, beneath his or her pillow, for example. The outer circle

Magic Circle for Love

*includes the names of God (*Eloy, pater*); around the star of David, we have the names of angels or demons (*Afreyneil, Barnael, *and so on); and around the branches of the star, an invocation is sketched out.*

We can compare the preceding example with the following extract from The Key of Solomon, *taken from a sixteenth-century Latin manuscript.*[14]

O Adonai, God most just and most high, you who have created all things in your leniency and righteousness, for it fills you, grant us to be deemed worthy so that this operation be consecrated and perfect in order; the light spilling from your most sacred Throne, O Adonai, thanks to which we may obtain favor and love. Amen.

Once that has been said, you should place [this prayer] in a clean piece of silk and bury it for one day and night at the crossing of four roads: each time you wish to obtain grace or favor, take it after consecrating it as necessary in accordance with the rules, place it in your right hand, and nothing you seek to obtain shall be refused to you. But if you do not act with care and accuracy, verily you shall not succeed in any way.

To obtain favor and love, write the following words:

Sator Arepo Tenet Opera Rotas Iah Iah Iah Enam Iah Iah Iah Kehter Chokmah Binah Gedulah Geburah Tiphereth Netzach Hod Yesod Malkuth Abraham Isaac Jacob Shadrach Meshach Abdenago, all be there to help me and obtain for me all that I desire.

Once these words are written as they should be, your desire will be realized.

An Old English charm employing magic words and characters, and requesting assistance from the apostles Matthew, Mark, and Luke. Tenth-century manuscript (Royal 12 D. XVII, folio 51).

7

THE PROTECTION OF HUMANS, LIVESTOCK, AND PROPERTY

Beliefs that related to time and the passage of time were quite prevalent in the Middle Ages. The Church classified these beliefs as superstitions, designating them as a whole by the phrase *observation temporum.* In the medieval worldview, everything was pregnant with meaning and it was necessary to pay close attention to signs. The two rules below permit the individual to know if the day that is dawning will be a propitious one or not. The dangerous or harmful days are referred to as "Egyptiacal." The first text offers a calculation method with two different memorization procedures; the second text valiantly lists the good and evil days of each month of the year.

99 ◈ THE CURSED DAYS[1]

> *Augurior decies, audito lumine clangor*
> *Liquit olens abies, coluit colus, excute gallum*

Remember this distich well! Each word corresponds to a month. The initial letter of the first syllable of each designates, by its place in the alphabet, the first harmful or Egyptiacal day of the month, but the first of the month should be set aside. The initial letter of the second syllable designates the second harmful day, but we must count starting from the last day of the month. The following table indicates those days upon which nothing, neither a task nor a journey, should be undertaken.

January	1	25	July	13	22
February	4	26	August	1	30
March	1	28	September	3	21
April	10	20	October	2	22
May	3	25	November	3	28
June	10	16	December	7	21

You can also use the following counting rhyme:

Jani I dies et XXVfine minatur
Februari IV dies et XXVI fine minatur, and so forth.

100 ◇ Auspicious and Harmful Days[2]

Here are the harmful days by reason of the evils and great perils that men must suffer. If someone must undertake an action, for example get married, consolidate a friendship, go off to war, build a house, or some other major work useful to man or other things similar to the things cited, and so forth. Here they are for each month:

For the month of January, these days are harmful: 2, 4, 6, 11, 15
For the month of February, these days are harmful: 16, 17, 19
For the month of March, these days are harmful: 14, 15, 16, 17
For the month of April, these days are harmful: 1, 6, 13
For the month of May, these days are harmful: 7, 14
For the month of June, these days are harmful: 11
For the month of July, these days are harmful: 12, 20
For the month of August, these days are harmful: 15, 16
For the month of September, these days are harmful: 1, 14, 15

For the month of October, these days are harmful: 1

For the month of November, these days are harmful: 16, 17

For the month of December, these days are harmful: 10

Here are the auspicious days:

During the month of January, 1, from the 2nd hour; 12, at the end
of the 11th hour

During the month of February, 4, from the 8th hour; 12, at the end
of the 10th hour

During the month of March, 1, from the 1st hour; 4 at the end of
the 2nd hour

During the month of April, 10, from the 1st hour; 11, at the end of
the [?] hour

During the month of May, 3, from the 6th hour; 7, at the end of
the 10th hour

During the month of June, 10, from the 6th hour; 16, at the end of
the 4th hour

During the month of July, 13, from the 11th hour; 11, at the end of
the 11th hour

During the month of August, 1, from the 1st hour; 2, at the end of
the 7th hour

During the month of September, 3, from the 7th hour; 8, at the end
of the 4th hour

During the month of October, 3, from the 5th hour; 10, at the end
of the 9th hour

During the month of November, 5, from the 8th hour; 2, at the end
of the 5th hour

During the month of December, 6, from the 7th hour; 10, at the
end of the 6th hour

Let us give thanks to God!

101 ◈ A VERY GOOD PHYLACTERY[3]

*Here is an amulet whose power essentially rests on names and adjectives taken
from the Holy Scriptures. First comes a series of divine names (from* Agios,
"saint," to o theos, *"O God"), followed by metaphors designating Christ*

(fountain, implying "of life," wisdom, force, Paraclete,[4] etc.), interrupted by fragments of phrases such as "I am that I am," taken from Exodus (3:14); compare charms no. 1–4. Following altabevare *at the end, the text becomes so garbled that it is unintelligible. The polyfunctionality of this phylactery, which promises its bearer escape from the most widespread dangers, is noteworthy.*

He who bears on his person the names of God the Father, the Son, and the Holy Ghost, with true and worthy faith, shall fear neither fire, nor water, nor war, nor court, nor prison; he shall not die by weapons, nor poison, nor by thunder or lightning, nor by storm, nor sudden death, nor by any other thing. And if a pregnant woman bears it, she shall not die in giving birth.

† Agios † Sator † Helyas † Hemanuel † orc adonay athanatos † otheos † Pentalon † fons † sapientia † virtus † paraclitus † sancto ego sum asum mediator † kyrieley † son † hension salvator † alpha et o principio genitus † principatione † rex † laus † potestas † glo † spem sine aticius † ejus vitulus † serpens † leo † vermis † ymago † gloria † sol † redemptor † et in nomine Christophori † altabevere † senetaras † iscretionis † bis sanctavita numiginem sancti bro † cadonis † digtoun † treba †virgo † adun hero

102 ◇ *The Brief of Pope Leo*[5]

The Brief of Pope Leo is a legend in its own right. The preamble is a fabrication, but the Brief *has nevertheless enjoyed huge and widespread popularity in various forms. It has been confused with the Charm of Saint Colomban, which itself was lumped in with that of Saint Coloman. The* Brief *consists of three parts: the first provides Leo's spell, which has yet to be deciphered; the second (*Christus vincit*) expresses the power of Christ presented by three verbs: "vanquish, rule, command" which makes him the* Pantokrator *(the Omnipotent); and the third is a new request for protection in the form of an orison that ends with an urgent petition that reflects the fear of a sudden death (a death that one has not had time to prepare for, and which is therefore an evil death that poses a risk of sending you to hell).*

Leo, Pope of the Romans, wrote and gave this to King Charlemagne. Whoever who bears these letters on his person and preserves them best shall fear neither enemies, nor sword, nor any potion, nor serpent, nor any [illegible].

† H. G. D. A. QQ. S. P. P. S. S. 9. F. G. A. S. s. N. Ł. H. t. X. ⏃ .
l a. a. O. V. ad P. p p p †

So that you shall fear no enemy, nor judge, nor evil spell, nor philter, nor potion, nor word, nor demon, nor plague.

Saint Colomban has drawn these characters and gave them to the king who was preparing to wage war:

Christus vincit, Christus regnat, Christus imperat. Amen

Father, aid me when I rise in the morning, when I move about during the day, and when I eat, and when I sleep. God almighty, by your grace and mercy, and by the merits of all the saints and their intercessions, forgive me my sins and give me time to pay true penance in this life and to be happy to serve you. Amen.

Extract from one of the briefs of Pope Leo, from the Sachet accoucheur.

103 ◇ ANOTHER BRIEF OF POPE LEO[6]

This other version of the Brief *contains two spells that are much more pagan, and the vestiges of the combination of different elements are quite evident: we have the* Himmelsbrief *(Heavenly Letter) brought by an angel to Pope Leo III, elected pope in 795, or to Saint Gregory (the text makes this unclear), and the one given directly to Charlemagne. Note that the* Enchiridion *of Pope Leo, printed in Rome in 1848, also opens with a dedication to Charlemagne.*

In the first spell, Sotha *must represent Sother, and* sebeth, *Saboath, both of which are names of God, as are* Adonay, prinseps *(prince), and* Emmanuel. Petrulol *could be the diminutive form of Petrus (Peter). In the second spell, the five words at the end are extremely distorted divine names:* Sother, Theos, *perhaps* Christum, Theos, *and* On.

The Lord Leo, Pope of the Romans, sent it to Charlemagne, emperor of the Franks. The angel of the Lord indicated to Saint Gregory that all good Christians should carry it (on their person) to persevere in good works so that they may be saved. Amen. In the name of the Father and the Son and the Holt Ghost. Amen.

† Petrulol la Sabina. Sotha. Adonay. Tereta ala demmanos prinseps. Emanuel. Ratam yden hoy may hanay linay ar y. Saday ased. Anila sebeth denua.

Whoever carries these characters upon him shall remain in life. Indeed, the angel of the Lord brought them to King Charlemagne, who was preparing to go off to war. You shall fear no enemy, nor evil spell, nor deadly herbal potion, nor demon, nor serpent, nor plague.

Hoscaraa Rabri milas filio. Anabonac. Baracha. Baracha abeba asar mesonor florem bethel behon. Sethen. Theon. Yham. Tehos † an.

God almighty, spare your servant.

104 ◇ AGAINST PERILS AND EVILS[7]

The following passage, taken from the Livre des Secrez de nature, *which was inspired by the* Kyranides, *is based on alphabetical magic. In the text of the* Kyranides, *the stone is called* aetitis, *"eagle stone," the bird* Aquila *and the plant* ampelos lifki, *all the names begin with the letter A, which reforges a chain of sympathy and increased the power of the ring considerably. All that is missing is the* anguille *[eel], cited in the* Kyranides, *for the chain to be complete.*

Take the aquillianus stone,* carve an eagle on top with over his claw a bryony seed harvested under the rising sun when it is in Gemini, add a bit of an eagle's wing and place all inside a ring that you will wear. It will protect you from every peril and every evil. And if you are in a dispute or in council, all shall respect you and hold you in honor.

105 ◇ AN EXCELLENT AMULET[8]

Any Christian who carries these characters on his person with devotion, fidelity, and purity, will fear no adversary, nor evil spell, nor deadly potion, nor plague, nor enemy, with the help of God.

N. X. K. Y. C. Θ. E. B. Q. T. _. Θ. M. N. Y. 𝕎 . C. X. TT. Et. Y. A. Y. _. X. G. Y. N. N. Θ. G. R. Q. L. C. I. א . R. Θ. S. X. H Q AL ℧ Christ Jesus. Filii Gibini savior of the world, save me, your servant N. Amen.

F. X. S. R. P. O. KT. K. Χ. S. s. S. t. P. M. K. C. K. CK. C. t. B. t. R. B. I. M. K. S. C. R. R. H. K. m. P. V. ti . TI. e. n. e. k. C. Q. N. R. t. R. N. ω NN. ND. Q. V. e. C. Y. N. P. M. Q. N. N. f. Q. A. ☦. K. .A. E. φ. E. P. O. N. O. N. t. A. N. V. M. A. E. B. a . a . o . a .v . T. XA. V. e. P. C. O. Sed. De. Deign to free me from the POWER of the Prince of darkNESS and do not permit me against him V. C. O. [ ] E. P. a. e. X. e. p. R. [ ]. P. [ ] you who live and reign in the centuries of centuries. Amen.

106 ◇ AN EXCELLENT PHYLACTERY[9]

This phylactery is based on biblical allusions and brings about the intervention of an angel—Michael, the leader of the heavenly hosts—and the archangels Gabriel (literally "the man of God," who is also the spirit of the Moon and presides over the first hour of Monday), Raphael ("God has healed," cited five times in the Book of Tobias [Tobit]), and Uriel ("Light of God," named in Book of Ezra [2 Esdras], which is not part of the canon,

---

*In other words, an aethite.

and rules over the first hour of Wednesday). Barchiel is perhaps identical to Bachiel, the angel of Sunday invoked in the East; Tubiel and Tobiel should be the same figure, who is part of Jewish angelology.[10] *The principal activities of the day are passed in review and the supernatural figures are there to protect the bearer of the phylactery in specific circumstances.*

In the beginning Christ's divinity was combined with bounty. Those who carry this brief on their person shall have nothing to fear from fire, water, and poison, and if a pregnant woman carries it, she shall not die when giving birth.

By my name they drive off demons, they shall speak new languages, they will grasp snakes, and if someone drinks any kind of mortal poison, he shall suffer no harm. They will place their hands on the sick and those individuals shall be cured † I believe in God the Father almighty † in the name of the Father † the Son † and the Holy Ghost † Amen.

Turn your thoughts toward Michael when you wash your hands and when you leave your bed during the day. Turn them toward Gabriel when you are seated, and nothing shall harm you. Turn them toward Raphael when you receive bread and drink and you shall have all things in plenty. Turn them toward Uriel against your enemies and when you see their threats while on the road, nothing shall terrify you. Turn them toward Barchiel when you are in a trial or litigation, and all shall smile upon you. Turn them toward Tubiel and Barchiel when you come before lords or princes, and all shall go well. Turn them toward Uriel and Tobiel when you are in a boat and you shall travel without peril.

107 ◈ AGAINST YOUR ENEMIES[11]
This charm confirms Uriel's specialty, encountered above, in the protection of the individual who invokes him against his enemies.

If you wish to march against your enemies, keep in memory:
Saint Uriel, blessed friend of God ✡ Explicit.
May the name of God be blessed. Amen.
And that of the blessed Virgin Mary. Amen ✡

108 ◆ To Be Spared from All Kinds of Danger[12]

The following charm is entirely made up of fragments or initial lines of psalms, verses, prayers, hymns, and so forth, to be recited for protecting yourself. Arcum conteret et confringet arma, *for example, is borrowed from Psalm 45:10. The evocation of the Tau, a particular form of cross, entered into folk magic at an early stage.[13] In 546, when the plague was ravaging the south of France, Saint Gall, the bishop of Clermont, organized a solemn procession. A "T" suddenly appeared over the houses and churches, and the epidemic ceased. Since that time, the Tau has been a protective talisman for houses, and it sends enemies fleeing.[14] Here we find* Ananizapta *(see charm no. 45) again, as well as the usual more or less garbled divine names.* Pentagrammaton *should be correctly written as* Tetragrammaton, *and* Hagios *("saint") as* agios.

Arcum conteret & confringet arma, &c. Monstra te esse matrem, &c. Dextera Domini, &c. Miserator & misericors Dominus, &c. Sancte Deux, &c. Deus qui in tot periculis, &c. Deus autem transiens,[15] &c. Domine Iesu Christe Fili Dei vivi qui hora, &c. † Agla Pentagrammaton ✠ On ✠ Athanatos ✠ Anafarcon ✠ &c. ✠ Crux Christi salva me ✠ &c. Perscrutati sunt, &c. Ave Virgo gloriosa, &c. Hagios invisibilis Dominus, &c. Per signum X Domine Tau libera me, In nomine Patris, &c. Adonay Iob Magister dicit, 91. O bone Iesu, &c. ✠ Ananizaptam ✠ Ihozath ✠ L A Laus Deo semper, O inimici mei ad vos nemo, &c. In nomine Iesu, &c.

109 ◆ Against Fever[16]

The "magic words" here are the names of God. Hely *is the distorted form of* Elohim, *plural form of the Hebrew majesty designating the deity; the singular* Eloah *(Eloha, Eloy, Heloi) means "my God" and can be found earlier in the Greek magical papyri (Ελωε).*

Ye, Ya *come from the Hebrew* jod, *"the Lord, Jehovah" (Arabic* iod), *in Greek* ταω, *abbreviated to* Τα; *in Saint Jerome we find* Ja,[17] *in Martin of Arles* Ya Ya, *in Peter of Abano* Ja Ja. Iod *is the first letter of Tetragram (= Yahweh).*

Write this on four hosts:

    † Hely. †† Heloy. †

    † Heloe. † † Heloen. †

    † ye. † † ya. †

    † Sabaoth. † † Adonai. †

and add the name of the sick person on two or three hosts; if room remains, add:

    † IHESUS. † † Christus.

    And add this against the fever:

    † Alfa. † † _. †

    † principium. † † Finis. †

Wear this spell on your person against p . s . a . c . B . t . N . m . r .

110 ◆ To Preserve Your Health[18]

Here we find a condensed set of magical operations necessary to fashion an amulet: the choice of a sacred text, Psalm 86, a canticle to the city of God (Zion); the inscription of symbols (characters) with the help of blood, the vital fluid par excellence; and the censing of the object, parchment, or tablet, with the help of aromatic plants. All that remains is to wear the amulet as recommended. See also charm no. 108 above.

Fundamenta eius in montibus sanctis. Write this psalm and these characters with pigeon blood and cense them with mastic and aloe wood, then attach them to your right arm. Your health will be preserved and your business affairs will prosper.

111 ◆ Against the Devil[19]

*During the Middle Ages, "devil" was a generic term used to designate all manner of demons, which could just as well be a dwarf or a nightmare. Since the power of the God of Christianity was stronger than that of the gods and demons of paganism, a prayer of the type below—which reflects the piety of the common people and recalls the decisive facts of the life of Christ (essentially all those aspects that distinguish him from other men)— carried on the person, was alleged to be an effective cuirass (*lorica*).*

If you wish the devil to be unable to harm you, carry this document on your person.

> In the name of Our Lord Jesus Christ, living son of God, have pity on us. Amen. Lord Jesus Christ, you have come down from heaven and have leant upon the Virgin Mary, you have been made veritable flesh and been born, you bore a glaive in your hands and feet and a crown, your body was placed in the tomb wrapped in a shroud, your spirit went down into hell and despoiled it, you resurrected on the third day, rose into heaven toward your father, and you did all this for the sinners. By all your holiness, by the holy Virgin Mary, by the Cherubim and Seraphim whose voices never cease to cry out: holy, holy, Lord God Sabaoth. The heavens and earth are filled with your glory. *Osanna in excelsis.* Benedictus. Amen. Son of God who came in the name of the Lord. *Osanna in excelsis.*

112 ◆ Against the Attacks of the Devil[20]

As early as Classical Antiquity, strong perfumes and odors were reputed to send demons fleeing, this is why, for example, they were placed in the tombs so that the demon could not come take possession of the corpse and animate it for his own ends. Garlic, mallow, and fennel were regularly used in the concoction of philters against the devil. It was said that betony opposed the intrigues of the devil and dementia. Saint Hildegard von Bingen asserted it fought lust and evil dreams, that is to say nightmares, and, in more recent times, the Italians used it as protection against the evil eye.

Take buckthorn, garlic, lupin, mallow, fennel, hairgrass, and betony, sanctify these plants and pour the holy water into the beer. The beverage should be in the same room as the patient. Chant *"Deus in nomine tuo salum me fac"* three times over this beverage before he drinks it.

113 ◈ AGAINST LUST[21]
Beati quorum remisse sunt iniquitates. If someone is inclined to fornication, he should read this psalm over holy water in church during the Epiphany of the Lord and wash himself with it. Write these characters and fumigate them with incense and attach them to the arm.

114 ◈ A BALM AGAINST ELVES, SPIRITS WHO ROAM THE NIGHT, AND THOSE WITH WHOM THE DEMON COPULATES[22]
In medieval belief, the figures of popular mythology known as elves were originally benevolent beings to whom regular offerings were made in exchange for their good will or neutrality. The Church transmogrified them by conflating them with dwarves, perverse and malevolent creatures, and with all the "beings who roam the night"—the nocturnal demons, such as the nightmare itself. These entities make you sick by shooting invisible arrows.

Take hops, wormwood, mallow, lupin, verbena, henbane, cudweed, Viper's Bugloss, myrtle, leek, and garlic plants, cleaver seeds, corn cockle seeds, and fennel seeds. Seal these plants in a container, place them beneath the altar, and chant nine psalms over it. Next boil them in butter and suet, add blessed salt, and filter all of it in a white linen cloth. Next, cast the plants into running water. If an elf, or a night-roaming spirit attacks a man, coat his face with this balm, place it over his eyes and the afflicted parts of his body, fumigate him with incense, and bless him often with the sign of the cross. He will get better.

115 ◈ AGAINST A DWARF[23]

In this Old English charm from before the year 1000, the linguistic shift of the "dwarf" into a "demon" has not yet been accomplished. The suggested remedy relies on consecrated hosts, in other words, items invested with the supreme power of God. Upon these one draws the names of the Seven Sleepers (see charm no. 30), which should have a direct connection with the affliction that is affecting (in the words of the charm, "persecuting") the individual. The cure definitely must have lasted seven days, with one host ingested each day. The explanation for the dwarf riding the patient is simple: in all the Germanic languages, the word for "riding" also means "fever."

If a dwarf is persecuting a man, † Take seven small hosts, from those that are used at mass, and write on each:

Maximianus. Malchus. Iohannes. Martinianus.
Dionisius. Constantinus. Serafion.

Next, chant each incantation, first in the left ear, then in the right ear, and finally above the head (of the patient). A virgin should then come to him and hang them around his neck. This will be done for three days and the patient will get better.

A spider-shaped being comes in holding his harness in his hands. He says that you were his mount. He takes the bridle from around your neck. They leave.

Then in comes the dwarf's sister who says and swears that he will never afflict the patient, nor he who obtains this charm, nor the one who knows how to incant it. Amen. May it be so!

116 ◈ AGAINST POISONS AND POTIONS[24]

Carry this on your person against poisons and philters.

ele. erape. hebe. occentinmos. ioth. hey. a. io. hoccayethos. ya. salay. amorona. asar. sycon. goyces. Beley. latem. sanctus. anon. raba. mefenecon. oncantia. tol. fa. tel. Ella. Sabira. Sada. Adonay. aaa. camsi. ayada. Maus. princeps. veni. est. Emanuel. Adonay. Bethpha. Adonay. qm. hoy. hoy. aanai. Nanay. Sede Adonay. asamilias. Ehur.

117 ◆ AGAINST A WICKED WITCH[25]

The magic spell here is, for once, partially decipherable. We first have A(lpha) and O(mega); followed by verbum, *the word, the verb, in Greek letters; then the name of Veronica,* Berenike *in Greek, but spelled* Brrenike *here; followed by a group ETTANI which appears as a whole or in part in many charms and on a large number of magic objects, mainly rings.*[26]

To protect yourself from the evil spells of witches, write this in Greek letters:

118 ◆ TO DISPEL EVIL SPELLS[27]

Judica me Domine quoniam. If you seek to dispel enchantments and ghosts, recite this psalm and an enchanter can do nothing to you. And if you recite it in the midst of enemies or wrongful men, you shall be rid of them and they shall not be able to harm you.

119 ◆ TO DISMISS ENCHANTMENTS[28]

Si vere utique. If you wish to render charms and phantasmagoria ineffective, recite this psalm seven times and they shall not be able to harm you in any way if this psalm is turned against them.

120 ◆ FOR ONE WHO IS UNABLE TO KNOW HIS WIFE CARNALLY[29]

Sexual impotence was once regarded as the result of an evil spell called a "nouement* de l'aiguillette."[30] The aiguillette are the ties used to hold the pieces of garment together, mainly the doublet to the legwear. The expression "courir l'aiguillette," like "courir le guilledou," means "to lead a shameless life, to prostitute oneself." Jacob Sprenger and Heinrich tell how a witch in the Strasbourg diocese prevented an earl of Westrich from consummating his marriage. This man found out that one of his former concubines had spoken to an old woman, who then revealed this to him: "She boasted of bewitching your body so that you could not perform the carnal act with your wife at all. The sign is this: there is a well in your courtyard. At the bottom of the well, there is a cooking pot containing various enchanted things. She placed it there so that, as long as it remains there, you will be afflicted by conjugal impotence."[31] It was also possible for a woman to prevent a man from sleeping with her. To accomplish this, she simply needed to carry on her person a needle that had been first dipped in manure, then covered with mud from a grave and wrapped in a mortuary sheet.[32]

Eripe me de inimicis meis. If someone's breeches-strings have been knotted and he is unable to sleep with his wife, write these characters on a piece of parchment and read this psalm seven times over them. Next, place this parchment is his legwear and this man will be freed.

121 ◆ AGAINST DEMONS AND EVIL SPELLS[33]

Among the hundreds of recipes for protecting the home that have come down to us from the Middle Ages, those which make use of plants are quite numerous.[34] Such practices are of great antiquity, and Pliny the Elder offers examples of similar beliefs. Over a span of more than two thousand years, scant differences can be observed in the tradition.

---

*[The word *nouement* means "knotting," and thus *nouement de l'aiguillette* could be translated as a "knotting of the breeches-strings."—*Trans.*]

If you have St. John's wort at your home, all demons will flee. This is the reason many call it "demon chaser."

Mugwort placed or hung above the entrance to the house will thwart all evil spells.

122 ◆ AGAINST THE EVIL EYE[35]

The evil eye is sometimes a spell cast by an individual who wishes you misfortune and sometimes an evil spell that is issued by a person's gaze when he or she stares at you.[36] Until recently, people protected themselves against the evil eye either with gestures that countered its effects or by carrying amulets like this one.

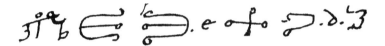

Conserva me domine quoniam speravi. If you fear being bewitched by the evil eye and suffering harm thereby, write this psalm on a piece of parchment with these characters and carry it on your person.

123 ◆ AGAINST THEFT AND THIEVES[37]

In the spell below, it should be noted that only the first three words are magical. This is revealed by the alliteration and the vocalic play that creates the rhythm of a monotonous chant. What comes after this must have been an abbreviated divine invocation, with God being named by means of his secret names (one of which is poorly spelled, on top of it all). In a conjuration collected in Denmark and dating from around 1700, the thief is bound by Abraham and Jacob.[38]

Sabor. † seles. † selas. † bo. † N. _ _ TretragramatoN

Write these three names and carry them on your person and you shall fear no robbers or thieves for they will not be able to harm you.

124 ◆ AGAINST A THIEF[39]

Several accounts like the following can be found in the scholarly treatises of the early Middle Ages. We have a charm together with its ritual. The purpose of the operation is to first hermetically seal the space so that no thief can gain entrance, and then to bind and obstruct the robber. The allusions are biblical: God bound Satan to Hell, Christ was nailed on the cross, therefore it will go the same way for the thief and for all the openings in the house. The reference to the five wounds of Christ is a bit startling when we see that it is essentially employed in formulas like "May the five wounds of Christ be my remedy!"

The magical operation comes next: the making of the candles, which are sanctified through prayer, and the recitation of the second part of the charm that now includes an expression of loathing—one wishes to bind the thief, of course, but one also wants to kill him.

The last part of the charm can be compared with extremely ancient beliefs relating to the doorsill and the hinges.[40] The dirt must be taken from beneath this sill because the threshold is sacred. By sprinkling the dirt over the hinges, they are made sacred or placed under the protection of the spirit of the threshold, and they are thus given the power evoked by the charm, which is then repeated.

Door, I turn you!
  Thief, I bind you!
  By the word that God himself has uttered,
  May all the doors be closed and locked,
  And may all the doors be nailed shut
  As God was upon the holy cross.
  May his five wounds help me to bind you, thief!
  May the holy Christ who was born in Bethlehem help me to
bind you!

Next say five Our Fathers. Then may a woman spin five threads without getting them wet. Place them on the sill that the thief has breached, and beneath the door he used, and turn your feet toward the room from which he took his loot. Make a wick of the five threads and a taper. It should measure the length from the elbow to the tip of the middle finger.

Make five candles from this taper and burn one each day while saying first a Credo, then an Our Father, as many as one can while the candle is still burning. When it has burned down, then say:

"Dear Saint Christopher, in honor of your holy hope,
grant that this thief be hampered in all his movements
as if he were bound by a belt around his waist.
God salutes you, death!
I beseech you to loan me your covering
in order to smother the breath of the thief and his tongue.
Just as I know not whether you be man or woman,
by the same token do not appropriate my property.
May the ban God placed on the dead help me!"

Next say three Our Fathers and three Ave Marias . . . then take some dirt from beneath the door the thief has breached, sprinkle it over the hinges, then open and shut the door three times while speaking these words:

Door, I turn you; thief, I bind you by the word; and so forth. Once this has been done, the thief will not be able to carry anything away.

125 ◆ For Preventing Fear of Thieves[41]

Usque quo domine oblivisceris. If thieves lay traps for you and you fear them, say this psalm three times and they shall flee far from you. If, then, when sleeping in a deserted place, you read this psalm three times up to *ne quando dicat inimicus meus prevalui adversus eum,* you shall fear neither death, nor thieves and their helpers.

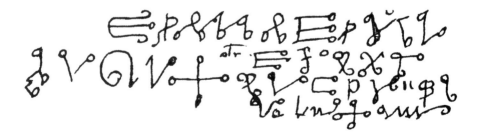

126 ◊ To Remove Fear of Animals[42]

Miserere mej Deus miserere. If you find yourself in the wild and you dread the ferocious beasts, recite this psalm seven times and they will not be able to harm you, with the help of God.

127 ◊ Against Bad Dreams[43]

The nightmare, which the ancients called a "nocturnal terror," was regarded in the Middle Ages as a spirit: the spirit of a dead person, or the double of a witch, which hurled itself upon you and smothered you.[44] It is therefore logical that people would protect themselves with a psalm requesting divine aid.

Dixi custodiam vias. If the dreams of a woman multiply, write this psalm on the right side of her face while saying nothing: she will no longer have nightmares.

128 ◊ Against the Storm[45]

It was formerly believed that the sound of bells drove off evil spirits, notably those of the air that allegedly brought storms. For this reason a Danish bell bears the following inscription: "My voice is a terror for all the evil spirits." Rhineland inquisitors noted that bells were rung "so that, like the consecrated trumpets of God, they put demons to flight and avert evil spells; and so that the awakened populace would invoke God against the tempests."[46] For the bell to become a true phylactery, however, it had be carved with signs and/or words.[47]

Carve these words upon a bell:
> *Dum turbor procul cedant ignis grandas tonitrua*
> *Fulgor fames pestis gladius Satan et homo malignus*

When you ring the bell, it will send storms, lightning, plague, Satan, and evil men fleeing.

129 ◊ Against Bad Weather[48]

The image described here is that of Aquarius. It forms part of the paranatellonta, which are the pictorial depictions of the planets and signs of the zodiac. The spell described amounts to healing evil with evil.

If you find a stone engraved with a man sitting on a leopard and holding a pitcher in his right hand pouring water, put it in an iron ring on
the first or the eighth hour of Saturday with this sign ♄

Here is the virtue of this stone: if you fear the storm striking the
land or over the city, stick this stone on an iron stake and plant it where
you fear the tempest will strike, and it will not cause any damage. And
if a man thinks ill of you, you will know it.

130 ◈ CONJURATION OF THE EAGLE[49]

Eagle! Eagle, God created you, Adam named you. I command you, in
the name of the Father, the Son, and the Holy Ghost, to not stretch out
your claws toward the falcon you pursue.

8

MAGIC RINGS

Magic rings bring sympathetic chains into play. Each planet rules over one or more stones and over one or more metals, and so on. In magical traditions of Greek origin, we have, for example, the following correspondences:

Sun	Chrysolite	Heliotrope	Carbuncle	Hyacinth
Moon	Aphroselenite	Chrysolith	Thaure	Galactite
Mars	Hematite	Sard	Emerald	Garnet
Jupiter	Ceraunia	Herbosa	Sard	Jasper
Venus	Medius	Egyptilla	Sapphire	Chrysolite
Mercury	Arabi	Hematite	Topaz	Chalcedony
Saturn	Ostrachite	Agate	Sardonyx	Sard/Sardonyx*

The figures that should be carved on the rings described in examples 131 through 136 are the fantasy representations of the personified planets, which are called *paranatellonta*. A large number exist for each planet, and for the signs of the zodiac and their decans. In the subsequent examples (137 through 146), the engravings are the same tradition but do not allow us to positively identify the celestial bodies whose

---

*For all these stones, see my book *A Lapidary of Sacred Stones,* Inner Traditions, 2012.

power they harness. Some of these texts can also be found in the lapidaries, mainly in the one attributed to John Mandeville.[1] Examples 147 and 148 are archaeological finds of actual rings.

"Rings," says Henry Cornelius Agrippa, "impress their virtue upon us, inasmuch as they do affect the spirit of him that carries them with gladness or sadness, and render him courteous or terrible, bold or fearful, amiable or hateful; inasmuch as they do fortify us against sickness, poisons, enemies, evil spirits, and all manner of hurtful things, or, at least, will not suffer us to be kept under them" (*Occult Philosophy*, I, 47). He also mentions the *Life of Apollonius of Tyana*, written by Philostratus between 217 and 245, in which we read: "Iarchas gave seven rings to Apollonius named after the seven stars, and that Apollonius wore each of these in turn on the day of the week which bore its name."[2]

The reader will note a recurring expression in these texts, which calls for a brief explanation: "If you find an image on a stone . . ." This shows that a clear distinction was made between stones on which an image had been carved by human hands and those that are "carved by nature." The ancients provided the following explanation. The celestial bodies cast their radiance on the stones, plants, animals, and so forth, which therefore individually receive a particular influence. Based on their observation of things, our ancestors noted that these images, signs, and seals were to be found on all the elements and they could thus be used as amulets and talismans. There are therefore images imprinted on stones by nature and dependent upon an astral causality; imitating them aims at achieving the same effects. In his treatise *De mineralibus* (On the Minerals), Albertus Magnus notes: "The first teachers and professors of natural philosophy counseled the carving of gems and metallic images with resemblance to the heavenly bodies, by observing the moments when the celestial force was proven to be strongest for that image, for example, when many of the celestial virtues were blended together in it, and they performed wonders with these images."[3]

131 ◈ RING OF SATURN[4]

Saturn rules over the stone of turquoise and over lead. So, then, at Saturn's hour on a Saturday when the Moon is in Capricorn, one carves on a piece of turquoise a man standing on a dragon, holding a scythe in his right hand and holding something like a rock with the signs of an egg in the middle of his (left) hand, and then when this is set in a lead ring—one will refrain, when wearing it, from eating meat in which there is a looseness (illness) and from entering dark places: the spirits that are active in shadows and darkness are sporting there—great secrets will be revealed to you; men, serpents, mice, and the reptiles of the earth will spare you; and all the works of Saturn shall smile upon you.

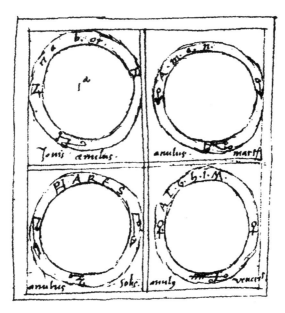

The rings of Jupiter and Mars (top row), and the Sun and Venus (bottom row). Fifteenth century.

132 ◆ RING OF JUPITER

Jupiter rules over tin and chalcedony. Thus, if on a Thursday, at the hour of Jupiter when the Moon is in Sagittarius, one carves on a chalcedony a man seated on an eagle, with the panels of his garments stretched out or raised, holding in his right hand an oramet [?], and if this is set in a ring of lead, the sons of men will find agreement with its wearer; eagles, vultures, and lions will spare you; and all the works of Jupiter will give you success.

133 ◈ RING OF MARS

Mars rules over the stone of iron. Thus, if on the hour of Mars on a Tuesday one carves on it a man wearing a breastplate that also covers one arm, one sword at his side, one sword in his right hand, and a man's head in his left, he who wears (the ring) into combat will be victorious; he will master elephants, lions, and vultures; and all the works of Mars will be favorable to him.

134 ◈ RING OF THE SUN

The Sun rules over the stone of diamonds and of gold. Thus, if on a Sunday at the first hour of the day, when the Moon is in Aries, one carves on a diamond the Sun standing in a quadriga, holding in his right hand a *marcha* [this is an Arabic word and designates a mirror or a fumitory plant] and a whip with knotted cords in his left hand, and with wax over his head, and one sets it in a gold ring and its wearer abstains from eating white meat and sleeping with a white woman, one will have the favor of the sons of men and of the great who will listen respectfully to what you say, and all the works of the Sun will ensure your success.

135 ◈ RING OF VENUS

Venus rules over the stone of bronze and copper. Thus, if on the hour of Venus on Friday when the Moon is in Libra you carve on the acuty [?] stone a woman standing upright, holding a comb in her right hand, and you set it in a ring of brass, and you refrain from sleeping with an old woman, its wearer will be pleasing to women and kings; birds, the forest animals, chickens, grasshoppers, and all the flying animals with fine plumage will be calm; and all the works of Venus will bestow their favor on him.

136 ◈ RING OF MERCURY

Mercury rules over quicksilver and the magnet stone. Thus, if on a Wednesday at the hour of Mercury when the Moon is in Virgo one carves upon a magnet a man sitting on a cathedra, having in front of him a tray holding a book, and men and disciples sitting at his feet listening to him, and if its wearer abstains from eating fish, he will understand things more profoundly and reflect upon them from a loftier state; rivers, seas, and all that lives in them will spare him; people will be friendly to him, and the works of Mercury favorable.

137 ◈ Against Spells and Poisons[5]

If you find a stone carved with a leopard that is holding a scepter in its right paw and a flying vulture in its left, with a crocodile beneath its feet, set it within an iron ring at the first hour of Saturday, or the eighth hour, and carve this sign on the setting ♄ and ♋. The one who crafts the ring must be clean and fasting. No enchantment or poison will be able to harm either the one who wears this stone or the place where it happens to be.

138 ◈ Magic Ring[6]

One who takes a ring of azari or a stone of alaquech, on which he shall carve these twenty-six figures and then wear it, when he comes before the king or any noble, he will be given the highest and warmest welcome, and all he may ask of one or the other shall be granted. But take heed that no character is missing from this figure! If one is missing, its effect will be null. This is one of the marvels of this art. Here are the figures:

∪⌐ 8 Χ Τ‹∪› 6 Ⴑ Ꮩ Ꮩꝿ⁄ Ꮩ⌐ ᵒ⎮ ⁄⎮Ꮩ
∪⌐ ꝯ Ⴈ ∪ ∪ ⊡ ⅂ ∪ ⌐

139 ◈ To Make a Magic Ring[7]

Look for a small stone on which the face of a man is depicted. Have a silver ring made in the name of the one for whom you are working. When the stone is set in the ring, put on a white vestment and go to an empty house and consecrate the ring with water and wine between two lit candles. You shall do this three times at dusk. When entering the house, say: "I come in peace to visit this dwelling." Pronounce the following names over the ring:

iandispar reffna. dardaneus. effreinel. sarbuniel.* gatintya. panzarenus

---

*Effreinel and Sarbuniel are the names of angels.

On the third day, a spirit will come forth and you will take great pains to avoid speaking a word to it. It will take the ring. When you return the next day, you will find it in its place. You will pick it up and keep it wrapped in a red cloth in a clean place.

When you wear the ring on the ring finger of your left hand, no one will refuse to answer your questions.

When you touch someone with the ring, that person will love you.

When you take it beneath the moon, you will be invisible.

If you slip it onto the finger of someone who is possessed, the devil will tell you what you wish to know.

When you fasten it around the neck of a possessed person, he or she will heal that very same day.

140 ◆ TO EARN THE GOOD WILL OF ENEMIES

Information about magic rings is often found scattered throughout the lapidaries because the gems, as we have seen, should be combined with a sympathetic metal that has a relationship to a planet. A certain Chael gathered together a number of engraved stones that, set within a certain metal, have astonishing virtues. The engravings are often the symbolic representation of a planet, its personalization. For other examples, see chapter 10 on the magic of images.

If one finds in any stone an image of Scorpio and Sagittarius in full combat, and one imprints this image in wax, and with this seal one touches malicious enemies, you will earn their good will. It must be fixed to silver.

141 ◆ TO BECOME INVISIBLE

If a hyacinth is engraved with a figure that is half-woman and half-fish, with a mirror in one hand and a branch in the other, set it in a gold ring and place it on your finger. For if you wish to become invisible, turn the ring on your ring finger toward the palm of your hand, close your hand, and you will be invisible.

142 ◆ To Summon Evil Spirits

If one carves in a diadochos the standing figure of a man, holding a small offering in his right hand and a snake in his left, with an image of the sun above his head and a lion lying by his feet, and if one attaches it to a lead ring along with a piece of mugwort and fennel root, and if you bear it with you to the bank of a river and summon evil spirits, they will answer your questions.

143 ◆ To Win Partiality

With respect to the following figure, it should be engraved in crystal or any other precious stone, then mounted in brass on a bed of musk and amber. This image is a man with a lion's face and the claws of an eagle, with a two-headed dragon at his feet and its tail stretched out. This man should be carrying a staff in his hand with which to strike the dragon's head. He who wears this stone will win the partiality of both sexes; he will obtain the obedience of spirits; he will increase his resources and accumulate vast wealth.

144 ◆ To Obtain Obedience

If one carves in a hyacinth or in a crystal an image of a woman whose hair falls over her breasts, as well as a man who has just appeared and is showing her some token of love, and one fixes this stone to gold, and if this stone carries amber, aloe, and that herb known as polium, the owner of this stone will obtain the obedience of all; and if you touch a woman with this stone, she will act in accordance with your will; and if you place it beneath your head when going to sleep, you will see everything you desire in dream.

145 ◆ To Find Treasure, Gain Victory, etc.

If you find in a stone the image of a long-faced, bearded man with curving eyebrows, seated on a cart between two bulls and holding a vulture in his hand, know that this stone is useful for planting trees and finding treasure, and that it will bring victory in battle. Serpents flee the presence of its owner. It cures epileptics and frees one of all the fear and torments that evil demons can inflict. It must be set on an iron ring and worn this way.

146 ◈ To Win the Obedience of All Spirits

If one finds in an amethyst the image of a man with a sword in hand seated on a dragon, and this stone is set in a ring of lead or iron, he who wears it will win the obedience of all spirits, and these latter will reveal treasures to him and answer any questions he may ask.

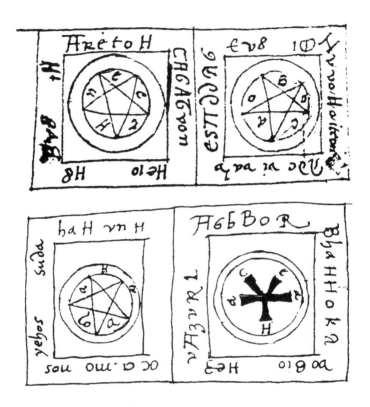

The Four Magic Rings[8]

147 ◈ A Magic Ring

In 1763, a square-sectioned gold ring was found near Amiens, France, that bore the following characters, mixed in with Roman and Greek letters, on each of its surfaces.[9] *Various divine names can be recognized, such as iothe (= iod), on, alpha ("beginning"), omoiga (= omega, "end"), Agla, and Adonai ("Lord").*

† OEGVTTA † SAGRA † HOGOGRA † IOTHE † HENAVEAET
† OCCINOMOC † ON † IKC † HOGOTE † BANGVES † ALPHA
† ANA † EENETON † AIRIE † OIPA † AGLA † OMOIGA † ADONAI
† HEIEPNATHOI † GEBAI w† GVTGVTTA † IEOTHIN

148 ◈ To Protect against Cramps and Spasms

In October 1904, a gold ring with square sections was discovered in Donauwörth (Bavaria) that dated from the final third of the thirteenth century.[10] It displays a clear kinship with the preceding ring with respect to the inscriptions

† GVGGVGBALTEBANI † ALPHA & ω
† EHERAVELAGAIHAEHRA † ENORAYA. ω
† GVT † GVNANIA † ADOSDE.B.E.L ω
† MELChAAGLA † AQTVO Lc Lo Mo—o I

Here we see AGLA again, combined with MELCHA ("a very sacred name; he that carries it on his person will be delivered from all peril," says a Munich manuscript). The word THEBALGVTGVTANI, sometimes written in Greek letters ΘΗΒΑLΓVΘΓVΘΑΝΙ, as on a ring discovered in 1846, is extremely common on magic rings. Comparison with a Latin charm against cramps or spasms suggests that a ring bearing this term protected the bearer from such an ailment.

In southeast Jutland, a twelfth-century ring was discovered bearing a similar inscription: † TH / EB / AL / GV / VT / HA N/.[11]

A magic ring, dating from around 1300, now housed in the Donauwörth Museum. The square section is fully engraved and among other things we can find on it the words Alpha and Omega, as well as Agla.

The magic circle offers protection to the magician who summons demons. Here we have Doctor Faust. Note the astrological symbols (planets and signs of the zodiac) in the perimeter of the circle.

9

MAGIC OPERATIONS

149 ◆ MAGIC CIRCLES[1]

The procedures for conjuring spirits are delicate and dangerous. Precautions must be taken to protect oneself, for no one truly knows what the reactions of the creature appearing to the magician will be: remember the end of Doctor Faust! The circle is the standard means of protection.

The pseudo-Agrippa goes on at length about this subject and his opinion is worth mentioning.

> Therefore when you would consecrate any Place or Circle, you ought to take the prayer of Solomon used in the dedication of the Temple and moreover, you must bless the place with the sprinkling of Holy-water, and with Fumigations; by commemorating in the benediction holy mysteries; such as these are: The sanctification of the throne of God . . . ; And by invoking divine names which are significant hereunto; such as the Place of God, the Throne of God . . . and such-like divine names of this sort, which are to be written about the Circle or place to be consecrated. (*Occult Philosophy,* IV, 55)

In the diagram below, the master (magister) stands in the center of the triple circle. The arrangement of the stars of David (called "pentacles of Solomon" in magical texts) forms a cross that divides the space in four, with each quarter placed under the dominion of an angel and a demon. The outer signs on the circles undoubtedly represent the secret symbols of the celestial bodies. The knife at the center of the circle, between the Latin words locus magistri, *"place of the master," is used to draw the circles and also possesses, like all iron metals, the power to repel demons.*

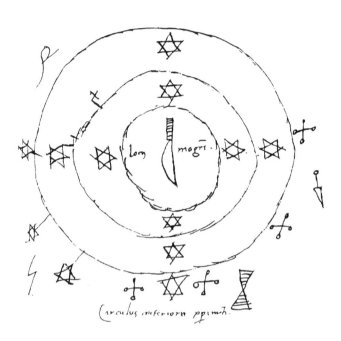

150 ◆ WHITE MAGIC CIRCLE

Here we see the same principle that governed the previous example, but this time the cross dividing the space is marked and the orientation—the four cardinal points—is indicated. Small crosses have replaced the pentacles of Solomon. God is the tutelary power represented by alpha and o(mega), the expression of the Whole (in Latin: principium et finis*). Thus, in contrast to the preceding circle, we may safely assume this represents a white magic circle. One novel feature here is the fact that the master stands in the eastern part, the direction of Jerusalem (the center of the world according to medieval cartography, which made this city the heart of Christ), and his disciple stands in the western part.*

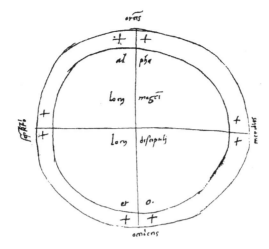

151 ◈ A Demonic Circle

Four demons—Sathan, Beelzebub, Lucifer, and Belial—are named in this new circle, as if each ruled over a quarter of the world, which is recalled by the notation of the cardinal points. The charms teach us that every conjuration is cast in the four directions. Two other demons are invoked: Appolin *and* Morraloth; *given their place in the circle, they are likely hypostases or servitors of Belial and Beelzebub. The central inscription cites the name of the master, Inloman (for Solomon?), labeled as "master of this order" (science?), and indicates that the name of the disciple must be inscribed within the circle.*

152 ◈ A Magic Rectangle

In this configuration, the master and his companion place themselves in the center, protected by the divine names Adonay, Eloy, Emmanuel, Sabaoth, Eloyn, and Eloe. The rectangle, which is a rare form in magic operations (although not in magic seals), erects an additional barrier against the spirits. We find some heavily distorted names and designations for God: Ayos *("saint"),* Yschiris *(Ischyros: "strong"), as well as a variation on a term that sounds Greek:* paneron. *The latter word appears in a sonorous interplay of variations, with* paneron, pancron, *and* pantaron *four times. It is possible that these words correspond to titles like* Panton *(All) or* Panstraton *(Head of the Armies), which we encounter in the lists of divine names. If the four stars of David are connected by lines, this creates a St. Andrew's Cross; if lines are drawn connecting the crosses, we get a larger Christian cross.*

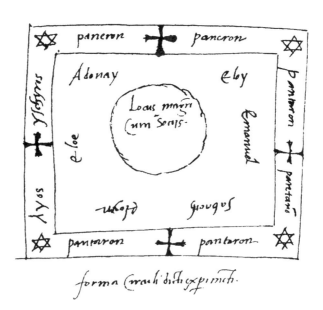

153 ◈ Another White Magic Circle

The last circle makes use of the composition principles that we have just seen above. God is represented by Adonay, *as well as* A *for alpha and* O *for omega, in accordance with the Book of Revelations (21:6). The inscription, in which we can read "E agra 9, Kor," is unintelligible, as are the three symbols. Finally, we might note that a cross in a quadrilateral is a sign that appears fairly often in the prescriptions.*

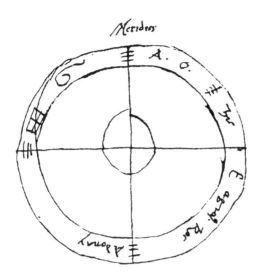

154 ◈ To Discover a Treasure[2]

Treasure hunting is an age-old pastime and in the nineteenth century a magic wand or pendulum was still used for this purpose. Here the search is carried out with the aid of a divinatory crystal, the ancestor of the famous crystal ball of our modern seeresses. The ritual consists first of the purification of the magician's body (fasting, chastity) and soul (confession), and it requires the presence of a child who represents purity and innocence, and the candle he holds in his right hand is the symbol of the true faith. Furthermore, he is protected by the stole, which approximates him to a priest celebrating his office, and the cross. Attending three masses and making an offering is one means of guaranteeing a spiritual defense.

It is Michael and Uriel who will confer their power to the crystal. We also know that this kind of crystal had to be blessed.[3]

You shall fast for three days on bread and water, you shall make confession, and you shall remain chaste, you shall then go to church accompanied by a child and attend Michaelmas, the Epiphany Mass, and the Mass of the Dead, and you shall give VI coins to the officiant.

Next you shall take an olive leaf that has been blessed as required and write the words Michael and Uriel on a crystal. The child should be facing east and standing with the help of a tripod in the middle of a circle.

The text surrounding the circle says: "Lord, judge the innocent so that they be not dragged into a fight. May those who think ill of me be confounded and less than dust in the wind."

Once this has been done, take a piece of crystal with your left hand and a lit candle that has been blessed in your right. This child should wear a long cassock with a stole knotted in a cross. Then recite the psalm *Deus in adjutorium meum intende,*[4] sprinkle it with holy water, then say: *Asperge Domine, locum istum isopo et mundabitur lavabis eum.*[5] Make a sign of the cross on the child with holy oil, and recite a psalm with great devotion and the four orisons "I conjure you, etc.," in which you ask Jesus to allow Michael and Uriel to appear in this crystal and show themselves to this innocent child N and show him where the treasure you seek is hidden.

A sixteenth-century manuscript of The Key of Solomon *provides another recipe titled "To Take Possession of a Treasure Owned by the Spirits." Its tone is quite different and the text is worth citing here.*

One Sunday, between July 10 and August 20, before sunrise, when the moon is in Leo, go to where you have learned—by interrogating the spirits or by other means—there is a treasure. You will draw a sufficiently large circle with your sword of the magical art and you will open the ground with it if the nature of the soil permits. During the day you burn three times the perfume corresponding to the day. Next, dressed as required for the operation, you will hang, using any kind of device, a lantern above the opening. The lamp oil will be mixed with the fat of a man who died in July, and its wick will be made from the shroud in which he was buried. You will light it with a new flame and you will strengthen your workers with a garland made from the hide of a freshly slaughtered goat, on which you will write these characters with the blood of the man from whom you took the fat.

A ⊖D⚡o Padous

You can then get down to work in all security and you will tell [the workers] to not let themselves be troubled by the ghosts they see and to boldly keep working. If you are unable to complete the work in one day, have the opening covered up again, every time you leave the location, with wood and six inches of dirt. You will then be able to continue the operation until the end, clad in the necessary garments and with the magic sword. Afterward, you shall say this prayer:

"Adonai Elohim El Ehaieh Asher Eheieh, prince of princes, being of beings, take pity on me and rest your eyes upon your servant N who invokes you with great devotion and beseeches you, by your sacred and terrible name TETRAGRAMMATON, to bestow your favor and command Your angels and Your spirits to come and stay here. O angels and spirits of the stars, O angels and elementary spirits, O all you spirits present before God, I, minister and loyal servitor of the Most High, I conjure you, God himself, being of beings, I conjure you to come and assist this operation. Amen.

Once the workers have filled in the hole, you shall grant the spirits leave to depart and thank them for the bounty they have shown you. You will say:

"O good and happy spirits, thank you for the gifts we have received from your generous bounty. Depart in peace to govern the element that God has given you as your home. Amen."

155 ◈ To Make a Magic Bell[6]

A magical bell, a handbell rather than a church bell, is one of the means to compel obedience from the spirits. The pseudo-Paracelsus tells us the following:

> I cannot pass over in silence, however, a very great miracle I saw performed in Spain by a certain Necromancer. He had a bell that weighed no more than two pounds. Every time he struck it, he could evoke and summon specters, visions of numerous and varied Spirits. When it pleased him, he inscribed several words and characters upon the inner surface of the bell, then he began swinging and ringing it, causing a Spirit to appear in the form and appearance he wished. With the sound of this same bell, he could attract or repel numerous other Spirit apparitions. . . . Every time, though, he performed a new work, he changed the words and characters.

Here the bell draws its power from the configuration of the heavens, the combination of metals that reflect that configuration, and the names inscribed upon it. The summoning (convocation) of spirits follows a precise ritual and takes place in a secret location. Every detail is important. For this reason the color of the ink used varies with each spirit: the Picatrix *(II,3) devotes much space to this and states, for example, that red ink should be used for Mars and green ink for Jupiter. Lastly we come to the evocation. The presence of divine names should come as no surprise if we recall the words of Luke (10:17): "Lord, even the demons submit to us in your name." By virtue of the names of God, the spirits should comply with the magician's commands.*

Here we can also clearly see how close magic is to religion. How much difference is there between this and the manufacture of Christian bells that also bear inscriptions? The procedure below takes into account the submission to an astral configuration and the correspondences of the alloys: gold is governed by the Sun, iron by Mars, and lead by Saturn, and so forth.

Start by noting the day of your birth and which day of the week it was. If the Sun is in Leo, Taurus, or Virgo, in ascension, the IVth, Vth, VIth, VIIth, XIIth, XIVth, XVth day, and the Moon is in Aries, Gemini, or Libra, and Saturn in Virgo, Taurus, or Sagittarius, in the East until the 13th or 14th degree, and when Leo and the Dragon's Head are in a good aspect.

Whatever the week may be, take two ounces of gold, one of silver, ½ of mercury, ½ of lead, ½ of tin, six of iron. But take one more ounce of the metal corresponding to the day of your birth. When you have blended this all together, have a bell cast. When it is ready, carve ADONAY on the clapper, and THETRA GRAMMATON on the outside, and JHESU on the handle. Next, keep it clean and store it in a clean place, because this is a secret of God and you have no need of any other names but these three.

When you wish to use this bell, prepare yourself six days beforehand, be chaste, and eat and drink modestly, pray, and put on new vestments. At night, make your way to a secret place so no one knows where you are. Set a table, cover it with a fine green or yellow cloth, and cover all the surrounding chairs. On the table place three handsome wax candles in a silver or copper candleholder, prepare an ink as I have indicated to you, and with a new goose quill that you have sharpened with a new knife, write the names of the spirits or planets that you wish, each with its color. Once this has been done, say: "O God, Thetragrammaton, Adonay, I, N! your creature, I implore you to oblige these spirits to reveal to me what I wish to know." Next, ring the bell while saying: "Spirit N! I wish that you appear to me at once." Repeat this three times and ring the bell three times. They shall appear.

Command them to sit by calling each of them by name and say: "I, N, I ask you—and you shall name the spirit of the planet—to tell and write what I desire."

156 ◆ To Make an Invisible Sword[7]

All the processes for manufacturing this sword take place under the sign of Mars, which is to be expected as Mars is a martial god. The wood that has been struck by lightning is connected to Jupiter, one of whose names is the Thunderer; the spoke from the torture wheel, just like the hangman's rope, is invested with supernatural power by virtue of its connection with death, and the same holds true for the execution-er's sword. The materials mentioned here are all sacred in nature and form a logical series. The snakeskin and that of the eel are protective: the texts inform us that they were once used for making shields and breastplates.

Buy a good blade in the hour of Mars (*in hora Martis*). The guard should be forged on a Tuesday (*scilicet dies Martis*).* Obtain some wood struck by lightning and shape it for the hilt *in hora Martis.* It you can find one, take the spoke of a wheel on which a man has been executed. Attach to the bare skin of your right arm a snakeskin covered by tanned eel hide. Next, have a sliver of iron cut from the sword of an execu-tioner, *in hora Martis,* and have it soldered on a gold, silver, copper, or brass ring, as you see on the image below.

---

*[Tuesday is *mardi,* "Mars' Day," in French. —*Trans.*]

When you must go into a fight, imprint the seal of this martial ring upon your forehead and wear it on the ring finger of your right hand. You shall triumph!

157 ◇ A MAGIC MIRROR[8]

The magic mirror, which has become especially renowned since it features prominently in the fairy tale Snow White, *has always been regarded as a means of communicating with the supernatural world. In the Middle Ages, for example, it was believed that if a steel mirror was smeared with mugwort juice, spirits could be summoned to appear in it.*

The prescription I provide here consists of two parts. In the first part, which is a bit enigmatic, the magician or a woman—the woman he loves? Whose love he desires?—will see what he should do. (As the "ingredients" used suggest, this could fall under the heading of love magic.) The second part of the prescription is where one procures power over supernatural beings and men. The use of human secretions foreshadows the sorts of operations attributed to witches two centuries later.

The names of the seven planets are given in Arabic and in the following order: Saturn, Jupiter, March, Sun, Venus, Mercury, and Moon. The names of the angels are more complicated. While Michael, Gabriel, and Raphael pose no problem, identifying the others is more difficult. Anael, or Haniel, is one of the spirits of Venus and "the seventh seal of Anael" was used to discover treasures. Samael is, according to the Hebrew Kabbalists, the planetary spirit of Mars.

In fact, to discover which spirits the author has in mind here, we have to refer back to the long lists of the angels, intelligences, and demons of the astral bodies. We then learn that the seven angels cited are those of the seven planets in the following order: Captiel (Zapkiel) for Saturn, Satquiel (Zatquiel) for Jupiter, Samael (Camael) for Mars, Raphael for the Sun, Anael (Haniel) for Venus, Michael for Mercury, and Gabriel for the Moon.

You make a mirror of gold and silver that you cense with the hairs [taken from] the comb of a woman and you anoint it with your seed. Next cense it with hairs [taken from] her clothing. While washing yourself, make what appears in the mirror take her shape and then yours, or first take your shape, then hers. This experiment is that of a certain Ptolemy of Bebil. Three Indian sages arrived from Egypt and recommended the crafting of a mirror like this when the Moon is conjunct with Jupiter, and to gild or polish it when the Moon is conjunct with Venus. I shall tell you the composition of this mirror, and how you should proceed, and what you should do to ensure that all the natures of man enter into it.

Dip the mirror into fresh, natural blood, then cense it. Next, write upon it the names of the seven stars, their seven figures, the names of the seven angels and the seven winds. The names of the seven planets are: Zohal, Musteri, Marrech, Xemz, Zohara, Hotarid, Alchamar. And the following figures should be written on the mirror's outer edge:

And they will be in a circle. Then write within the polished, gilded circle, the names of the seven angels: Captiel, Satquiel, Samael, Raphael, Anael, Michael, and Gabriel. Once this has been done, inscribe the names of the seven winds* on the unpolished part.[9] These are the powerful winds whose names are: Barchia, Bethel almoda, Hamar benabia, Zobaa marrach, Fide arrach, Samores maymon, and Aczabi. Then hang the mirror in the sarza [?] for seven days over water and cense it. It should be hung on a red rod. Cense it for three days through with good perfumes, better than those found in the Book of Moses. If you look into this mirror and take good care of it, know that by its virtue you shall resemble men, the winds, spirits, demons, the living or the dead. All shall obey you and be sent to you. To achieve

---

*Occultists maintain that four angels govern the winds and the four corners of the world.

your work, it requires seven human elements in the fumigation: blood, sperm, spit, earwax, tears, excrement, and urine. Fumigate with this, especially for the winds, and they will do your will. Keep this and understand what I tell you, and you shall have power over the winds,* men, and demons, and you can do whatever you wish. When you are bathed and clean, call them: they will come and obey you. The working must be carried out above a cauldron full of water or beneath a clean container filled with water. Then you shall see, and what you request will be achieved.

158 ◈ TO INTRODUCE YOURSELF TO A KING OR PRINCE[10]

Use of the psalms represents just one of the ways in which the Bible is used for magical ends. In the sixteenth century, the pseudo-Agrippa recommended: "If some verse from the psalms or some passage in the Holy Scriptures conforms with our desire, we can insert it into our prayers."[11] In the following, the reader will find numerous examples that are all constructed in the same fashion: a psalm, whose incipit *(first few words) is indicated, must be written out, followed by various procedures (censing, washing, burying, etc.). However, it is worth noting that there is practically no connection between the psalm referenced and the purpose to be achieved! This can be verified by reading any of the given psalms in their entirety.*

Confitebor tibi domine in toto corde me narrabo. If you wish to be honored by a prince or to be warmly welcomed by one in honor, write this psalm on a sliver of glass along with these characters, then dilute them with rose water that you will in turn rub over your face.

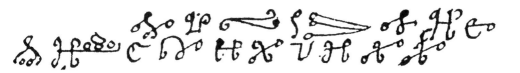

---

*This should be understood as *pneumata* or spirits.

159 ◆ To Destroy the House of Your Enemy[12]

In domine confide. Write this psalm on the hide of a gazelle, that is a wild goat of the forest, up to *ignis et sulfore et spiritus procellarum,* along with these characters using a pen or stylus of iron, fumigate it with pitch, and bury it in front of the feet of your enemy. Write another charter and present it to him.

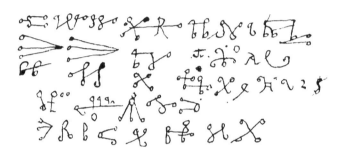

160 ◆ Against Your Enemy's House[13]

Exaudi Deus orationem meum. If your enemy is building a house and you wish the construction to advance no further, speak this psalm over its foundations and it will never be built.

161 ◆ Against an Enemy[14]

Domine deus salutis mee. If any enemy causes you harm, write this psalm on a pot, fill it with water from a spring or well that the sun has never cast its light on, and draw these characters on a sliver of glass and dilute them with a woman's bathwater, then put it in the above-mentioned pot and go pour it at the door of your enemy. Without a doubt, he will fall into great misfortune.

162 ◆ To Destroy Your Enemy[15]

Deus quis similis tibi erit. If someone is hostile to you, take a new pot, fill it with the water from a woman's bath, and read this psalm over it seven times, and he will be destroyed. But before filling the pot with water, write these characters on it.

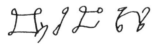

163 ◆ To Destroy an Enemy[16]

Noli emullari. Write this psalm and bury it in front of his door. His house shall be destroyed and his sons as well as his animals will die.

164 ◆ To Scatter Your Enemies[17]

Non ne Deo subjecta. Take the dust from beneath the altar after the masses have been said and the faithful have left the church. Read this psalm over it seven times, and then spread it in the house where your current enemies are gathered. You will come to the end and their house will be destroyed.

165 ◆ To Vanquish Your Enemies[18]

Exaudi Deus orationem meum. If you have enemies, read this psalm over these characters and attach it to your arm: you shall overcome them.

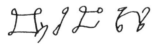

166 ◆ To Soothe an Enemy[19]

Salva me domine quoniam. If you wish to counter the enmity of someone who slanders you, write this psalm with these characters

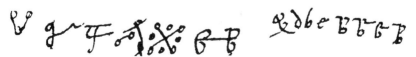

on a plate, cense it with styrax, read this psalm again over the water and then dilute the characters with it, and pour it on the door of your enemy.

167 ◆ TO BE FEARED BY ALL[20]

Dixit insipiens in corde suo. It you wish to obtain great things and honors from someone, read this psalm over clean water and salt up to *quoniam in generatione iusta est.* Write these characters and fumigate them with mastic, musk, and incense, then wash and dilute them with the aforementioned water and spill that over the door of whoever you choose. Speak the psalm cited—*insipiens*—and a second, *Quare fremuerunt gentes,* until *tunc loquatur ad eos in porta sua.*

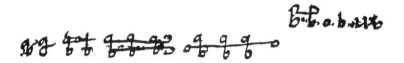

168 ◆ TO NOT GET LOST WHILE TRAVELING[21]

Dominus regit me et nihil mihi deerit. If someone begins a journey while ill, or however he is feeling, he should speak this psalm seven times and he shall have nothing to fear from his enemies. If he goes astray while en route, he should read this psalm over a good oil and anoint his face with it: he will find his way again.

169 ◆ TO ENTER A CITY OR A PRINCE'S HOME[22]

Domine quis habitabit. If you wish to enter any city or the home of a prince, read this psalm from its beginning, write these characters, and carry them on your person.

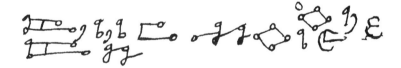

170 ◆ TO BE FREED FROM WANT[23]

Judica me Domine nocentes. If you fall into distress, recite this psalm seven times and you shall be saved. And if you wish to enter the home of a prince or an enemy, write it, and attach it to your arm, and God will deliver you.

171 ◇ For a Loan[24]

Verba mea auribus percipe. If you would like to borrow from a lender, read this psalm over a good oil until the end, anoint your face with it, write these characters, and he will give you all that you need.

172 ◇ To Avoid Scandal and Discord[25]

Exaudi domine. If you wish to avoid scandal and discord, write this psalm on a piece of parchment up to *animam meam ab impis* accompanied by these characters, fumigate them with mastic, and carry them on your person.

173 ◇ To Enjoy Good Fortune[26]

Benedixisti Domine terram tuam. Write this psalm on laurel leaves, fumigate them with mastic and saffron, blend them with rose oil, and anoint your face with the mixture: you will be lucky in all that you do.

174 ◇ For Incarcerated Individuals[27]

In te Domine speravi. If someone is imprisoned in a dungeon, he should read this psalm three times a day and three times a night until *miserere mej Domine quoniam tribulor,* and he should write these characters on an apple and eat it. He will get out of his prison cell immediately.

175 ◇ To Open All Locks[28]

There are numerous ways for opening closed doors, for example, by using a particular plant. Here is one that relies on a plant and the word Jesus spoke when healing a deaf-mute, ephphatha, *"be [thou] opened!" (Matthew 7:34). In the text I have translated, this is written as* effata *and repeated three times.*

Take some yarrow harvested on a Friday before the rising of the sun, place it within a consecrated pot, and have three Friday masses said over it. Touch the locks with it while saying: "Be opened! Be opened! Be opened!"

176 ◈ IF YOU WANT SOMEONE WHO HATES YOU TO FEAR YOU[29]
While he is sleeping, carefully place these characters and he will dread you.

† p . h . t . k . v . c . p . p . q . q .q . n .

177 ◈ BATTLE AMULET[30]
If you find a stone on which is carved a horse or wings, whoever carries it will benefit from it on the field of battle and his horse will never fall ill.

The engraving represents Pegasus, the horse of Bellerophon, which refers us to the constellation of the same name in the northern hemisphere.

178 ◈ TO SPEAK WITH THE SPIRIT OF A DEAD PERSON[31]
In the ancient past, the dead were never truly the departed and they could be summoned to learn whatever one desired. In the Bible, the witch of Endor summoned the specter of Samuel (1 Samuel 28), and in The Pharsalia, *Lucan describes a Thessalian witch who raised a corpse back on its feet. A distinction was made between two kinds of necromancy: necromancy, which raised the corpse and required blood; and sciomancy, which was satisfied with summoning the shade of the deceased. Most often it was those who died badly who were addressed, meaning those who had died without absolution or a grave, and those whose lives were prematurely cut short.[32] It was believed possible to attract the dead by burning incense in the places they visited most often, cemeteries, and the places where criminal executions took place. In the prescription below,*

the ritual is reduced to its simplest expression: all that remains is a rite of purification and a spell.[33]

The purification with hyssop has several possible explanations. In Judaism, a branch of hyssop is used to sprinkle the blood of sacrificed animals or holy water. According to the Bible, when Jesus was on the cross and said "I thirst," a sponge soaked in vinegar was attached to a hyssop branch and raised to his mouth (John 19:29). This is why hyssop was considered to be holy and even pious during the Middle Ages. In southern Europe, hyssop was long used as a defense against spirits.

Go to the tomb of the dead in the fourth hour of the night and sprinkle it with water blended with hyssop and the sap of the plant called costus.[34] Say three times:

> *Surge! Surge! Surge et loquere mihi!*

The spirit of the deceased will then appear and tell you what you wish to know.

179 ◈ To Prevent Dogs from Barking[35]

While making the sign of the cross over yourself, say:

> † Ray † Roy † lamitabat † cassamus

180 ◈ For Understanding the Song of Birds[36]

Man has always dreamed of understanding the speech of animals and this has given birth to all kinds of legends, such as those that maintain animals talk on Christmas night. In a remote past, it was thought that shamans and sorcerers could speak with animals. The most famous example from literature comes from the legend of Siegfried; after putting his finger covered with the blood of the dragon Fafnir in his mouth, Siegfried could understand the songs of the birds.[37] *In the ritual below, the acquisition of this gift is childishly simple and assumes a strong dose of naiveté!*

Take the tongue of a bird you wish to understand, put it in a pot of honey, and place it on your tongue. You will understand what it says.

181 ◇ To Give Someone a Fever[38]

It has always been believed that it is possible to transmit disease. To heal oneself, the illness would be transferred to the trees, for example—a practice that could still be found in the nineteenth century. In the charm below, the coded name of the tree could refer to an aspen or a laurel tree. The first hypothesis is the correct one, however, because we are in the presence of an analogical relationship: so-and-so is trembling with fever like an aspen!

Have three nails made that are like those that nailed Our Lord Jesus Christ and go close to the tree called *lspm* and stick these nails into it while saying: "Just like this *lrbrr* shivers, may this man, or this woman, shiver and be feverish as long as these nails are planted in this *lrbrrn.*"

182 ◇ Conjuration of Satan[39]

To conjure up the devil to obtain his obedience or some advantage is the central theme of the story of Faust, a figure who has many "colleagues" in the Western world. In Poland, for example, his equivalent is Pan Twardowski. The magician protects himself with a moral and physical purification, and then goes to a notorious malefic place, the crossroads, which is well known as a gateway to hell. It is on account of such beliefs that suicides and condemned persons are buried there—thus they will gain direct access to Satan's kingdom. This is also the place where one draws a magic circle in the middle of the night for invoking the spirits.[40] The conjuration is based on alliterations and the use of an anaphora that gives the words added force.

After taking communion and hearing the mass of the Holy Ghost, you will wash your hands and garb yourself in clean, white vestments, then make your way to the crossroads at the fall of night; you will draw there the necessary circle, and you shall say:

> Satan oro te pro arte te spero
> O Satan oro e te rapta reportes
> Satan ter oro te opera praesto

Satan oro te reo portas patere
Satan ter oro te reparato opes
Satan pater oro stare te pro eo
Satan pereo apro restat oro te
Satan oro te et appare e rostro.

183 ◇ To Conjure Belial[41]

Here is a fine example of the crafting of a voult *or* dagyde, *in other words, a figurine that serves as the support for a magical operation such as an evil spell.*

The ritual aims at giving life to the figurine so that it can serve as a medium for Belial. One combines the force of the planets with the vital fluids; one carries on one's person the Seal of the Sun, another element necessary for life; and the image is then censed, which is a consecration.

When the Sun is setting in the west and the moon is rising on the day of Mercury, make the image of a man with his feet turned behind out of virgin wax. Sprinkle it with water that has been poured through a silver flask for three days. Before the end of the fourth day, smear the image with the blood of a young chicken, first the head, then the chest, then the feet, and do this for three days in a row. Then draw the Sigillum Solis on its chest.

On the chest:

On the back:

Cense the image on the third day and pour running water over it for two more days with an old coin and lay four crowns of [?]. Let the image rest for the next three days. At their conclusion, return to the place it is kept and sprinkle it with the blood of a pigeon that, in March or January [several illegible words]. Amiably ask it what will happen and it will answer you in a friendly way.

Or else!

After making this figure, you will say: "Belial, by the supreme king, by Ariel and Daniel,[42] by Trion and Ymon!" Then strike it with a year-old hazel wand, and three times it will answer you in its own language and its own voice, and you will learn all that you wish to know. Carry it on your person and place it in a clean and secret place in your house or somewhere else, and take precautions so that no one else knows about it. And the figure will respond to as many questions as it pleases you to ask it.

This is one of the most secret spells and one of the best in the world, and better cannot be found. Never reveal it to anyone. That which has been proven is true.

184 ◇ To Invoke a Spirit[43]

The rituals for invoking a spirit all exhibit a common structure that is subject to outer variations. The fixed elements are: the purification of the magician, his protection, the conjuration, and the summons. In the magic circle below, the Latin inscription in the center reads: "Come down and show yourself to me, in my palm, and reveal to me what I ask of you, by the God who created you and in whom you believe and who is feared by heaven and earth. Amen." This circle is particularly interesting because it shows us the characters that belong to the "gods" of the days.

You shall remain chaste for three days, you shall wash your hands with the water that you shall cast in the air in honor of the gods of the planets and the days of the week. Be clean in your body, wash it well, and put on clean, white vestments! You shall next attach the following design to the palm of your left hand.

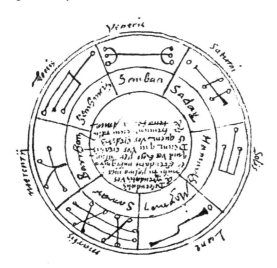

All these words, signs, and characters should be written starting with the Lord of the day on which this experiment shall be performed. If it is Saturday, you shall write Saday with the sign of the god of the day above it. If it is Tuesday, Maymon with the sign as indicated in the design. Next, take rue mixed with virgin oil and smear it on the design, which should shine like tin. You shall recite this conjuration no less than twenty-three times.

Hyr hensym caulesym schemin beneim lechelimurietin cellen hierfaucim Elfiramhi faraym mynclmensy henycaly letu metemie ylle calle.

Then you shall call each of the gods of the days, one after the other, those whose names are located in the inner circle, starting with the day on which you are performing this working. If it is a Sunday, you shall say:

O, Hamarth, turn toward me, approach and show yourself in my palm and unveil to me without lying what I ask of you. Furthermore, I command you instantly by the supreme majesty and by the God who created you and in whom you believe, and by the heavens, the earth, and the sea, and all that is found therein.

When the spirit appears, question him about what you wish to learn!

185 ◈ For a Fearful Man or Woman[44]
Bind this around their neck:
> *abre et abremon et abrende et consecramina**

186 ◈ To Remove Fear of Evil Folk[45]
Deus Deus meus respice in me. If you fall into the hands of your enemies or unjust men, and you are in fear of their malicious acts, read this psalm seven times and you will be delivered from them.

Write these characters on a small sliver of glass, cense them with mastic, then dissolve them with clean water that you will next pour on the door of your enemy: he will distance himself from you.

187 ◈ If Someone Has Fallen From Grace with His Lord[46]
If you have justly or unduly lost your lord's grace, bear these characters written on your left hand and you will be reconciled.

---

*"Abrende" is a distortion of *abremonte,* a magic word.

B. O. K. n. f. G. R. S. P. b.
C. O. H. D. A. A. l. q. P.
9 gg G ††† H. D. S. p. s. F. F. A. I. O.
ω Gleon y y † .R. R. R. O-S Cˢ C. t o r R

These names of Jesus Christ among the Hebrews [ ] iga ardens.

188 ◊ To Retain the Good Will of One's Lord[47]

Exaudiat te Dominus in die tribulationis. If you read this psalm every day, you shall retain your lord's affection. Write these characters, cense them with mastic, and carry them.

If you read the aforementioned psalm over a seriously ill man, he will recover if he is meant to live, otherwise he will die at once.

189 ◊ To Be Well Received[48]

Domine in virtute tua letabitur. If you wish to be received by any order,* or else be held in honor, read this psalm seven times over rose oil while at the same time writing these characters, then anoint your face with it. You shall receive a great honor.

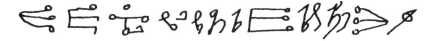

190 ◊ Another Version[49]

Deus stetit in sinagoga. Write these characters and read this psalm over them seven times, dilute them with rose oil, and anoint your face with it. You will be granted a grand and excellent welcome.

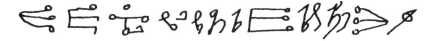

---

*The word "order" means "social class."

191 ◆ In Order Not to Lose the Grace of One's Lords[50]

This prescription mobilizes the four Apostles, the three Kings, six names of God (including the three most powerful), and a number of angels (who are identifiable by the –el ending of their names). After the invocation comes the consecration by means of the Masses and the wax of the Easter candle. By inscribing the names of the four Apostles, one encompasses the entire world as each of them stands at one of the cardinal points, and by attending a Mass to the Dead, one is seeking to propitiate them.

Write these following names on a piece of paper:

† lucas † marchus † matheus † johannes † jasper † melchior † balthesar
† on † onon † agla † tetragramaton † ely † eloy †
　Christus vincit † Christus regnat † Christus imperat †
Christ! Protect and guard your servant here and elsewhere
　† orebon † Michael rabeth affryel confryel luciel anaratri
　aynel

These names protect N., God's servant. In the name of the Father, the Son, and the Holy Ghost. Amen.

Have three Masses performed: one for the Four Apostles, one for the Three Kings, and one for the Departed. Fold this note and bury it secretly in the wax of the Easter candle, then carry it.

192 ◆ To Develop Your Memory[51]

Take pumpkin seeds, bury them in a man's skull, and smear them with human brain. Care for them protectively until they have germinated and borne fruit. He who eats the meat of these pumpkins will see an infinite development of his mental faculties. He will retain everything he hears and can carry to its conclusion any task he takes on.

193 ◆ Conjuration of Bees[52]

Bees! By the ineffable name of Our Lord Jesus Christ, I conjure you not to leave. By the very holy mother of Our Lord Jesus Christ, may our bees not flee from this field. Father, paraclete, consoler, Advocate. And speak this verse:

Lord, our lord, may your name be admired throughout the world.

194 ◈ To Drive Flies Away[53]

Draw this figure on a copper strip when the first decan of Leo is rising—it represents the sign of the Lion—and put it in the place from which you want to drive away the flies.

Draw this figure on a strip of tin when Scorpio rises in its third decan. The flies will abandon the spot where you place it.

195 ◈ For Planting the Vine[54]

Deus illuminatio mea. If you wish to plant a vine, write this psalm at the new moon and dilute it in the spring that waters your vine. It will be rid of all parasites, with the help of God.

196 ◈ For Pressing Wine[55]

Inclina domine aurem tuam. Read this psalm twenty-one times over the wine press and write these characters and put them in the press: a divine blessing will come down upon the wine.

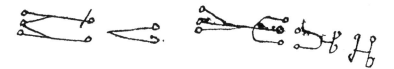

197 ◈ Wolf Spell[56]

Christ lived before the wolf. Christ must be understood as the Savior. Christ deliver these dogs or these other animals from the jaws of the wolves, the hand of thieves, and all your enemies!

198 ◈ Weapon Spell[57]

Barnasa ✠ Leutias † Bucella † Agla † Agla †
Tetragrammaton † Adonai

Admirable Lord, Abba, Father, Son of God, take pity on me! Protect your Servant N from all the kinds of weapons with which the saints were martyred. I command you, weapons of all kinds, to not have the power of slicing my flesh, nor spilling my blood, nor wounding me! By the cross of Our Lord Jesus Christ. Amen.

199 ◈ To Be Eloquent

He who carries this image on his person will have splendid eloquence.

10

THE MAGIC OF IMAGES

"So great is the extent, power, and efficacy of the Celestiall bodies, that not only naturall things, but also artificiall when they are rightly esposed to those above, do presently suffer by that most potent agent, and obtain a wonderfull life, which oftentimes gives them an admirable Celestiall virtue," says Henry Cornelius Agrippa when he explains to us how the heavenly bodies leave their mark on all the elements of nature. He goes on to say more precisely that the celestial bodies give more effective virtues to images "if they be framed not of any, but of a certain matter, namely whose naturall, and also specificall vertue is agreeable with the work, and the figure of the image is like to the Celestial."[1] An appropriately crafted image, that is, one crafted under the ascendant of the astral body and at the right moment, is then capable of fulfilling its celestial duties. As the reader will soon see, however, the engravings correspond to the traditional subjective representations of the planets. The god of war, Mars, appears as a warrior, and so forth. There are countless such images, which vary according to the texts. Each planet or constellation possesses several of them. Regarding Venus, for example, Albertus Magnus notes: "Nothing can be said of this in a few words since two thick books of magic, which deal only with her images, have been written on the subject."[2]

200 ◇ IMAGES OF MARS FOR DOING AS YOU WILL FOR GOOD OR EVIL[3]

On a magnet stone, depict Mars in the form of a man riding a lion, holding a bare sword in his right hand and a man's head in his left. You will do this at the hour of Mars when Mars is rising into the second decan of Aries. Whoever carries this stone shall be powerful in good as in evil, but more powerful in evil.

And if you wish your appearance to be dreadful and terrifying, depict Mars in the form of a standing man, wearing a breastplate and holding two swords, one resting on his throat and the other blade bare in his right hand. You will do this at the hour of Mars when it is in its house, on one of the martial stones. Whoever carries this stone shall be feared by all those who see him and nothing will happen to him.

To staunch the blood coming from any place, give Mars the form of a lion with these figures or signs in front of him

on the aliaza stone [= onyx] at the hour of Mars when it rises into the second decan of Scorpio. Whoever carries this image will be staunched at that place of his body from which it is flowing.

201 ◇ IMAGES OF THE SUN

1. If you wish the king to dominate all other kings and be victorious, depict the Sun on a ruby or another balas stone in the form of a king seated on a cathedra, wearing a crown with a crow in front of him and these signs beneath his feet: b o| o, when the Sun is rising into its exaltation. The king who bears this stone will vanquish all the kings that oppose him.

2. If you wish for someone to avoid defeat, accomplish all he undertakes, and have no nightmares, depict the Sun on a ruby in the form of a lion with the four aforementioned figures over him, when the Sun is in the ascendant of Leo and the nefarious [stars] are mov-

ing away and not looking at him. Whoever bears this stone will never be vanquished by another and all he undertakes will succeed, as I have said earlier.

3. If, when the Sun is in its exaltation, you depict it on a diamond in the form of a woman seated in a quadriga, holding a mirror in her right hand and a staff in her left, with seven candleholders above her, he who bears this image will be feared by all those who see and oppose him.

4. If, on the sedina stone [hematite], you depict the Sun by these signs below when it is rising into the first decan of Leo, he who bears this image on his person will be protected from any epilepsy that comes from the combustion of the Moon.

$$\text{ı } \text{ʃ } \text{ʯ30} \text{C } \text{ʒ}$$

202 ◈ IMAGE OF VENUS[4]

1. If you depict Venus in the form of a woman with a human body but with a bird's head and the claws of an eagle, holding an apple in her right hand and, in her left hand, a comb resembling a wooden tablet upon which is written these figures: O _ O I _, he who bears this image will be warmly welcomed and found pleasing by all.

2. If, when Venus rises into the first decan of Libra, you depict it on a white stone in the form of a woman holding an apple in her right hand and a comb in her left, he who bears this image on his person will always feel gay and lighthearted.

3. If, at the hour of Venus, you depict Venus on a lapis lazuli in the form of a naked maiden holding a chain on her neck and around her, with a man at her side and, behind her, a small child raising a sword, he who bears this image will be found pleasing by women and can do with this whatever he wishes.

4. If, on a crystal or beryl, you depict Venus in the form of a serpent with the image of a tarantula above it and gushing water in front, Jupiter being in its exaltation, he who bears this image will not be bitten by snakes, and he who washes it in any kind of liquid and gives it to someone to drink, it will heal the bite.

5. If, at its hour, you depict Venus by these signs

but in another book they are

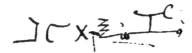

then take all those you wish—all children will love and follow you.

6. If, on the almehe [?] stone, you depict Venus at its hour and when it is in its exaltation, as a seated woman with wings and braided hair tossed behind her head, with two children in her lap, he who bears this stone will move about easily without any pitfalls.

7. If, on a crystal, you depict Venus at its hour by three people bound together, he who bears this stone will be lucky in business affairs and draw benefits from them.

8. If, on a coral stone, you depict Venus in the form of two cats and a mouse, at its hour, when Venus is rising into its exaltation, no mouse will be able to stay wherever you place said stone.

9. If, on the alaquech stone [carnelian], you depict Venus in the form of a fly in flight, and the hour of Venus when it is in its exaltation, no fly can remain wherever this image may be.

10. If, on one side of a dehenech stone [malachite], you represent Venus in the form of leeches, and if you make two leeches on the other side, the head of one touching the tail of the other, at the hour of Venus and beneath its ascendant, and if you make a seal of this image in wax or some similar thing, and you throw the seal where you please, a place where there are leeches, none will remain in this place.

11. If, on a crystal, you depict Venus in the form of a standing woman with an idol in front of her, also standing, at the hour of Venus, when it is in its ascendant, he who bears this stone will be found pleasing to women.

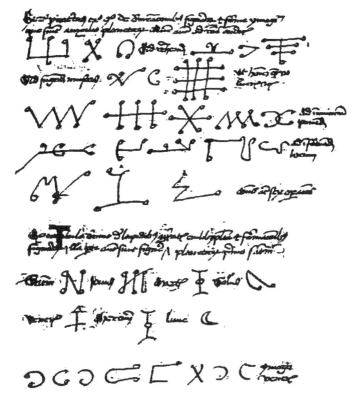

Characters of the planets as shown in the Picatrix latinus, *Vienna manuscript (National Library, Codex 3317, folio 113 v°).*

203 ◆ IMAGE OF MERCURY

1. If you depict Mercury on an emerald as a baron seated in a chair with a rooster's head above him, and feet like those of an eagle, and to his left there is a kind of fire and these signs are at his feet:

If, then, you make this at the hour of Mars when it is in its exaltation, the prisoner carrying this stone will be delivered from his bonds.

2. If, in connection with the operations of Mercury, you draw these signs on an emerald, when Mercury is in its ascendant, the stone will be useful to copyists, notaries, and all the merchants that carry it.

3. If, in connection with the operations of Mercury, you draw the image of a frog on an emerald when Mercury is in its hour and in the ascendant, no one will offend you; one will speak well of you and of all your works.

4. If, in connection with the operations of Mercury, you draw the form of a lion on an emerald and another in the form of a lion's head, at its hour and when Mercury is in the ascendant in the sign of Gemini, and if you write an "*a*" above its head, and a "*b*" below, he who carries this image will be delivered of his illnesses, will be feared, and people will speak well of him.

5. If, in connection with the operations of Mercury, you draw the form of a scorpion on an emerald, at its hour and when Mercury is in its ascendant, the pregnant woman who carries this image on her person will give birth easily and without danger for either herself or her progeny.

6. If, in connection with the operations of Mercury, you draw on stone of marble the hand of a man holding a set of scales, in its hour and when Mercury is in its ascendant, and if you seal this image with dirt or another substance that lends itself to this, and you give it to someone who is ill, he will be healed immediately, whatever the nature of his disease, and this is demonstrated by fevers.

204 ◊ IMAGES OF THE MOON

If you depict the Moon in the form of a man with a bird's head propping himself up on a staff, with something that looks like a flowering tree in his hand, at the hour of the Moon and when it is in its exaltation, he who bears this image on his person will never be fatigued whatever path he pursues.

If, on a lapis lazuli, you depict the Moon by these signs, at its hour and in its ascendant, and you wash this image in any liquid and give it to two or more men to drink, they will get along famously and nothing will be able to separate them.

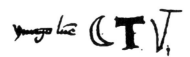

205 ◈ Talismanic Seals of the Days of the Week*

Sunday

Monday

Tuesday

Wednesday

Thursday

Friday

Saturday

*The six planets correspond to the Arabic numerals 851585.

206 ◆ THE IMAGES IN THE STONES

The Seals or Images According to Hermes[5]

The work of Hermes referred to here is called Quadripartitus *because in its four parts it deals with fifteen stars, fifteen stones, fifteen plants, and fifteen images.[6] There are five extant manuscripts of this pamphlet; two of these are from the thirteenth century and a revised version exists in two fourteenth-century manuscripts. Comparison of them with our example reveals that the name of the star and that of the plant were removed. Here, for example, is what corresponds with our number 5: the planet is Canis Major, the stone is the beryl, the plant is the savine, after which the means for crafting the ring is then given: "You shall set down a bit of mugwort, a little dracontea, and serpent tongue beneath the beryl when the Moon is in Canis Major; whoever wears this ring will be graced by the spirits and will forge peace between the Great Ones as well as between the husband and wife. Its engraving looks like a hare or a beautiful young woman."*

Hermes, in his small book titled *Quadripartitus,* mentions fifteen images: as it is possible to come across them, I shall mention them, too.

1. A man's head with a long beard and some blood around his neck, engraved upon a diamond, you should know, brings victory and audacity, and it protects the body from wounds. It also permits winning the favor of kings and princes.

2. A virgin, a young girl, or else a torch engraved on crystal, you should know, possesses the power to protect life.

3. A man in the middle of an argument engraved upon a ruby, you should know, will bring honors and wealth.

4. A sapphire, on which a man wishing to play a musical instrument is depicted, raises its owner to honorable estate and wins him the favor of all.

5. A greyhound sculpted on a beryl helps in attaining the highest honors, renown, and goodwill.

6. An agate decorated with a rooster or three young girls wins its owner the favor of other men, it enables him to dominate the spirits of the air, and it is useful in the art of magic.

7. A lion or a mouse catcher depicted on a garnet brings wealth and honors, causes the heart to rejoice, and drives melancholy away.

8. A crow or a viper, carved on an onyx, you should know, gives its owner courage, subjugates and gathers demons, and sends them fleeing; and it calms the evil winds.

9. An emerald on which a man who looks like a merchant bringing his goods to sell is depicted, or a man sitting beneath a centurion,* provides wealth, brings victory, and protects one from evil and perilous situations.

10. The owner of a magnet decorated with a bull or a calf can go wherever he pleases in complete safety and with no worries; it also frees one from all enchantments and artifices, and shifts them to another object.

11. A jasper decorated with a horse or a wolf soothes fever and keeps the blood in.

12. A crowned man raised in the air depicted on a topaz makes its owner good, friendly, and esteemed by men, and brings him honors and consideration.

13. An armed man, with a sword in hand, carved on a sardonyx or an amethyst procures its owner a good, reliable memory, and gives him wisdom.

14. A stag or a goat carved on a chalcedony has the power to increase wealth, if it is kept in a money box.

207 ◇ RAGIEL, *THE BOOK OF WINGS*

The authorship of The Book of Wings *has been attributed to Ragiel (Raziel), an angel whose name means "God's secret," and who is the personification of divine wisdom in the Kabbalah. In this book, a lapidary (which draws from the same sources as do the lapidaries of Solomon and Hermes) teaches us about the powers of several engraved gemstones.*

---

*The meaning here is obscure because none of the texts makes it possible to see whether Leonardo made a mistake or not. Perhaps the word centurion designates a tree, perhaps an eglantine.

1. If one finds in an onyx the image of a camel or two goats among the myrtles, it has the power to call up demons, gather them together, and enslave them; if one carries it on one's person, it has the power to cause terrible dreams.

2. If one finds the image of a Vulture in a chrysolite, its power is to enchain demons and winds, contain them, and gather them together; it protects the place where it is found against demons and their ravages; and demons will obey the person who carries it with him.

3. If the image of a Bat is sculpted into a heliotrope, it gives its owner power over demons, and it is useful for incantations.

4. A man with a sword in hand carved on a carnelian has the power to protect the place it is found against storms and lightning, and to guard its owner against vices and enchantments.

5. The image of a Bull in a prase [stone] thwarts, it is said, evil spells and brings the leader recognition.

6. A Bear figure carved in an amethyst has the power to send demons fleeing, and to protect and guard the individual from intoxication.

An image of an armored man carved in a magnet has the power to combat enchantments and bring its owner victory in war.

208 ◈ SOLOMON'S LAPIDARY

1. If a green jasper is topped by a head and neck, fix it upon a gold or silver ring, carry it on your person, and you shall escape all deaths. Write the following letters on the ring: B.B.P.P.N.E.N.A., and your entire body will be spared from all disease, especially fever and hydropsia, and the stone will greatly help in hunting birds. And you will be reasonable and honest in all things, in times of war and in times of peace, and this stone helps women conceive and give birth; it brings peace, harmony, and several other good things to the person who carries it; in their behavior, though, these individuals should be just and honest.

2. If you find the image of a man carved on a diadochos holding a small offering in his right hand and a snake in his left, keeping a lion at his feet, with the sun above this man, and if one fixes this stone to a lead ring along with a root of mugwort and a root of Greek fennel,

bring the ring to the water's edge, invoke evil spirits as you please, and they will answer all your questions.

3. If you find in a hematite an image of a man standing on a dragon and holding a sword in one hand, mount it on a ring of lead or iron, and all the spirits that dwell in darkness shall obey you and with a sweet charm reveal to you where treasures are hidden, and they will show you how to hunt them down.

4. If you find carved on a crystal the head of a lion or a two-headed dragon with a short tail, or a man with a staff in his right hand that is striking the head of the lion or the heads of the dragon, affix it to orichalcum with musk and amber placed beneath the stone. If you carry it on your person, all will obey you, and your riches will increase. Imprint this stone in wax and give this seal to the person of your choice, and he or she will have the same powers.

5. If a pyrite is decorated with a horseman with girded sword holding the reins in one hand and a bow in the other, and if this stone is affixed to a gold ring, its owner will be victorious in combat, and no one will be capable of resisting him. And if someone dips this ring in musk-scented oil, and dampens his face with this same musk-scented oil, all those who see him shall be in fear of him, and none shall be able to resist him.

6. If any kind of stone is decorated with a standing man in a cuirass with a helmet on his head and an unsheathed sword in his hand, and if it is mounted on an iron ring equal in weight to this stone, none shall be able to resist its owner in battle.

7. If one finds the image of a naked man standing in a magnet, with a naked young woman standing to his right, with her hair gathered up around her head, and the man has his right hand resting at the throat of the young woman and his left hand on his chest, and he is gazing at the face of the young woman, while she is looking at the ground, this stone must be affixed to a ring equal in weight to it. The stone must be placed upon a hoopoe tongue, myrrh, alum, and as much human blood as required to equal the weight of a bird's tongue. None, upon seeing him, shall be able to resist the owner of this ring, whether in war or some other context; no thief or ferocious animal will be able to enter

the house in which said stone is to be found. And an epileptic who drinks of the water in which this stone has been steeped will be cured. Imprint this stone on red wax, hang it from the neck of a dog, and as long as this stone is in this location, it will not be able to bark; all persons who carry the seal in question in the midst of thieves, dogs, and enemies shall be spared by them.

11

ORISONS

An orison is a magic prayer. It can be distinguished from the ordinary Christian prayer by the use of noncanonical elements such as obscure words and apocryphal references. The first example below is an extremely beautiful expression of a form of popular piety blended with paganism. This kind of paternoster was being used up into the twentieth century.[1] It involves protecting oneself from everything that might happen during sleep. It is a common belief that the eruption of malefic beings tends to occur when darkness has fallen, so some kind of protection is called for. In medieval literature, the legend of Merlin testifies to what can happen when one is not protected: the enchanter's future mother forgot to sign herself with the cross one night, the devil slipped into her bed, took advantage of her, and fathered Merlin.

209 ◈ White Paternoster[2]
Little white paternoster that God made, that God said, that God put in paradise. In the evening when going to bed, I find three angels sleeping in my bed, one at the feet, two at the headboard; the good Virgin Mary in the middle who tells me that I can go to sleep, there is nothing to doubt, the good Lord is my Father, the good Virgin is my Mother, the three Apostles are my brothers, the three virgins are my sisters. My body is wrapped in the shirt inside which God was born; the Cross of

St. Margaret is written on my chest. Milady goes out into the fields crying aloud to God, and meets Milord S. John. Milord S. John, from where do you come? I come from Ave salus. If Lady trusts he is in the tree of the Cross, his feet hanging, his hands nailed, a small hat of white thorns on his head.

Whoever says this three times in the evening, three times in the morning, will reach heaven in the end.

210 ◈ Orison[3]

All powerful lord God, by your name Jothe, save me, your servant, here and in eternity, and take me far from the demons and grant me prosperity by your very name Jothe. Amen.

211 ◈ Orison for the Falling Sickness[4]

Oremus, Praeceptis salutaribus moniti &c. Pater noster, &c.

212 ◈ The Beard of God[5]

Sinners male and female come speak to me, my heart should tremble strongly in my belly like the leaf on the aspen, like the *Loisonni* when she sees that it is necessary to come onto a small plank, which is neither larger nor thicker than three hairs of a woman put together. Those who God's Beard will know over the plank shall pass, & those who do not will know at the end of the plank shall sit crying, braying, my God, alas, unhappy are they, like a small child is what God's Beard teaches me, a sole God you shall worship, and so forth.

213 ◈ The Holy Virgin's Passport of Immaculate Conception[6]

Holy Mary, mother of my Savior Iesus-Christ, who was conceived without original sin, pray for me now & at the hour of my death. Pray for my conversion, protect me in all my undertakings: be ever my consolation; take care of my salvations; I have placed all my trust in you, mother of mercy, who never had any stain of sin. Tota pulchra es Maria, & macula non est in te.

214 ◆ ORISON TO THE PLANETS

To get a true sense of the orisons to the planets, one must first realize that each celestial body has angels and spirits. For example, if we can place our trust in the Picatrix *(IV, 9), the planet Saturn's angel is Quermiex (or Rredimez); at its top stands Toz, at the bottom Herus (or Corez), at its right Quenis (or Deytuz), at its left Dius (or Deriuz), in front of it is Tamines (or Talyz), and behind it is Tahytos (or Daruz). Macader (or Quehinen) gives impulse to its movement. The same is true for each planet, with the names following a similar distribution. The seven orisons below, which are conjurations, strengthen the invocations to the planets when the aid of the latter is requested for a magical operation that involves the purification of the officiating magician, attention paid to the day and to the hour, and the burning of incense.*

Orison of Saturn[7]

Quermiex, Tos, Herus, Quemis, Dius, Tamines, Tahytos, Macader, Quehinen; Saturn! Come at once with your spirits!

Orison of Jupiter

Bethniehus, Darmexim, Maciem, Maxar, Derix, Tahix, Tayros, Deheydex, Mebguedex; Jupiter, Bargis! Come at once with your spirits!

Orison of Mars

Guebdemis, Hegneydiz, Gueydenuz, Magras, Herdehus, Hebdegabdis, Mehyras, Dehydemes; Red Mars, Baharam! Come at once with your spirits!

Orison of the Sun

Beydeluz, Demeymes, Adulex, Metnegayn, Atmefex, Naquirus, Gadix; Sun! Come at once with your spirits!

Orison of Venus

Deydex, Gueylus, Meylus, Demerix, Albimex, Centus, Angaras, Dehetarix; Venus, Neyrgat! Come at once with your spirits!

Orison of Mercury

Barhuyex, Emirex, Hamerix, Sehix, Deryx, Meyer, Deherix, Baix, Faurix; write, Mercury! Come at once with your spirits!

Orison of the Moon

Guernus, Hedus, Maranus, Miltas, Taymex, Ranix, Mehyelus, Degayus; Moon! Come at once with your spirits!

Orison

Lord Jesus Christ, you who are in heaven and on earth, give us our bread.

12

MAGIC ALPHABETS

Magic has always sought to preserve its secrets in order to prevent just anyone from using them without mastering the accompanying science. The legend of the sorcerer's apprentice is well known: he set in motion a process that he was unable to stop. Over the course of the centuries, magicians and sorcerers have created a multitude of alphabets—some of which are yet to be deciphered.

Signature of the demons, from Le Véritable Dragon rouge
(Avignon, 1522, 1822).

215 ◊ THE ALPHABETS OF TRITHEMIUS

In 1508, the abbot Johannes Trithemius, whom we met in the introduction, wrote a study of cryptography titled Polygraphiae,[1] *in which he examines the combinations of words and letters of the Bible, the names of spirits, and* alphabets. *In the folio edition of 1518 he reproduced: 1. The alphabet of the Franks, by a certain Doracus; 2. The alphabet he found in the Grammar of the Alsatian monk Otfrid of Weissenburg; 3. The alphabets used as ciphers (secret codes) at the time of Charlemagne; 4. An alphabet of his own composition; 5. A secret alphabet accompanied with advice to those who wished to compose their own. It so happens that in this last alphabet, the letters m, M, q, z, ch, and y show great similarities with certain characters from the magic prescriptions cited in the preceding chapters and which open with the first verse of a psalm. The reader may therefore attempt to decipher some of the encrypted spells by using these alphabets.*

SECRET ALPHABETS

⊖	a	z	g	ȝ	n	o	t
ı	b	ψ	b	9	o	q'	v
ç	c	∞	l	x	P	q	x
6	d	ϒ	k	H	q	⅋	y
R	e	8	l	V	r	s	z
y	f	ʌ	m	φ	s	ð	w

δl	a	q	g	x	m	n	q	†	.
ɣ	b	ɴ	b	ƀ	n	b	r	ⴲ	w
α'	c	φ	i	ᴦ	o	y	r	ⴘ	x
ɣ'	d	⅄	k	E	p	y	sc	X	z
⧺	e	x	l	ᴇⱼ	ph	y	sch	ⴗ	ch
λ	f	ⵝ	m	Ɇ	pr	ꜧ	t	ꝗ	y

216 ◈ THE ALPHABET OF HERMES

In the tenth century, an Arab scholar named Ibn Wahshiya compiled a treatise titled The Long Desired Knowledge of the Occult Alphabets Finally Revealed, *in which he reproduced eighty-seven alphabets, the majority of them occult and attributed to illustrious figures including Socrates, Hermes, Plato, and Democritus. His treatise is of interest because he informs us that there were alphabets for the planets and signs of the Zodiac. They were used for making amulets and talismans as well as for writing the magic spells we find in some fifteenth-century manuscripts. Knowledge of the alphabets in the West is attested by Athanasius Kircher (1601–1680), the Jesuit scholar who wrote treatises in Latin on the occult sciences, such as* The Underground World *(1664) and* The Egyptian Oedipus *(1652–1654).*

Below I reproduce the alphabet of Hermes, which was preceded by the following note:

The alphabet of Hermes abu Thoth the philosopher. He wrote on the noble art of the philosophical secrets. In Upper Egypt he built treasure rooms and erected stones containing magic inscriptions that he sealed and protected by the charm of this alphabet originating in the regions of darkness.[2]

The Arabs were quite impressed by the hieroglyph-covered remnants of Ancient Egyptian civilization, and they interpreted these symbols as being magical signs. One example of this is The Summary of Wonders, *written in the tenth century by the mysterious Ibrahim Ibn Wasif Shah, half of which is devoted to the marvels of Egypt and describes a multitude of magicians and talismans.*[3] *The two alphabets read from left to right.*

ي ط ح ز و ه د د ج ب ا

ق ق ف ص ف ع س ن م ل ت

غ ظ ض ذ خ ث ت ش ر

217 ◈ The Alphabet of Colphoterios

Here is the alphabet of the philosopher Colphoterios. The note by Ibn Wahshiya says:

He was extremely versed in the knowledge of spirits and Kabbalistic charms, in talismans, astrological aspects, and in the art of black magic. Philosophers and learned men have used this alphabet in their books and writings, in preference over others, on account of its various extraordinary qualities.

ط ح ز و د د ه ب ا

ف ق خ س ن م ل ي ك ت

ض غ ظ ت ش ر ص

غ ظ ض

218 ◆ The Planetary Alphabet of Hermes

This alphabet attributed to Hermes, extracts from which I reproduce here, is introduced as follows:

> This alphabet has been used on the obelisks, the pyramids, the tablets of inscriptions, and the stones, the temples and other ancient buildings, since the times of the first pharaohs. It does not consist of a series of letters like other alphabets but in expressions composed in accordance with the arrangement made by Hermes the Great.

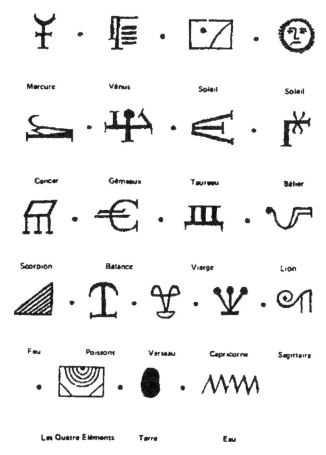

219 ◆ The Secret and Sacred Alphabets of Pietro d'Abano

Pietro d'Abano (Petrus De Apono or Aponensis; 1250–1316), a philosopher,[4] professor of medicine at the University of Padua, and alchemist of Pope Honorious IV, was the author of Elements for Working in the Magic

Sciences, *the manuscript of which is housed at the Arsenal Library. Other works of magic were also attributed to him. Put on trial because of his neoplatonic and Averroist beliefs, he was incarcerated by the Inquisition and died in prison.*[5] *He recorded four alphabets that were later used by Henry Cornelius Agrippa.*

The first of these alphabets came from the Theban Honorious. The second is the "Script of Malachim or Melachim," which is to say it came from the angels; the name of the third alphabet is the "Script from Beyond the River"; and the final alphabet is called the "Celestial Script" by the Hebrews because it was found drawn in the constellations. The small circles or balls in the characters depict the stars. Readers may entertain themselves by comparing these last three alphabets with those I introduced earlier, and by attempting to decipher the magical spells with their aid.

The Alphabet of Honorius

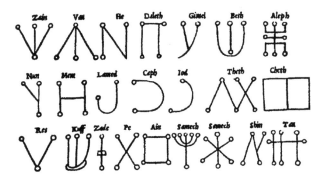

The Script of Malachim

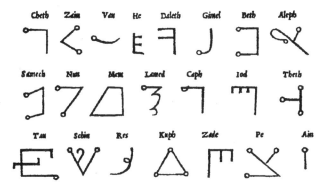

The Script from Beyond the River

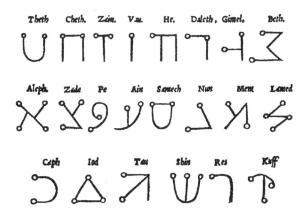

The Celestial Script

PART TWO

From Scholarly Magic to Folk Magic

Romanus-Büchlein

vor

GOtt der HErr bewahre meine See-
.le, meinen Auß und Eingang;
von nun an bis in alle Ewig-
keit, Amen. Halleluja.

Gedruckt zu Venedig.

Cover page of the Little Book of Roman (Romanus-Büchlein).

13

THE *ROMANUS-BÜCHLEIN*

In Germany, the *Romanus-Büchlein* (*Little Book of Roman*) was one of the most widely distributed grimoires from the seventeenth to the end of the nineteenth century. Adolf Spamer has made a very enlightening study of it to which I shall refer,[1] but of all the editions he surveyed, the one at my disposal was unknown to him.

The title is the *Little Book of Roman* and its flyleaf says:

> May the Lord God guard my soul, my comings and goings, henceforth and for eternity, amen. Hallelujah!

It also includes the false assertion that it was "Printed in Venice." This fictional printing place was intended to deceive the censors. The booklet in question contains forty-seven pages glued into a handmade, brown-leather binding that is devoid of any information. The booklet contains eighty-one prescriptions. A very large number of these concern protection against all manner of weapons; there are also prayers and orisons, and benedictions and protections against all kinds of evil spells. Occasionally we come across an amusing magic spell, such as one for enchanting a staff so that it will strike a person's victim. The printing and the language indicate that this edition was produced in the seventeenth century, although it is impossible to date it more precisely. The text contains gaps where certain magical inscriptions and figures have not been reproduced. Here is the first part, which has never before been translated.

220 ◆ MATIN PRAYER TO SAY WHEN EMBARKING ON A JOURNEY AND WHICH IMMEDIATELY PROTECTS THE MAN FROM MISFORTUNE

I (your name), I wish to leave today, I wish to follow the divine route and paths, those that He traveled, those that our dear Lord Jesus Christ took as well as our beloved Virgin with her cherished infant, with his seven rings, with his true objects, O my dear Lord Jesus Christ, I am your serf, so that no dog may bite me, so that no wolf may bite me, so that no murderer comes near me! My God, protect me from sudden death! I am in the hand of God, I am attached to it, I am bound to His hand by the five sacred wounds of Christ, so that no gun and any other weapon may wound me, no more than the virginity of the Virgin Mary was by the favor she received, by her infant Jesus. Recite three Our Fathers, three Ave Marias, and a Credo.

221 ◆ ANOTHER PRAYER

Jesus of Nazareth, king of the Jews, king of the entire world, protect me, N.N., today and tonight so that I may be neither captured nor bound. May the holy Trinity prevent any projectile, any gun shot, any lead from striking me! May these projectiles be as the tears and sweat of the agony of Jesus Christ. In the name of God the Father, the Son, and the Holy Ghost. Amen!

222 ◆ ANOTHER PRAYER

My God and Lord, powerful judge, I beseech you, by your rosy blood that sprang forth from your sacred side and your five holy wounds, to protect me, N.N., so that no misfortune befalls me and no wrong be done to me. May Christ protect me from all manner of weapons. May Jesus Christ accompany me and be with me, and be before me, and be at my sides. May Jesus Christ be my head and my guardian, in the house and in the yard, in the forest and in the open field, protecting me from all thieves and murderers, whether they be visible or invisible. Christ, be my protection, my guard, and my shield. Lord, you have yourself sanctified your holy cross with your rosy blood! Christ, help me and protect me day and night from any projectile and all weapons, in all places and from a shameful death. My Lord and my God, I pray you and exhort by your great martyrdom and innocent death that you have suffered on the wood of the holy cross for me, poor sinner, because you are the A[lpha] and the O[mega], the beginning and the end. The virtue of Christ goes to the end of all. God willing henceforth guard me and protect me for eternity. Amen.

223 ◆ WHEN A MAN SUFFERS FROM A DISEASE OF THE MOUTH, WHEN THIS IS SPOKEN, IT SHALL SURELY AID HIM

Job traveled the land with a staff in his hand. He met the Lord God who said to him: "Job, why do you complain so much?" Job answered: "Ah God, why wouldn't I? My throat and my mouth are going bad." God replied: "Below in this valley, there flows a spring." N.N. it will heal you in the name of God the Father, the Son, and the Holy Ghost. Amen.

Say this three times every morning and every evening, and when you say "it will heal you," blow three times into the mouth of the child.

224 ◆ A SURE CHARM AGAINST FIRE, WHICH ALWAYS WORKS

In the suffering and bitter death of our dear Lord Jesus Christ, fire, wind, and blaze, you who possess the power of the elements, I command you by our Lord Jesus Christ, who has spoken over the winds and the sea, which obeyed the powerful words that Jesus has spoken, I command you, fire, I threaten you and announce that you must calm down immediately with your elemental force, you flame and inferno, by the sacred rosy blood of our dear Lord Jesus Christ. Fire, wind, and burning blaze, I command you as God has commanded through his holy angel so that the three saints Sadrach, Mesach, and Abednego would remain unscathed by what occurred. Do the same, fire and flame and blaze, extinguish yourself as the all-powerful God has spoken when he created the four elements as well as heaven and earth, saying: *Fiat fiat! Fiat!*, which is to say: that this is achieved in the name of God the Father, the Son, and the Holy Ghost. Amen.

225 ◆ THE ART OF EXTINGUISHING FIRE WITHOUT WATER

Write the following letters on each side of a plate and cast it into the fire, it will harmlessly go out at once.

S A T O R
A R E P O
T E N E T
O P E R A
R O T A S

226 ◆ FOR DIVERTING FIRE

Take a black chicken in the nest, either morning or evening, slit its throat and toss it on the ground, tear out its stomach, but do nothing with it, leave it near the body, then seek to obtain a piece of a shirt that was used for the menstruations of a young girl who is still a pure virgin. Take a plate, when the time comes that there are many, and wrap these two pieces together, paying close attention that you do not use an egg laid on the Thursday of Palm Sunday. Wrap these three things together with the wax, then place them inside a rabbit, cover them, and bury them beneath the threshold of your house, with the help of God, so long as one beam remains standing, when fire has already taken the front and back of your home, the inferno will cause no harm, neither to you nor to your children. It is invested with divine power that is sure and true.

If a violent fire suddenly breaks out, arrange to obtain the whole shirt used by a young girl when menstruating, or a cloth in which a woman gave birth to a child, throw it rolled up into the fire in silence, for certain this will help you.

227 ◆ TO PLACE IN THE STABLE AS PROTECTION FROM WITCHES THAT ENCHANT LIVESTOCK, OR TO WRITE ON BEDS FOR PROTECTION AGAINST ILL-INTENTIONED MEN OR SPIRITS

**WHO AFFLICT YOUNG AND OLD AT NIGHT, WHICH WILL
FREE AND SPARE THEM**

Witch, I forbid you my house and my yard, I forbid you my horses and stable! Go afflict another house! Start by crossing every mountain, by counting all the stakes of the hedges, crossing over all the waters until cherished day enters my home. In the name of the Father, the Son, and the Holy Ghost. Amen!

**228 ◈ TO PLACE IN THE STABLES SO THAT EVIL FOLK CANNOT
DO ANYTHING TO THE LIVESTOCK**

Take wormwood, black cumin, cinquefoil, and asafoetida, two pieces of each, take swamp bean stalks, the ordure from behind the stable animals, and a little salt. Make a small packet from this and place it inside a hole you will make in the threshold over which the animals cross when leaving and entering, and seal it with a peg of alder.

229 ◈ HOW TO HELP A BEWITCHED MAN OR BEAST

Three false tongues have bound you; three holy tongues have spoken in your favor. The first is that of God the Father, the second that of God the Son, and the third that of God the Holy Ghost. They give you flesh and blood, and peace and courage. Flesh and blood have grown on you, and were born with you. If a man has bewitched you, you have lost them. May God bless you and Saint Cyprien, too! If a woman has bewitched you, may God and Mary bless you! If a man-servant has bewitched you, I bless you in the name of God and the heavenly kingdom. If a maid or a girl has done you malice, may God and the heavenly bodies bless you. The sky is above you, the earth is below, and you are in the middle. I bless you against curses. When our dear Lord Jesus Christ was dying in bitter suffering, all that the evil Jews had wrongly said shivered. Look how the sons of God shiver as if they had fever. Our Lord Jesus Christ said: "I do not have fever, no one shall have it. He who helped me bear my † and my complaints, I shall deliver him from fever." In the name of God the Father, the Son, and the Holy Ghost. Amen.

230 ◈ Against Ghosts and All Kinds of Evil Spells

I.

N. I. R.

I

Sanctus   Spiritus

I

N. I. R.

I.

May all be spared, here from this time, and in the beyond eternally! Amen.

The spell that forms part of this is: *God bless me, here at this moment, and in the beyond for eternity! Amen.*

231 ◈ For Driving Away Misfortune and Danger in the House

Saint Matthew, Saint Mark, Saint
Luke, Saint John
Ito, alo, Massa Dandi Bando, III. Amen
J. R. N. R. J.

Our Lord Jesus Christ entered the hall where the Jews were quarreling. Today, those who denigrate me wrongly with their pernicious tongues must face me, give praise to God, shut up, keep their silence, be scared and be criticized, forever and without end, and also propagate the laws of God. May I.I.I. help me always and for eternity! Amen.

232 ◈ A Phylactery to Carry on Your Person to Protect You from the Arts of the Gypsies, Break Mortal Dangers, and Protect Men at Every Moment

Just as the prophet Jonas, God's forerunner, remained hidden for three days and three nights in the belly of a whale, may all-powerful God see to guarding and paternally protecting me from all danger. I.I.I.

233 ◈ To Carry On Your Person To Shunt Distress and Death from Your Path

I know that my Savior lives and that he will resurrect me from the earth.

234 ◈ Against Swellings

Three pure virgins were on their way. They wished to examine a swelling and an illness. The first said: "It is." The second declared: "It is not." The third said: "Now then, it is not. May our Lord Jesus Christ come forth and speak in the name of the holy Trinity!"

235 ◈ Against All Hostility and All Kinds of Quarrels

Force, Hero, Prince of Peace, I.I.I.

236 ◈ How to Help a Cow Whose Milk Has Been Stolen

Give the cow three spoonfuls of fresh milk. Address yourself to spots of blood. If someone asks where you put the milk, answer: "The woman who took it has come and I ate her in the name of God, the Father, the Son, and the Holy Ghost. Amen." Then say the prayer of your choice.

237 ◈ A Second Version

I. The cross of Jesus Christ spilled milk.
I. The cross of Jesus Christ spilled water.
I. The cross of Jesus Christ spilled good.

These words should be written on three notes. Then take the milk of the ailing cow and the three notes. Grate a little from the skull of a poor sinner, place it all in a pot, blend it well, and strain all of it. The witch will die. You can also take the three notes, recopied, in the mouth, go out in front of the rain gutter, speak these words aloud, then give them to the animal to eat. In this way you will not only see all the witches but you will heal the animal.

238 ◈ Against Fever

Begin by praying early in the morning, then turn your shirt inside-out starting with the left sleeve while saying, "Reverse yourself, shirt, and turn aside fever"; next, speak the name of the person who is feverish. "I inflict this penitence upon you in the name of God the Father, the Son, and the Holy Ghost. Amen." Say these words three days in a row, the fever will vanish.

239 ◈ To Cast a Spell on a Thief That Will Force Him to Stay (This Spell Must Be Spoken Early Thursday Before the Rise of the Sun, and in the Open Air.)

May God the Father and the Son and the Holy Ghost reign! Amen. Thirty-three angels were seated together, come with Mary who they were taking care of. The good Saint Daniel said: "Believe me, dear Lady, I see robbers coming who seek to steal your dear child. I cannot conceal it from you. Our Lady said to Saint Peter: "Saint Peter, bind! Bind!" and he answered: "I have bound with one hand, with the hand of Christ, the thieves are trussed by the very hands of Christ when they seek to make off with wine, in the house, in the tavern, in the meadow or fields, in the woods or in the plowed land, in the tree, the grass, and the vines, or else everywhere they wish to steal the wine." Our Lady said: "May he who wishes to steal, steal, but when this occurs, he must become still as a goat, as rigid as a staff, and count all the stones that are upon the earth and all the stars in the sky. I permit you, I order you, Spirit, to be the master of every thief, by Saint Daniel swiftly, to bear as a burden all the goods of the earth, and you must consider that you cannot stir from here as long as my eyes see you not and as long as my tongue of flesh does not permit you to. I command you by the Holy Virgin Mary, Mother of God, by the force and the power of he who created heaven and earth, by all the hosts of angels and by all the saints, in the name of God the Father, the Son, and the Holy Ghost. Amen.

If you wish to free him from this charm, command him to leave in the name of Saint John.

240 ◈ Another Version

Thieves, I command you to obey as Christ obeyed his Father, even on the cross, that you should remain before me and not vanish from my sight. In the name of the Holy Trinity, I command you by the divine force and incarnation of Jesus Christ to not vanish from my sight ††† and to remain like the Lord Christ at the edge of the Jordan when Saint John baptized him. Like him, I conjure you, horse and man, to remain there and not disappear from my sight, just as Christ remained nailed to the wood of the holy cross and the Father delivered him from the power of Hell. Thieves, I tie you with these bonds! Like Christ has bound hell, be bound ††† Whatever the words may be, be released!

241 ◈ A Very Rapid Fastening

Horseman, foot soldier, there you are! Beneath your hat, you are surely covered with the blood of Jesus Christ. By the five sacred wounds, may your rifle, your carbine, and your pistol be bound. May your saber, your dagger, and your knife be banned and bound, in the name of God the Father, the Son, and the Holy Ghost. Amen!

You must say this three times.

242 ◈ Suppression of the Charm

Horseman, foot soldier, I come to conjure you! Leave in the name of Jesus Christ! By the word of God and the treasure of Christ! All disappear now!

243 ◈ In Order to Compel a Thief to Bring Back What He Stole from You

Go before sunrise to a pear tree and bring with you the nails taken from a bier for a dead or a new horseshoe; hold the nails out toward the east and say:

"Robber, I bind you by this first nail that I plant in your forehead and your brain so that you bring the stolen property back to where you found it! May it cause you pain equal to that it caused to the man and place from whom you stole it, as it befell Judas when he betrayed Jesus. I plant the second nail in your lung and your liver, [and] your brain, to ensure you return the stolen goods to their place. May it cause you as much pain as it caused him whom you stole it from and the place from which it was stolen, like Pilate suffering infernal pains! Thief, I plant the third nail in your foot and your brain so that you return the stolen goods to where you found them. O robber, by the three holy nails that pierced the sacred hands and feet of Christ, I compel you to return the stolen property to the place from which you took it. †††."

It is necessary to smear the nails with the fat from a poor sinner.

244 ◆ To Give to Livestock to Protect Them From Sorcery and Evil Spells

```
S A T O R
A R E P O
T E N E T
O P E R A
R O T A S
```

245 ◆ A Charm for Everything

Jesus! I am going to get up. Jesus, accompany me! Jesus, enclose my heart in Your own! Allow me to entrust my body and soul to you! The Lord is crucified. May God keep my senses so that evil enemies do not strike me down! In the name of God the Father, the Son, and the Holy Ghost.

246 ◆ For Always Winning Games

Attach the heart of a bat with a red thread to the arm that deals the cards and you shall win.

247 ◆ Against Fire

Our sweet Lord Jesus Christ went over mountains and valleys. He spied a fire: Saint Laurence was roasting on a grill. Our dear Lord Jesus Christ went to him to offer aid and consolation: he raised his divine hand and blessed it, he blessed the fire so that it would devour no more and spread no further. May this fire be blessed in the name of God the Father, the Son, and the Holy Ghost. Amen.

248 ◆ Another Version

Go away, fire, do not come in! Whether you are hot or cold, do not burn anymore! May God keep your blood, your flesh, your marrow, and your bones. In the name of God, may all your veins, small or large, be protected from hot or cold fire and remain unscathed. In the name of God the Father, the Son, and the Holy Ghost. Amen!

249 ◆ To Prevent Any Kind of Wound

Say this: "I dress the wound by the three names so that you may carry away fire, water, vertigo, swelling, and all that can aggravate the swelling, in the name of the holy Trinity."

You will say this three times. Circle the wound three times with a thread, place it in a corner in the east, and say: "I put you down †††, so that you may carry off flowing, swelling, or pus, and all that can poison the wound. †† Amen!"

Recite an Our Father, and may God take action.

250 ◆ To Remove the Pain of a Fresh Wound

Our sweet Lord Jesus Christ had many contusions and wounds, but none had been dressed. They did not get deeper nor get worse, nor become infected. Jonas was blind, I say, child of heaven, as true as the five wounds that were inflicted. They did not suppurate nor ulcerate. I draw from them all the water and blood that heals all the evils of the wounds. Sanctified by he who can heal all ills and wounds! ††† Amen.

251 ◆ When One Has Worms

Peter and Jesus went out in the field and drew three furrows, from which emerged three worms. One is white, the second black, and the third red. Here are three dead worms, in the name †††. Speak these words three times.

252 ◆ Against All Malignancy

Lord Jesus, may your red wounds guard me from death!

253 ◆ To Obtain Justice in Court

Jesus Nazarenus Rex Judeorum

Begin by carrying on your person this phrase as it is written, then say the following words:

"I, N.N., present myself before the house of the judge. Three dead men are hanging from the window. The first has no tongue, the second has no lungs, the third is ill, blind, and mute." It is [for] when you appear at the tribunal or argue a case at court and the judge is not favorable to you. Then say the charm above when approaching the judge.

254 ◈ To Stop a Hemorrhage, Always Effective
Once you have been cut and bruised, say: "Blessed wound, blessed hour, blessed be the day on which Jesus Christ was pierced! In the name †††. Amen!"

255 ◈ Another Charm
On a note, write the name of the four major rivers of the world, those that flow from paradise, to wit, Pisahn, Giho, Hedekiel, and Pheat, presented in the Book of Moses, second chapter, verses 11, 12, 13, there where you opened it. It is effective.

256 ◈ Yet Another
Or else blow on the patient three times, recite the Our Father until the "on earth," three times, and the blood will quickly cease flowing.

257 ◈ Another Absolutely Certain Spell
When a person has a hemorrhage or injured vein, place the note on top and the blood will cease flowing. He who does not believe this should write the following letters on a knife and stick it into a dumb beast; the animal will not bleed and he who carries it on his person shall be able to resist all his enemies.

I.m.L.K.I.B.I.P.a.x.v.ss.St. vas I.P.O. unay. ⌐it.Dom.mper vobism.*

When a woman is suffering the pains of childbirth or has a heavy heart, she should take the note and all will turn out well.

---

*The conclusion abbreviates *Dominus semper vobiscum* ("The Lord always be with you").

258 ◆ A Specific Charm That Is As Good for Men As It Is for Animals
The compiler, or printer, failed to provide the text under this heading.

259 ◆ When You Must Defend Yourself, Carry This Sign On Your Person
The sign was not drawn and the manuscript is blank here.

In the name of God, I attack! May my savior aid me! I entrust myself to the holy help of God with all my sore afflicted heart. May God help us all! Jesus, be blessed!

260 ◆ Protection of the House and Farm
Beneath a blank area in which a sign should have been printed, we read:

I am delivered from all the assaults of my enemies beneath your shield. J.J.J.

261 ◆ A Phylactery to Carry On One's Person
If I bear these words on me, nothing can afflict me: Annania, Azaria, and Misaël. Praise the Lord because he has delivered us from hell and has helped us against death, and he helps us in fire. May the Lord watch over so that none start a fire.

I.
N.I.R.
I.

262 ◆ To Stop All Enemies, Robbers, and Murderers
Brothers, may God greet you! Be humble, thieves, robbers, murderers, horsemen, and soldiers, because we have drunk the red blood of Christ! May your guns and firearms be stopped up by the holy drops of the blood of Jesus Christ! May all your knives and swords by bound by the five wounds of Christ!

Three red roses were laid on the heart of Christ. The first is good, the second is powerful, and the third represents His divine will. Thieves, you should submit and cease for as long as I desire and I conjure you in the name of God the Father, the Son, and the Holy Ghost!

263 ◆ A Protection Against All Weapons

Jesus, man and God, protect me, N.N., from all projectiles, and all arms long and short, and guns of all metals and shots! Hold your fire like Mary kept her virginity before and after birth! May Christ bind all weapons as he is attached to humanity—full of humility! May Christ urge all the guns like Mary, mother of God, received a husband! May the three drops of blood that Jesus discharged at the Mount of Olives protect me! Jesus Christ, protect me from murder and blazing fire! Jesus, do not let me die, and even less be damned, without having received holy communion. May God the Father, the Son, and the Holy Ghost help me. Amen!

264 ◆ To Stop Shot, Weapons, and Animals

Jesus crossed the Red Sea and looked out over the land. In the same way all bonds and ropes should break, fray, and be unusable so should all the arquebuses, guns, and pistols! May all the false tongues be silenced! May the blessing that God gave extend over me for all time since he created the first man. May the blessing God gave when he commanded Joseph and Mary in a dream to flee to Egypt with Jesus, remain on me. May it envelope me without end, may the holy † remain beloved and valorous in my right hand. I traverse the extent of the country and no one is robbed, murdered, or beaten. No one can cause me suffering, no dog can bite me, no animal can rend me, everywhere I protect my body and my blood from sin and the false tongues, that go from earth to heaven, by the power of the four Apostles, in the name of God the Father, the Son, and the Holy Ghost. Amen!

265 ◆ Another Version

I, N.N., by the spear that pierced the side of God and opened him so deeply that blood and water flowed from him, I conjure you, rifle, saber, and cutlass, as well as all weapons so that you may not cause me, the servant of God, any harm! In the [name] of †††, I conjure you, by Saint Etienne who was stoned by the Jews, to not afflict the servant of God, who I am. In the name of †††. Amen!

266 ◈ **AGAINST BULLETS AND THE BLOWS OF POINT AND BLADE**
In the name of J.J.J. Amen! I, N.N., [say] that Jesus Christ is the true Savior. Jesus Christ rules, governs, annihilates, and vanquishes all enemies, be they visible or invisible. Jesus, help me everywhere, always and for eternity, on all the roads and paths, on the waters and on earth, over mountains and valleys, at my home and on the farm, in the entire world wherever I happen to be, wherever I happen to stand, go, ride, or circulate, sleep or wake, eat or drink! Be present, O Lord Jesus Christ, always, sooner or later, at each hour and every instant, whether I am entering or leaving! O Lord, Jesus Christ, may your five red wounds redeem all my sins, be it manifest or concealed, and may they not overlook me one whit, so the rifle can neither wound or harm me! ††† that God helps me, protect me, and keep me. Guard me, N.N., always from daily sins, of wrongs down here, injustice, spite, plague, and other illnesses, fear, martyrdom, and suffering, from all evil enemies, false tongues, and old gossips! May ††† help me so that no projectile strikes my body! That no thief, not the bohemians, the robbers of the main roads, the arsonists, sorcery, or other deviltries slither into my house or into my farm! May the less powerful still enter there! May this be guaranteed by dear lady Mary and all the children around God in his heavens, who gives me the comfort of the divine glory of the Father in eternal joy, may the wisdom of God the Son illuminate me, may the virtue and grace of the Holy Ghost strengthen me, henceforth and for eternity! Amen.

267 ◈ **SO THAT NO EVIL BEING CAN DECEIVE, ENCHANT, OR BEWITCH ME, AND SO THAT I MAY BE BLESSED WITHOUT END**
Like the chalice and the wine and the communion our sweet Lord Jesus Christ offered to his disciples on holy Thursday and so that, in day and night alike forever, no dog may bite me, no beast can rend me, no tree can crush me, no water can carry me off, no firearm can touch me, no steel

or iron weapon can touch me, no fire can burn me, no liar can judge me falsely, no rogue can irritate me, and so that I might be protected from all evil enemies, sorcery, and magic, O Lord Jesus Christ, defend me! Amen.

268 ◇ For Paralyzing Rifles and Weapons

The benediction that came down from heaven when Jesus Christ was born, may it fall upon me, N.N.! The blessing that Lord God gave when he created the first man, may it fall on me! The blessing that occurred when Christ was captured, bound, whipped, maliciously crowned, and struck, then gave up the ghost on the cross, may it fall on me! The benediction that the priest gave over the body of Jesus Christ, may it fall on me! May I be aided by the constancy of holy Mary and all the saints of God, the three magi Kings, Caspar, Melchior, and Balthazar! May the four Apostles, Matthew, Mark, Luke, and John, give me their aid! May the archangels assist me! May Saint Uriel assist me! May the twelve messenger saints of the Patriarchs assist me, and the entire celestial army, all the saints whose number is inexpressible! Amen.

Rapa. R. tarn. Tetragrammaton Angeli
Jesus Nazarenus Rex Judeorum

269 ◇ Another Version

May the holy Trinity protect me! May it be and remain by my side, me, N.N., on the waters, on earth, over the water or in the fields, in the towns or in the villages across the entire world, wherever I may be! May the Lord Jesus Christ protect me from all my enemies, known or hidden! May the eternal deity protect me through the bitter sufferings of Jesus Christ! May the rosy blood he spilled on the wood of the holy cross assist me! J.J. Jesus was crucified, martyrized, and succumbed, these are true words. All these words should thus have all their strength, those that are written here, and those I speak and pray. May they help me to not be captured, bound, or defeated by any person whatsoever! May all the guns and weapons be unusable and stripped of their power toward me! Rifle, hold back your fire, in the name of the all-powerful hand of God. All weapons should be bound, ††† as the right hand of Jesus

Christ was attached to the wood of the cross. Just as the Son obeyed the Father until his death on the cross, may divine eternity protect me! By his rosy blood that escaped his five sacred wounds that he received on the holy cross, may I also be blessed and as well protected as the chalice and the wine and the true precious bread that Jesus distributed to his twelve apostles on the evening of holy Thursday. J. J. J.

270 ◈ For the Voyage

May I be touched by divine grace and mercy, me, N. N.! I am going to leave or depart, I am going to gird myself, surround myself with a sure belt, if God in heaven wishes it so. May he wish to protect me, my flesh and my blood, all my small veins and my limbs, today and the night that awaits me! Whatever the number of my enemies, may they be silenced and all transformed into a death white as snow! May no one fire on me, nor strike me, nor cast projectiles and defeat me! Whether he has in hand rifle or steel, or any other metal, as the cursed weapons and knives are called, may my rifle come forth from heaven like the lightning and may my saber slice like a razor! Our lady went up onto a high mountain and cast her gaze into a very dark vale. She saw her dear child among the Jews, so hard, so hard that he was captured, so hard that he was tightly bound: may our dear Lord Jesus Christ protect me this way from all that could harm me, †††. Amen.

271 ◈ Another Similar Version

I am leaving this day and night, do not let all my enemies and all the thieves come near me; they shall bring his rosy blood in my chest; if they do not bring me what has been consecrated* on the holy altar, when God the Lord Jesus Christ ascended living into heaven, O Lord, may this benefit me today and tonight, †††. Amen.

272 ◈ Yet Another Version

In the name of God, I am leaving. May God the Father be over me! May God the Son be before me! May God the Holy Ghost be at my side! May he who is stronger than these three persons address himself

---

*I have corrected a typographical error in the original: *gehandelt* for *gewandelt*.

to my body and my life! He who is less strong than these three persons,* may he leave me in peace. J. J. J.

273 ◈ A Good Means for Stopping Bullets
May the peace of Our Lord Jesus Christ accompany me, N.N! In the name of the powerful prophet Agtion and of Ely, stop yourself bullet, and do not slay me! O bullet, stop yourself! I order you by heaven and earth, by the last judgment, so that you have no wish to hurt a child of God, †††. Amen.

274 ◈ Another Version
Swords, daggers, and knives and all that is harmful and inflicts wounds upon me, by all the prayers of the priest, by he who guided Jesus to the temple and said that a cutting sword will pass by your soul, I order you to not wound me, I, a child of God! J. J. J.

275 ◈ A Very Rapid Binding
I, N.N., conjure you, saber, knife, and all the weapons, by the spear that pierced the side of Jesus, and opened it so thoroughly that water and blood poured out, do not allow me to be wounded, I, a servant of God. †††. Amen.

276 ◈ To Definitively Stop Thieves
Three lilies stood on the tomb of our God. The first represents his courage, the second his blood, the third his will. Stop, thief! Just as Jesus Christ did not come down from the †, just shall you be unable to flee from here! I command you by the four apostles and the four elements of heaven, in the river or in the shot, at the court or on the face [?]† I conjure you by the last judgment to stop and go no further until I see all the stars in the sky and the sun spreads its glow, I stop you in your course and in your bounds. I command you in the name †††. Amen.

You will say this three times.

---

*The text reads "eight persons" here, which makes no sense.
†The rhyming expression that appears here, *"im Fluß oder im Schuß im Gericht oder Gesicht,"* lacks any clear sense and seems to represent an example of verbal magic.

14

THE DOCTOR OF THE POOR

The Doctor of the Poor is the title of a peddler's chapbook that formed part of what is called the blue library of Troyes. In use in the country-side from the seventeenth to nineteenth centuries,[1] *The Doctor of the Poor* gives us a very clear picture of what became of the ancient pre-scriptions. Because this small book was copied again and again by the healers, I reproduce here the most significant extracts.

The twelve-page booklet in my possession was printed in Troyes by Baudot, but does not include any date.

277 ◇ PRAYER FOR STOPPING TOOTHACHE

Saint Apollonia sat on a stone of marble. Our Lord passing by asked her: Apollonia, what are you doing there? I am here for my head, for my blood, for my toothache.* Apollonia, look back; if it is a drop of blood it will fall and if it is a worm, it will die. Five Our Fathers and five Ave Marias in the honor of and aimed at the five wounds of Our Lord Jesus Christ. The sign of the cross on the cheek with the finger, facing the pain one feels, and in a very short time you will be cured.

---

*St. Apollonia's teeth were broken and torn out during her martyrdom.

LAISSEZ DIRE
ET FAITES LE BIEN.

LE MÉDE IN DES PAUVRES.

Christus regnat. Christus imperat. Christus vincint :

J. C. règne, J. C. commande, J. C. est vainqueur.

EN DIEU LA CONFIANCE.

PRIÈRE
pour arrêter le Mal de Dents.

Sainte Apoline assise sur une pierre de marbre, Notre Seigneur

Se trouve à Troyes chez Baudot, libraire.

278 ◈ For Stopping the Blood from Any Kind of Cut, and All Kinds of Wounds

God was born on Christmas night at midnight: God is dead: God is resurrected: God has commanded that the blood stop, that the wound close, that the pain pass away, and that no matter nor scent nor rotten flesh shall enter as did the five wounds of Our Lord Jesus Christ. *Natus est Christus, mortuus est, et resurrexit Christus.* These Latin words are repeated three times, and each time one blows in the form of a cross on the wound, while naming the name of the person, saying: God has healed you, so let it be.

One will next begin the novena on an empty stomach, aimed at the five wounds of Our Lord Jesus Christ.

279 ◈ For Rheumatisms and Other Pains

The blessed Saint Anne, who gave birth to the Virgin Mary; the Virgin Mary who gave birth to Jesus Christ: God heal you and bless you, poor creature, N. of rheumatism, wound, break, hindrances, and all kinds of ailments, in honor of God and the Virgin Mary, like Saint Como and Saint Damian have healed the five wounds of Our Lord.

Speak three Paters and three Aves: during nine days, every morning, on an empty belly, in honor of the agonies that Our Lord Jesus Christ suffered at Calvary.

280 ◈ Prayer for Ringworm

Paul, who is seated on the marble stone, Our Lord passing by him, said: Paul, what are you doing there? I am here to heal the pain of my head. Paul stand up and go find Saint Anne, so she may give some kind of oil, you will lightly apply it on an empty stomach once a day, and during one year and a day he who does this will have neither wrath, nor scabies, not ringworm, nor rabies.

281 ◈ Orison for Healing and Breaking of Fevers[2]

When Jesus carried his cross, a Jew named Mark Antony came upon him and said: Jesus you are shivering. Jesus told him: I am neither shivering nor trembling; and he who pronounces these words in his heart shall never have fever or shakes. God commands the tertian fever, the agues, the intermittent fevers, the purple fevers, to leave the body of this person.

(*Name the person.*)

Jesus, Mary, Jesus.

It is necessary to say a novena on an empty stomach, aimed at the person, in the memory of the sufferings endured by Our Lord Jesus Christ at Calvary.

282 ◈ ORISON FOR PROMPTLY HEALING COLIC

Put the big finger of your right hand directly on the pain and say: Mary who is Mary, or colic passion that is in my liver and my heart, enter between my spleen and my lung, stop, in the name of the Father, the Son, and the Holy Ghost, and say three Paters, and three Aves, and name the person, saying: God has healed you. Amen.

283 ◈ ORISON FOR HEALING ALL KINDS OF BURNS

Three different times, you shall blow upward in the form of a cross and say: Fire of God, lose your heat, like Judas lost his color when he betrayed Our Lord in the Garden of Olives, and name the name of the person, saying: God has healed you with his power. Without forgetting the novena aimed at the five wounds of Our Lord Jesus Christ. So be it.

284 ◈ ORISON FOR THE THORN

Points on points. May God cure this point like Saint Como and Saint Damian have healed the five wounds of Our Lord Jesus Christ in the Garden of Olives.

(*And speak the name of the person.*)

Natus est Christus, mortuus est resurrexit Christus.

285 ◈ ORISON

To Saint Anthony of Padua, for recovering the losses and other needs we have each day.

Father and Patron, Saint Anthony of Padua
Who invokes you, if necessary save you,
Perils of death and calamities,
Leprosy, fevers, and other ailments,
Remedy to sudden death and plague.
On earth and sea cease lightning and storm,
For recovering all things lost,
Good causes are defended by you;
And quite often the innocent poor,
Make it so that all trials satisfy all.
Young and old who have recourse to you,
To their needs you give all assistance.
Pray for us who in leaving this world
Joyfully into heaven, lasting peace,
Ever delectable rest.
So be it.

286 ◆ PRAYER FOR DISPELLING EVIL SPIRITS

Each morning on rising, say: "O father almighty! O mother, the gentlest of mothers! O admirable example of feelings and the tenderness of all mothers! O son; the flower of all the sons! Firmest of all the firm, soul, spirit, harmonies! O number of all things, keep us, protect us, guide us, and be propitious for us in all times and all places!"

Then say three times: "My God, I place my hope in you, the Son, the Holy Ghost, and in myself."

287 ◆ ORISON FOR EYE COMPLAINTS[3]

Blessed Saint John, passing by three virgins on his path, asked them: What are you doing here? We are healing cloudy vision. Heal, virgins, heal the eye or eyes of N., making the sign of the cross and blowing into the eye, one says: film, inflammation of the cornea, or whether it be nail, seed, or spider, God commands you to have no more power over this eye than the Jews on Easter had over the body of Our Lord Jesus

Christ; then make another sign of the cross while blowing into the eyes of the person while saying: God has healed you.

Do not forget the novena to say to the blessed Saint Claire.

288 ◈ Precious and Perfect Healing Orison for Anthrax

Jesus, my Savior, true God and true man, I firmly believe that you spilled your blood for us, I believe in the Eucharist; after having suffered for us, spread your blood precious with your grace, and do not overlook me in your holy grace, for the illness about which I implore our patron to intercede for us. So be it.

At the foot of the altar, it is necessary to ensure the intervention of the patron of the place where the patient is, and next you shall take ivy, the closest to the ground, and soap that had not been used, and beat it all together with fresh cream, you shall apply this with the orison and one wll be promptly cured.

289 ◈ Prayer for Healing the gripes of Horses

Black or gray horse, for it is necessary to distinguish the hair color of the animal belonging to N., if you have inflammation of the parotid in any color. Or red tranchées, or one of thirty-six other ills, whatever the case may be, God heal you and the blessed Saint Eligius.*

In the name of the Father, the Son, and the Holy Spirit. So be it.

And you will say five Paters and five Aves to thank God for his grace.

290 ◈ Precious Orison for Saving Us from Swarms

The following orison was found on the sepulcher of Our Lady in the Valley of Josaphat and has so many virtues and properties that he who reads it or has it read once a day, or who carries it on his person in good will and devotion, cannot die, neither by fire nor water, nor in battle, and will have fortune and victory over his enemies; none can harm or trouble him, and he will have so many advantages that if a person has

---

*St. Eligius is the patron saint of horses.

fallen into mortal sin, God will give him the grace to remove it before his death; he shall see the Virgin Mary come to give him aid and comfort. It is to be repeated three times as it has three different properties.

Glorious Virgin Mary, mother of God, Lady of the Angels, benign and pure hope, and the comfort of all good creatures.

May it please you, lady and mother of the Angels, to keep our body and soul! We pray your precious son, that it is his wish to keep us safe from all peril and danger, and enemy, hell, and temptation, by the merits of his bitter passion; make this mortality cease, war, and preserve the fruits of the earth, so that we may live in concord, O mother of God, full of mercy, have pity on poor sinners, and protect us from infernal torment, and lead us to the kingdom of heaven, where we will all find ourselves before God, the foremost father, to whom we kneeling ask forgiveness, and may it be his pleasure to forgive us, like Magdalene and the good thief, when he asked forgiveness on the tree of the cross!

A woman in the pain of childbirth, on whom the aforementioned orison is placed, will deliver immediately.

291 ◈ AGAINST BURNS
In another more recent edition of the Doctor of the Poor *(Mâcon: Imprimerie Romand, 1875), we find different recipes such as this one, for example, against burns.*

Our Lord went out with Saint Peter
To say a novena, into a field,
He found three worms, one white, one red, and one black.
Devouring worms, I forbid you
To any longer trouble the blood of N.
Say three Our Fathers, and so on.

A nineteenth-century edition of La Poule noire
(The Black Hen), *with no place or year of
publication given.*

15

EXTRACTS FROM VARIOUS GRIMOIRES

292 ◈ Amulet[1]

Vahos, a nostro noxio Bay gloy, apon, agia, agios, Ischyros.

These are the words that Adam spoke when he was in hell or in limbo on the banks of the Acheron: if someone carries them in war on his person, he will not be slain or wounded by anyone whoever; the same will be true of the traveler who carries them on his person and says them in the space of seventy days, he will never be taken on the road, nor wounded or attacked by thieves, and will have the time to be heard in confession by a priest, and given remission of his sins; it is also of great virtue for those voyaging by sea; it spares he who bears it with devotion from peril; the words should be written on a paper, and carried while on his way.

293 ◈ For Striking a Thief, Witch, or Enemy with Magic[2]

On a Saturday before sunrise, cut a shoot from a hazel tree of that year while saying these words: Shoot, I break you in the name of the one I wish to beat and hurt. Then cover a table with a cloth while repeating three times: "Droch, Myroch, Esenaroth † Betu † Baroch † Ars † Haaroth. It. O holy Trinity, punish the thief who has stolen (or the witch who has cast an evil spell) and carry him away by your great justice. † Eson † Elion † Emain alesege. And knock on the table three times."

294 ◆ To Be Freed[3]

If someone has been incarcerated and bound in iron chains, he should be shown this scapular in gold. On the day and at the hour of the sun; his bonds will fall off immediately and he will be at liberty. May their sword enter into their heart and may their bow be broken.

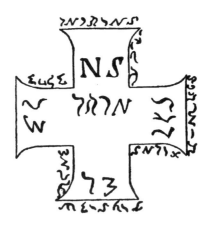

295 ◆ For Love[4]

Take virgin wax and fashion an image with it. Three Sundays in a row, before sunrise, go plunge this image into running water. Give it the name of the one you desire. On the image's chest write these characters at the level of the heart: ff † b † O † 2 † d, then cast it immediately into the fire. The hotter the image becomes, the more rapidly the woman will hurl herself upon you.

296 ◆ For Love[5]

To obtain the love of someone, it is necessary to write these words on a virgin parchment:

Sator Arepo Tenet Opera Rotas Jah, Jah, Jah, Enam Jah, Jah, Jah, Ketler, Chokmah, Binah, Tedulah, Teburah, Tiphereth, Netzah, Hod, Jesod, Malkouth, Abraham, Isaac, Jacob, Shasrach, Meshach, Abdenago.

297 ◇ For Bending a Woman to Your Will[6]

Take an egg that was laid on a Saturday when the moon was full that same night, and write upon it the following: † esa † his † masmo † caldi † male † am † es †, then cast it into the fire while saying: "I conjure you, N., by the power and force written on this egg, to desire me as passionately as this egg in the fire so that you will know no rest until you come to me and do my will."

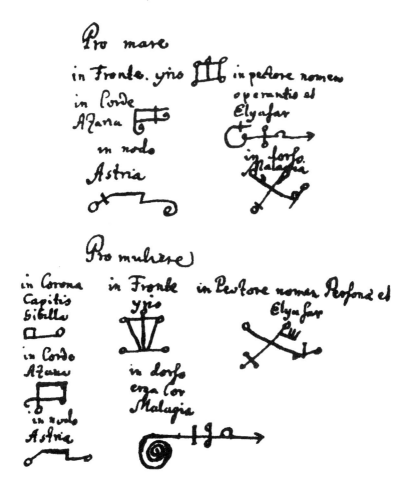

To Cause a Thief to Return.
To be written on certain parts of the body of a wax figurine with a stylus
when the sun is in Leo during the period of the full moon. Magia de Furto,
folio 15 r (eighteenth century).

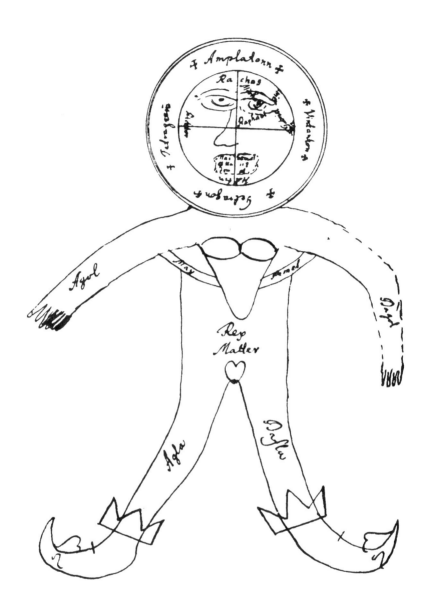

298 ◆ To Blind a Thief in One Eye[7]

One takes a needle with his left hand and places it on the eye while saying: "† Amplotonn † Rachas † Vriel † Vintarton † veh † Gabriel † Tetragon † Holltin † Raphael † Tetragon † Richtor † Michael †" and recites three Our Fathers and three Ave Marias while adding: "O

Lord Jesus Christ, who, by the intervention of your servant Joshua, has ordered and held court in Jericho for the theft of Achan, O Lord, grant me that this thief, N., who has robbed me, N., who has robbed Our Lord, will have suffering in his eyes and feel stings ceaselessly so long as this needle is stuck in the drawn eye; grant me by the praise, the honor, and the glory that has been attributed to you for all eternity."

This must be said three times and, at each time, thrust the needle more deeply into the eye. It must be done where the theft took place. One writes the figure with crow feathers and soft charcoal, or with the charcoal of a tree struck by lightning.

299 ◈ FOR UNCOVERING A THIEF[8]

℞ ☿ vivi, from the white of an egg laid that same day, and draw this circle that day on the wall, as follows, and say: "God almighty and eternal, you who have permitted by your servant Joshua that Achan was discovered, he who had stolen in the city of Jericho despite the royal prohibition, make the thief appear before the community so that we may know who he is. By the Christ Our Lord."

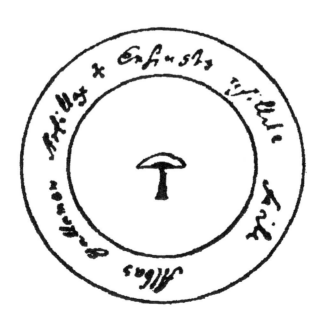

300 ◆ Charm of the Three Marys[9]

> *The Three Marys set off*
> *Beyond the mountains*
> *To seek healing*
> *Of film on the eye and pimples.*
>
> *They met Our Lord Jesus Christ*
> *Who asked them, Marys, where are you going?*
> *Lord, we are going beyond the mountains*
> *To seek Healing*
> *Of film on the eye and pimples.*
>
> *Our Lord told them: Mary, Marion,*
> *Return to your homes*
> *For film on the eye and pimples*
> *You shall find a cure.*

301 ◆ Seal of Aries[10]

Take ½ ounce of iron, ¼ ounce of gold, 1 dram of silver, and ½ of copper. Melt these four metals together over a high flame at the hour and on the day when the Sun is in the sign of Aries, or March 10, when the Sun enters its first degree. The iron in the filings needs to have been reduced, otherwise the fire will not liquefy it. When all is melted and ready, it is necessary to carve the seal on a Tuesday, when the Moon is in Aries as it travels through the months, toward the 9th or 10th degree of Aries, and hang it when Mars is in the 11th house of the heavens, in *octavo coelo* [in the eighth heaven]. Here is this seal.

It is good against the flux, it purges the brain and dries the humors of the skull. Arrange it in such a way that—worn day or night—it touches your head; the sign of Aries should always be facing the brain.

302 ◆ MONDAY CONJURATION TO LUCIFER[11]

This experiment is performed at night, from eleven o'clock to twelve, and from three o'clock until four. It requires charcoal from willow wood, or the fire to make it, for writing the words that are around it. It requires a mouse to give to him, the master must have a stole and holy water for beginning the conjurations with a light heart but bitterly as a master should be to his servant, with all manner of threats, and before beginning, it is necessary to draw the circle and sanctify it with incense, like the others that follow that one might wish to make.

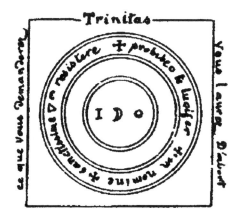

I conjure you Lucifer, by the living God, by the true God, by the holy God, and by the God who spoke and thus all things were created; I conjure you by the ineffable names of God Alpha and Omega, El, Eloy, Elion, Ya, Saday, Luso, Omogie, Rex salus, O Adonay, Messias, I implore you and exorcise and conjure you by the letters Y V E L and by the names Geary, Iol, Iel, Agla, Eizazeris, Oriston, Arphetice iphaton, Gesmon yegeron, Isilion, Agiron, Egia, Sperato, Smagon, Anol, Genaton, Sothea, Tetragrammaton, Puermaton, Tionem pengaron, Yraras, Yaras, Ton salaton on chiros iron voy pheron, Simulaton, penta rinum masone, and by the ineffable names of God Gabin, Gauldanum, in godon, o bei Englabus, that you have to come or that you send me N. in beautiful human form, without any accident or ugliness, to answer the true will of all that I ask of him without having any power to harm either my body or soul.

303 ◇ Wednesday Conjuration to Astaroth[12]

This experiment is performed at night from ten o'clock until eleven: it is for gaining the good graces of the king and others. One will write the following in the circle: Come Astaroth, come Astaroth, come Astaroth.

I conjure you Astaroth, wicked spirit, by the words and virtues of God, and by the powerful God, Jesus Christ of Nazareth to whom all demons are subject, who was conceived by the Virgin Mary through the mystery of the angel Gabriel; I conjure you once again in the name of the Father and the Son, and the Holy Ghost, in the name of the most glorious Virgin Mary and the very holy Trinity, in whose honor all the archangels, thrones, dominations, powers, patriarchs, prophets, apostles, and evangelists ceaselessly sing Holy, holy holy, the Lord God of the years, who was, who is, who will come like a river of blazing fire, so that you ignore not my commands, and you do not refuse to come. I command you by he who will come all in fire to judge the living and the dead, to whom all honor, praise, and glory is due. So come then promptly, obedient to my will, to pay homage to the true God, the living God, and all his works, and do not fail to obey me and pay homage to the Holy Ghost: it is in his name that I command you.

304 ◈ THE SEVENTY-TWO NAMES[13]

Here are the seventy-two names of Our Lord. Whoever carries them on his person shall have no fear of any misfortune or danger.

Hon, Trinity, holy, God of the Armies, Hemon, Adonai, Eloi, Usion, savior, alpha and omega, first-born, beginning, end, way, truth, life, wisdom, virtue, Paraclete, I am that I am, mediator, lamb, calf, ram, lion, snake, worm, mouth, prophet, priest, immortal, king, Christ, Jesus, spirit, saint, merciful Father-God, charity, eternal, almighty, creator, redeemer, God in four letters,* first and last, verity, good sovereign, gratias. Amen. Door, stone, house, glory, image of the Father, living, unique, God, Trinity in the One and One in the Trinity.

Fountain [of] life and rest.

305 ◈ CONSECRATION OF THE GRIMOIRE

There are two seventeenth-century works that indicate the grimoire needs to be consecrated before it is used. First here is the operation according to The Key of Solomon,[14] *next in accordance with* The Occult Philosophy,[15] *the fourth volume of which is not by Henry Cornelius Agrippa.*

1.

Make a small Book containing the Prayers for all the Operations, the Names of the Angels in the form of Litanies, their Seals and Characters; this being done thou shalt consecrate the same unto God and unto the pure Spirits in the manner following: Thou shalt set in the destined place a small table covered with a white cloth, whereon thou shalt lay the Book opened at the Great Pentacle which should be drawn on the first leaf of the said Book; and having kindled a lamp which should be suspended above the centre of the table, thou shalt surround the said table with a white curtain; clothe thyself in the proper vestments, and holding the Book open, repeat upon thy knees the following prayer with great humility.

---

*In other words, Tetragrammaton.

ADONAI, ELOHIM, EL, EHEIEH ASHER EHEIEH, Prince of Princes, Existence of Existences, have mercy upon me, and cast Thine eyes upon Thy Servant (N.), who invokes Thee most devoutedly, and supplicates Thee by Thy Holy and tremendous Name Tetragrammaton to be propitious, and to order Thine Angels and Spirits to come and take up their abode in this place; O ye Angels and Spirits of the Stars, O all ye Angels and Elementary Spirits, O all ye Spirits present before the Face of God, I the Minister and faithful Servant of the Most High conjure ye, let God Himself, the Existence of Existences, conjure ye to come and be present at this Operation, I, the Servant of God, most humbly entreat ye. Amen.

After which thou shalt incense it with the incense proper to the Planet and the day, and thou shalt replace the Book on the aforesaid Table, taking heed that the fire of the lamp be kept up continually during the operation, and keeping the curtains closed. Repeat the same ceremony for seven days, beginning with Saturday, and perfuming the Book each day with the incense proper to the Planet ruling the day and hour, and taking heed that the lamp shall burn both day and night; after which thou shalt shut up the Book in a small drawer under the table, made expressly for it, until thou shalt have occasion to use it; and every time that thou wishest to use it, clothe thyself with thy vestments, kindle the lamp, and repeat upon thy knees the aforesaid prayer, "Adonai Elohim," and so forth.

It is necessary also, in the Consecration of the Book, to summon all the Angels whose Names are written therein in the form of Litanies, which thou shalt do with devotion; and even if the Angels and Spirits appear not in the Consecration of the Book, be not thou astonished thereat, seeing that they are of a pure nature, and consequently have much difficulty in familiarizing themselves with men who are inconstant and impure, but the Ceremonies and Characters being correctly carried out devoutedly and with perseverance, they will be constrained to come, and it will at length happen that at thy first invocation thou wilt be able to see and communicate with them. But I advise thee to undertake nothing unclean or impure, for then thy importunity, far from attracting them, will only serve to chase them from thee; and it will be thereafter exceedingly difficult for thee to attract them for a pure end.

2.

For this Book is to be consecrated, a book of evil spirits, ceremoniously to be composed, in their name and order: whereunto they binde with a certain holy Oath, the ready and present obedience of the spirits therein written.

Now this book is to be made of most pure and clean paper that hath never been used before; which many do call *Virgin-paper*. And this book must be inscribed after this maner: that is to say, let there be placed on the left side the image of the spirit, and on the right side his character, with the Oath above it, containing the name of the spirit, and his dignity and place, with his office and power.

Moreover, there is to be observed the circumstances of places, times, hours, according to the Stars which these spirits are under, and are seen to agree unto, their site, rite, and order being applied.

Which book being so written, and well bound, is to be adorned, garnished, and kept secure, with Registers and Seals, lest it should happen after the consecration to open in some place not intented [sic], and indanger [endanger] the operator. Furthermore, this book ought to be kept as reverently as may be: for irreverence of minde causeth it to lose its vertue, with pollution and profanation.

Now this sacred book being this composed according to the maner already delivered, we are then to proceed to the consecration thereof after a twofold way: one whereof is, That all and singular the spirits who are written in the book, be called to the Circle, according to the Rites and Order which we have before taught; and the book that is to be consecrated, let there be placed without the Circle in a triangle. And in the first place, let there be read in the presence of the spirits all the Oathes which are written in that book; and then the book to be consecrated being placed without the Circle in a triangle there drawn, let all the spirits be compelled to impose their hands where their images and characters are drawn, and to confirm and consecrate the same with a special and common Oath. Which being done, let the book be taken and shut, and preserved as we have before spoken, and let the spirits be licensed to depart, according to due rite and order.

There is another maner of consecrating a book of spirits, which is more easie, and of much efficacie to produce every effect, except that in opening this book the spirits do not always come visible. And this way is thus: Let there be made a book of spirits as we have before set forth; but in the end thereof let there be written Invocations and Bonds, and strong Conjurations, wherewith every spirit may be bound. Then this book must be bound between two Tables or Lamens, and in the inside thereof let there be drawn the holy Pentacles of the Divine Majestie . . . then let the first of them be placed in the beginning of the book, and the second at the end of the same.

This book being perfected after this manner, let it be brought in a clear and fair time, to a Circle prepared in a cros way, according to the Art which we have before delivered; and there in the first place the book being opened, let it be consecrated to the rites and ways which we have before declared concerning Consecration. Which being done, let all the spirits be called which are written in the book, in their own order and place, by conjuring them thrice by the bonds described in the book, that they come unto that place within the space of three days, to assure their obedience, and confirm the same, to the book so to be consecrated. Then let the book be wrapped up in clean linen, and buried in the middle of the Circle, and there fast stopped up: and then the Circle being destroyed, after the spirits are licensed, depart before the rising of the sun: and on the third day, about the middle of the night, return, and new make the Circle, and with bended knees make prayer and giving thanks unto God, and let a precious perfume be made, and open the hole, and take out the book; and so let it be kept, not opening the same. Then you shall license the spirits in their order, and destroying the Circle, depart before the sun rise. . . . But the Operator, when he would work by the book thus consecrated, let him do it in a fair and clear season, when the spirits are least troubled;

and let him place himself toward the region of the spirits. Then let him open the book under a due Register; let him invoke the spirits by their Oath there described and confirmed, and by the name of their character and image, to that purpose which you desire: and, if there be need, conjure them by the bonds placed in the end of the book. And having attained your desired effect, then you shall license the spirits to depart.

NOTES

INTRODUCTION.
THE SIX KINDS OF MAGIC

1. Cf. Servais, *La Tchalette et autre contes de magie et de sorcellerie;* Comes, *Silence,* and *La Belette.*

2. Paracelsus, *Philosophia sagax,* 110ff.

3. Ibid., 112–14.

4. Cf. Mathers, *The Key of Solomon.*

5. There is a *Book of Raziel (Sepher Raziel)* in Hebrew, attributed to Eleazar of Worms and published in Amsterdam in 1701. A manuscript exists in the British Library (Sloane ms. 3826).

6. Thiers, *Traité des superstitions,* 247.

7. The best study on this figure is Arnold, *Johannes Trithemius (1462–1516).*

8. A manuscript of 148 folios preserved in Ghent under the shelf mark 1021 A. I should also mention the Halle manuscript, Landesbibliothek, 14 B 36, fol. 160 v°, 170 r°, 260 v°, 265 v°, with a wealth of figures and including various astrological treatises (*Liber ymaginum, Ymagines super septem dies ebdomade et sigilla planetarum, Tractatus de imaginibus, Thetel, Thebit, Ptolemy,* etc.).

9. Cf. Thorndike, "Traditional Medieval Tracts Concerning Engraved Astronomical Images," 229–38. Another important example is the Plut. 89 Sup. 38 manuscript in the Florence Biblioteca Medica Laurenziana in which we have Thâbit's *Tractatus de proprietatibus quarundam stellarum et convenentia earundem quibusdam lapidibus et herbis,* fol. 1 r°–3 v°; the text was edited in Carmody, *The Astronomical Work of Thabit ibn Qurra,* 179–97. The manuscript also contains *Tractatus de imaginibus,* fol. 3 v°–8

230

v°; *Ptolomei Tractatus de imaginationibus,* fol. 9 r°–17 r°; and *Theyzelius Quedam imaginum secundun planetas* (!) *extracte de quodam libello,* fol. 282 v°–294 v°. Cf. also manuscript II iii 214 (fifteenth century) in the National Library of Florence.

10. Cf. Thorndike, "Traditional," 256–61.

11. Cf. Paniagua, *Studia Arnaldiana;* Weill-Parot, *Les images astrologiques au Moyen Âge et à la Renaissance,* chap. 8.

12. Cf. C. Thorndike, "Traditional," 242–43. Note that an initial identification was proposed with Balinas, the pseudo-Apollonius of Tyana.

13. For comparison, the text from the Halle ms. 14 B 36, fol. 160 v°–170 r°; 260 v°, 265 v°.

14. Trithemius's text is replicated in Peuckert, *Pansophie,* 47–55 (= *Antipalas maleficiorum* I, 3).

15. Delatte, ed., *Textes latins et vieux français relatifs aux Cyranides.*

16. The extremely long title is quite interesting: *Traitant de l'inclination de l'homme & de la femme, suivant les mois où ils sont nés. Avec un traité de la complexion & des maladies qui arrivent, de leur inclination; du bien & du mal qui accompagnent leur jours. Où est ajouté la connoissance de la bonne or mauvaise fortune d'un chacun.* This is all by Sinibal de Spadacine of New Castle, Astrologer of the State of Milan.

17. Cf. Morin, *Catalogue descriptif de la Bibliothèque bleu de Troyes,* 405–7.

18. Joly, *Les Ardennes.*

19. Cf. Harmening, "Okkultkommerz—vermarktete Texte magischer Traditionen," in Harmening, ed., *Hexen heute, magische Traditionen und neue Zutaten,* 103–14, at 105.

20. For more on all this, cf. Harmening, ed., *Hexen heute,* 103–14.

21. *The Malleus Maleficarum of Heinrich Kramer and James Sprenger.*

22. Franz, *Die kirchlichen Benediktionen im Mittelalter.*

23. Cited in Bartsch, *Die Sachbeschwörungen der römischen Kirche,* 7327.

24. *Registrum libra,* V, 3.

25. Cf. Franz, *Die kirchlichen Benediktionen,* 426–27.

26. Schönbach, *Studien zur Geschichte der altdeutschen Predigt: Zeugnisse Bertholds von Regensburg zur Volkskunde,* 134: *clerici vel religiosi, qui contra febres vel alia infirmitates scribunt in oblatis, in pomis vel cedalis, vel phylacteria.*

27. Thiers, *Traité des superstitions,* 29.

28. Le Braz, *La Légende de la mort chez les Bretons armoricains,* 370.

29. Bodin, *De la démonomanie des sorciers.*

30. Bodin, *De la démonomanie*, 79 v°.

31. Ibid., 235 v°.

32. Thiers, *Traité des superstitions*, 417. The last quote is borrowed from John 19:34.

33. Montaigne, *Essais*, vol. 2, 173. I have modernized the sixteenth-century language.

34. Bodin, *De la démonomanie*, 152 v°.

35. Ibid., 55 v°.

36. Ibid., 17 v°.

37. Here is the spell for wax: "Extabor, Hetabor, Sittacibor, Adonai, Onzo, Zomen, Menor, Asmodal, Ascobai, Comatos, Erionas, Profas, Alkomas, Conamas, Papuendos, Osiandos, Espacient, Damnath, Eheres, Golades, Telanter, Cophi, Zades, angels of God, be present because I summon you in my operation so that it can be realized and achieved through you. Amen." Next recite Psalms 131, 15, 102, 7, 84, 88, 87, 133, 113, 126, 46, 47, 22, 51, 130, 139, 49, 110, 53, and say: "I exorcize you, O wax creature, so that by the sacred name of God and by his holy angels you may be blessed and sanctified and receive the virtue I expect. By the very holy name Adonai. Amen." London, British Library, ms. Add. 10862.

38. Bodin, *De la démonomanie*, 220 v°.

39. Cf. Grabner, "Ein Arzt hat dreierlei Gesicht."

40. Schulz, *Magie oder die Wiederherstellung der Ordnung*, 336. The Royal Manuscript 12 D.VXII (London, British Library), fol. 116, gives: "The Cunning One has bound, the angel has healed, the Lord has saved" (*Malignus obigavit, Angelus curavit, Dominus salvavit*).

41. Pseudo-Paracelsus, *Archidoxis magicae*, bk. 1.

42. Ms. Harley 585, fol. 12.

43. Daniel 3:11–30.

44. Cf. Dornseiff, *Das Alphabet in Mystik und Magie*. In the seventeenth century, Hans Michael Moscherosch (*Wunderliche und Wahrhafftige Satyrische Gesichte Philanders vom Sittewald*, 701) put these words into the mouth of one of his characters: "When I awake in the morning . . . I recite the entire alphabet; all the world's prayers are included in it."

45. Agrippa, *Occult Philosophy*, III, 29.

46. Pseudo-Paracelsus, *Archidoxis magicae*, bk. 1.

47. *Malleus Maleficarum*, 354 (see also page 394).

48. Ibid., 354.

49. Cf. Weill-Parot, "Causalité astrale et science des images au Moyen Âge."

50. Agrippa, *Occult Philosophy,* III, 47.

51. Pseudo-Paracelsus, *Archidoxis magicae,* bk. 1.

CHAPTER ONE.
NAMES AND SIGNATURES

1. *Saturnales,* III, 9, 10.

2. Exodus 20:7.

3. The ninety-nine names can be found in Weber, *Petit Dictionnaire de mythologie arabe et des croyances musulmanes,* 254–57.

4. Maalouf, *Le Périple de Baldassare,* 20.

5. Cf. Lecouteux, "Agla, Sator. Quelques remarques sur les charmes médicaux du Moyen Age."

6. *Sachet accoucheur,* 326.

7. Hon = on; Eleu = Eloy.

8. *Sachet accoucheur,* 346. *Pe* should stand for *petra* ("stone"), *ontes* for *fontes* ("source, spring"), and *ovid* for *ovis* ("lamb").

9. *Sachet accoucheur,* 327.

10. Ibid., 329. Certain phrases are recognizable, such as: "I place my body and soul in your hands" mixed in with a list of all the possible names designating God (flower, calf, lamb, voice, salvation, and so on), *hischiros (ischyros)* means "strong" in Greek.

11. *Sachet accoucheur,* 336. This list does not correspond in any way with the one found in Genesis!

12. Cf. Lecouteux, "Trois hypotheses sur nos voisins invisibles."

13. Paris, Bibliothèque nationale, Cod. Greek, 2419, fol. 243 v°, 246 r°. I have left out the prologue and the list of days that indicate which planets govern the hours. Here is one example: The day of Séléné (Monday), hour 1: Moon; 2 Saturn; 3 Jupiter; 4 Mars; 5 Sun; 6 Venus; 7 Mercury; then we find this progression twice, the three final hours of the day being under the patronage of the Moon, Saturn, and Jupiter. On Monday, the Moon therefore rules over the 1st, 8th, the 15th, and the 22nd hours. I would like to thank Emmanuelle Karagiannis-Moser (Montpellier) and Guy Saunier (Sorbonne) for their help in translating this text.

14. This can be compared with the orisons of the planets, charm no. 214.

15. Florence, Biblioteca Medica Laurenziana, ms. Plut. 89 Sup. 38.

16. *Picatrix latinus,* I, 5.

CHAPTER TWO.
THE MAGICAL CHARACTERS OF THE PLANETS

1. Cardano, *Hieronymi Cardani Mediolanensis medici de Rerum varietate libri XVII*, bk. XVI, chap. 91. Cardano reproduces these *caracteres* and analyzes them.

CHAPTER THREE.
DEMONS AND ILLNESSES

1. Cf. Lecouteux, *Les Nains et les Elfes au Moyen Âge*, 152ff.
2. Other versions of this text will be found in F. G. Conybeare, ed. and trans., "The Testament of Solomon," *Jewish Quarterly Review* 11 (1898): 1–45; and Chester C. McCown, *The Testament of Solomon*.
3. Fahd, "Anges, demons et djinns en islam," 183–84.
4. Migne, *Patrologia graeca* 122, col. 1316ff.

CHAPTER FOUR.
MAGICAL HEALING

1. Berlin, Preußische Staatsbibliothek, Codex Germ. 244.
2. Brussels, City Archives, Vieux fonds, liasse 829 (3), fol. 49 r°.
3. Ulric von Pottenstein, *Decalogue* (circa 1411–1412), Vienna, National Library, Codex 3050.
4. Cf. for example Ohrt, *Danmarks trylleformler*, vol. 2, 39 (no. 1167), in which Jesus meets Peter suffering from toothache.
5. King, "Talismans and Amulets," 227.
6. Paris, Arsenal Library, ms. fr. 2872, fol. 39 v°: *Le Livre des secrez de nature* (sixteenth century).
7. Florence, Biblioteca Medica Laurenziana, ms. Plut. 89, Sup. 38, Psalm 28.
8. Ibid., Psalm 29; this is an action of grace after a mortal danger. The verse reads: "I praise thee, God, for [thou have raised me back up]. [This and subsequent references to the Psalms are numbered in accordance with the Vulgate, not the King James Version of the Bible. —*Trans.*]
9. Cambridge, Pembroke College, ms. 87.
10. Maastricht, Gemeentearchief, ms. 85, fol. 115 r°.
11. London, British Library, ms. Harley 273.
12. *Sachet accoucheur*, 346.

13. Like Pax Max urnax, Pax † Fax † Max †, Pasai † pax † Max; cf. Ohrt, *Danmarks trylleformler,* vol. 2, 121.

14. London, British Library, ms. Harley 273.

15. Cf. Lecouteux, "Agla, Sator," 19–34.

16. London, British Library, ms. Sloane 146, fol. 48 v°.

17. London, British Library, ms. Royal 12 D.XVII, fol. 202 v°.

18. *Onhael,* "patient," *gruth,* "curdled milk," *struth fola,* "flow of blood."

19. *Sachet accoucheur,* 346.

20. Written Greek for Veronica; cf. the London manuscript, British Library, ms. Royal 12 D.XVII, fol. 53 r°.

21. Florence, Biblioteca Medica Laurenziana, ms. Plut. 89, Sup. 38, Psalm 80, "cry with joy for God!"

22. Florence, Biblioteca Medica Laurenziana, ms. Plut. 89, Sup. 38, Psalm 55, "take pity on me, Lord, for I am harassed!"

23. Meyer, "Recettes médicales en français," 367.

24. Florence, Biblioteca Medica Laurenziana, ms. Plut. 89, Sup. 38. This is Psalm 24, "I raise my soul toward you, Lord."

25. Ghent, University Library, ms. 697, fol. 35 v°.

26. London, British Library, ms. Harley 273.

27. *De Gloria martyrum,* I, 95.

28. There are too many Eugenes to know which one this might be; Denys is undoubtedly the Aeropagite (second century) and Etienne a pope named in 254. Quiriace is famous for slaying a dragon called "the Lizard." Prochasius might be a distortion of Protasius (Protais). I have not been able to identify the others.

29. Florence, Biblioteca Medica Laurenziana, ms. Plut. 89, Sup. 38, Psalm 8, "Lord, our God."

30. Ibid., Psalm 62, "Lord, my God, I am seeking you . . ."

31. Ghent, University Library, ms. 697, fol. 125 r°. This is one of many variants of the charm of Job.

32. Cf., for example, Graz, University Library, ms. 1501, fol. 63 v°; and Heidelberg, University Library, Codex Pal. Germ, 367, fol. 173 v°.

33. Bang, *Norske Hexeformulare og Magiske Opskrifter,* no. 1087. Cf. also Ohrt, *Danmarks trylleformler,* vol. 2, 114, in which a spiked horse is healed by writing *Magula Magula kom stata* on a note that is then slid into the animal's right ear.

34. London, British Library, ms. Sloane 84. The text is written in a mixture of Latin and ancient French.

35. Niedermann, *Marcelli de Medicamentis Liber,* XV, 102.

36. Ms. Sloane 84. For more on this saint, see Nux, "Sainte Apolline, patronne de ceux qui souffrent des dents," and Bulk, *St. Apollonia, Patronin der Zahnkranken.* Cf. also Ohrt, *Danmarks trylleformler,* vol. 1, 244–45 (no. 392 and no. 393).

37. Cf. Camus, *Paroles magiques, Secrets de guérison,* nos. 65–70.

38. London, British Library, ms. Royal 12 G IV.

39. London, British Library, ms. Add. 15236.

40. For example, Copenhagen, Royal Library, ms. GKS 1657, fol. 35 v°, 36 r°.

41. Florence, Biblioteca Medica Laurenziana, ms. Plut. 89, Sup. 38. The beginning of Psalm 17, a victory canticle, does not conform to the text of the Vulgate, which has: *Diligante, Domine, fortitude mea.*

42. Cf. Lecouteux, *The Tradition of Household Spirits,* 37–39.

43. Psalm 2, "Why do the nations rage."

44. Ghent, University Library, ms. 1272, fol. 148 v°.

45. *Sachet accoucheur,* 324.

46. Cf. the charms collected by Ohrt, *Danmarks trylleformler,* vol. 1, 269 (no. 269) and 302 (nos. 603–5).

47. Müller, *Aus mittelenglischen Medizintexten,* 107.

48. *Sachet accoucheur,* 346.

49. London, British Library, ms. Sloane 73, fol. 189 v°.

50. For other uses, see Ohrt, *Danmarks trylleformler,* vol. 1, 200 (nos. 262–63).

51. Florence, Biblioteca Medica Laurenziana, ms. Plut. 89, Sup. 38.

52. Alpha and Omega (Revelation 1:8).

53. *Sachet accoucheur,* 346.

54. Ibid.

55. Ibid., 334.

56. Researchers have deciphered this term that is derived from the Hebrew *Ha-Brachaks,* "blessed," and *dabberrals,* "say." The meaning is therefore: "Say the blessed name," i.e., the name of God, *Tetragrammaton.* Another palindrome can be found in the Greek texts, ABLAGANAGALBA, which means: "You are our father."

57. Ghent, ms. 697, fol. 10 v°, 11 r°, in Middle Dutch.

58. The same manuscript (fol. 146 r°) furnishes us another variation: † adabra † drabra † rabra † abra † bra † ra † a, followed by "May God grant my prayer!"

59. Berlin, Preußische Staatsbibliothek, ms. Germ. Folio 751, pt. 6, fol. 28 r°.

60. Cf. Hunt, *Popular Medicine,* 85 and 184; Braekman, *Middeleeuwse witte en zwarte magie,* 125.

61. Ghent, University Library, ms. 697, fol. 6 r°. The Cotton Caligula manu-script A.XV (London, British Library), fol. 129 r°, a: Eax. Filiax. Artifex. Amen; and another from Cambridge (Corpus Christi College 367, fol. 52) writes: † Ire. † arex. † x°e. † ravex. † filiax †.

62. In the *Ritual of High Magic,* attributed to Henry Cornelius Agrippa, we find the phrase *Omax Opax Olifax,* which should be written on the pieces of a pancake to uncover a thief.

63. London, British Library, ms. Add. 15236, fol. 47 v°, 48 r°. This piece is from the end of the thirteenth century.

64. *Sachet accoucheur,* 325.

65. London, British Library, ms. Sloane 2948, fol. 22 r°.

66. "Three angels walked on Mount Sinai and met Nessia, Nagedo, Stechedo, Troppho, Campho, Gigihte, and Paralysis. They asked them where they were going and were answered: 'We are going to the home of God's ser-vant N, to torment his mind, pull on his nerves, suck out his marrow, break his bones, and completely dissolve the ligaments of his limbs.' The angels replied: 'We implore you Nessia, Nagedo, Stechedo.' Troppho, Campho, Gigihte, Paralisis [...] to cause no harm to God's servant N, nor to his head, veins, marrow, nor to his bones, nor to any part whatsoever of his body. Amen.'" (Engelberg, Stiftsbibliothek, ms. 3/2, twelfth century)

67. Cf. Lecouteux, *Mondes parallèles,* 103, text from a brief in which the sisters are named Ilia, Restilia, Fagalia, Suafoglia, Erica or Frica, and Iulica, with the seventh incomprehensible. According to a sixteenth-century version of the same charm, the names of the sisters are: Ilia, Reptilia, Folia, Suffugalia, Affrica, Filica, and Loena or Ignea; cf. Ohrt, *Danmarks trylleformler,* vol. 2, 31.

68. *Sachet accoucheur,* 125; cf. Braekman, *Middeleeuwse witte en zwarte magie,* 125, and Storms, *Anglo-Saxon Magic,* 306. Cf. charm no. 52 above.

69. Berlin, Preußische Staatsbibliothek, ms. Germ. Folio 751, fol. 28 r°.

70. Ibid.

71. Ghent, University Library, ms 697, fol. 34 v°.

72. Coulon, "Curiosités de l'histoire des remèdes comprenant des recettes employées au Moyen Âge dans le Cambrésis," example no. 53, which repro-duces this: "Write these letters on parchment in two places and bind them to the thighs of he or she who has a hemorrhage and the blood shall stop: h

b c v o x a g. And if you wish to test it, write them on a knife to be used to kill a pig; no blood will come out."

73. Cambridge, Trinity College ms. 0.12.0.

74. Ghent, University Library, ms. 697, fol. 6 v°, 7 r°.

75. Cf. Ohrt, "Zu den Jordansegen."

76. Copenhagen, Royal Library, ms. GKS 1657, fol. 13 r°.

77. Florence, Biblioteca Medica Laurenziana, ms. Plut. 89, Sup. 38. Psalm 32, a hymn to Providence, which begins with "Rejoice in the Lord, ye righteous."

78. Ibid. This would be Psalm 18 where it says "the heavens extol the glory of God," to be written out until verse 9.

79. *Sachet accoucheur.*

80. Lecouteux, "Agla, Sator," 19–34.

81. London, British Library, ms. Sloane 3160, fol. 169 r°.

82. Florence, Biblioteca Medica Laurenziana, ms. Plut. 89, Sup. 38, Psalm 35. In the Bible, this is the prayer of a righteous individual suffering persecution.

83. Ibid., Psalm 39: "Hear my prayer O Lord, and give ear unto my cry."

84. Ibid. The quote, "Blessed be he who doth not seek out impious counsel," comes from Psalm 1, the first three verses of which should be written out.

85. Cambridge, Trinity College ms. 0.8.27.

86. The Hague, Royal Library, ms 133 M 27, fol. 125 v°.

87. Ludvik, *Untersuchungen zur spätmittelalterlichen deutschen Fachprosa*, 150–51.

88. This is sometimes lumped together as is the case in the Charm of the Three Brothers and, as can be seen in an example transcribed by Ohrt, *Danmarks trylleformler*, vol. I, 167–68 (no. 145).

89. Longinus was a Roman soldier who converted to Christianity at the death of Paul; cf. Peebles, *The Legend of Longinus in Ecclesiastical Tradition and in English Literature.*

90. Cf. Lecouteux, *Charmes, Conjurations et Bénédictions*, 79. An English manuscript includes this charm: "Just as Longi(n)us pierced the side of our Lord with his spear and this wound neither bled nor oozed, may this wound neither bleed nor ooze" (London, British Library, ms. Add. 33, 996, fol. 109 v°). According to legend, Longinus converted and was later martyred and canonized: St. Longinus's feast day was September 1.

91. London, British Library, ms. Sloane 962, fol. 135 v°.

92. Cf. Lecouteux, *Charmes, Conjurations et Bénédictions,* 27; Camus, *Paroles magiques,* nos. 77, 79, 81, 88–89.

93. Copenhagen, Royal Library, ms. GKS, fol. 234, 221–22.

94. See the entry "Nicodemus" in Vigouroux, *Dictionnaire de la Bible,* vol. IV.

95. Braekmann, *Middeleeuwse witte en zwarte magie,* no. 104.

CHAPTER FIVE.
REMEDIES TAKEN FROM THE HUMAN BODY

1. *Picatrix latinus,* III, 11. The text is attributed to Geber of Seville.

CHAPTER SIX.
LOVE MAGIC

1. Florence, Biblioteca Medica Laurenziana, ms. Plut. 89 Sup. 38. It is necessary to read Psalm 23, "The Earth is the Lord's and the fullness thereof," until verse 9.

2. Ibid.

3. Burning the cloth can be explained by referring to a prescription collected by Anton Birlinger in the nineteenth century in Brandeburg. It says this: "Take an egg hatched on Saturday when the moon that night is new, and write this on it † esa † his † masmo † caldi † male † am † es †, and put it in the fire while saying: "I conjure you, N, by the power and force inscribed upon this egg, to burn for me like this egg in the fire, so that you shall know no rest until you come to me and do my will." Cited in Spamer, *Romanusbüchlein,* 266.

4. *Sachet accoucheur,* 346.

5. Ibid.

6. *Picatrix latinus,* III, 10.

7. Florence, Biblioteca Medica Laurenziana, ms. Plut. 89 Sup. 38. Psalm 60. This operation is today called "returning one's feelings."

8. *Picatrix latinus,* IV, 9.

9. The Hague, Royal Library, ms. 133 M 27, sixteenth century, fol. 145 r°.

10. London, Wellcome Historical Medical Library, ms. 517, fol. 80 v°.

11. Brussels, Royal Library, ms. IV 9588, fol. 12 r°.

12. London, Wellcome Historical Medical Library, ms. 517, fol. 22 r°.

13. Florence, Biblioteca Medica Laurenziana, ms. Plut. 89 Sup. 38.

14. London, British Library, ms. Add. 10862.

CHAPTER SEVEN.
THE PROTECTION OF HUMANS,
LIVESTOCK, AND PROPERTY

1. The distich and the counting rhyme are taken from the *Rationale officio-rum,* VIII, 9, by William Durand, Bishop of Mendes from 1285 until his death in 1296. The cursed or harmful days are generally called "Egyptiacal Days." The list of days comes from the German manuscript 106 (Paris, National Library), as does the illustration.

2. Giles, ed., *The Miscellaneous Works of Venerable Bede,* vol. 6, 350.

3. *Sachet accoucheur,* 324.

4. Isidore of Seville gives two interpretations of *Paraclitus*: lawyer and consola-tion, cf. *Isidori Hispalensis Episcopi Etymologiae,* VII, 2.

5. *Sachet accoucheur,* 331.

6. Ibid., 325–26.

7. *Le Livre des secrez,* Paris, Arsenal Library, ms. 2872, fol. 39 r°.

8. *Sachet accoucheur,* 328. The passages between the brackets are illegible.

9. Ibid., 325–26.

10. Cf. Lecouteux, *Charmes, Conjurations et Bénédictions,* 26–27.

11. Ibid.

12. Thiers, *Traité des superstitions,* 405.

13. Cf. Gaerte, "Beschriftete Thau-Amulette aus dem Mittelalter."

14. Cf. Lecouteux, *Tradition of Household Spirits,* 55–56.

15. Luke 4:30.

16. Paris, National Library, ms. New Latin Acquisition 7743, fol. 251 r°.

17. Re-used by Isidore of Seville, who listed ten names of God; cf. *Etymologiae* VII, 1.

18. Florence, Biblioteca Medica Laurenziana, ms. Plut. 89 Sup. 38. Psalm 86, "its foundation on the holy mountains."

19. *Sachet accoucheur,* 345.

20. London, British Library, ms. Royal 12 D.XVII, fol. 125 v°, 126 r°. The psalm to sing is Psalm 53.

21. Florence, Biblioteca Medica Laurenziana, ms. Plut. 89 Sup. 38, Psalm 31, "Happy are those who are absolved of their sins."

22. London, British Museum, ms. Royal 12 D. XVII, fol. 123 r°–v°. In Ohrt, *Danmarks trylleformler,* vol. 2, 68 (no. 1259), one can find a fine conjura-tion of male and female elves.

23. London, British Museum, ms. Harley 585, fol. 167 r°–v°.

24. *Sachet accoucheur,* 345.

25. London, British Library, ms. Royal 12 D.XVII, fol. 52 v°. It was Anne Berthouin-Matthieu who first succeeded in deciphering a large part of the phrase; cf. *Prescriptions magiques anglaises,* 468–69.

26. Cf. Lecouteux, *Charmes, Conjurations et Bénédictions,* 65 and 111.

27. Psalm 25, "Judge me, Lord!" The incantations of sorcerers (*venefici*) are mentioned in the sixth verse, which could be the reason this prayer of the innocent is used in this context.

28. Psalm 57, "is it true." In verse 14, it is said, "Destroy in your anger, destroy! That your enemies may be no more!"

29. Psalm 58, "deliver me from my enemies!"

30. In his *Autobiography* written around 1115, Guibert de Nogent mentions (I, 12) in these terms what latter centuries would call the "knotting of the breeches-strings": "Taking place for more than seven years then were the curses by which means the consummation of a natural and legitimate bond was prevented. [. . .] This is a frequent practice among the common people and extremely ignorant individuals have the art of doing it. But finally an old woman brought an end to these evil tricks, and my mother submitted to the duties of the conjugal bed." See Guibert de Nogent, *Autobiographie,* 85.

31. *Malleus Maleficarum,* 314.

32. Agrippa, *Occult Philosophy,* I, 46.

33. London, British Library, ms. Harley 3.

34. Cf. Kropatscheck, *De amuletorum apud Antiquos usu capita duo,* 45–70. Kropatscheck lists more than seventy plants and provides their properties.

35. Florence, Biblioteca Medica Laurenziana, ms. Plut. 89 Sup. 38. Citation from Psalm 15, "protect me Lord, for I have placed my hope [in you]."

36. Cf. Seligmann, *Der böse Blick und Verwandtes.*

37. *Sachet accoucheur,* 346.

38. Cf. Ohrt, *Danmarks trylleformler,* vol. 1, 407 (no. 924): Abram † liguit † Jabob † religuit † Jsaag † ad dominum † redurit.

39. Ulrich von Pottenstein, *Decalogue* (circa 1411–1412), Vienna, National Library, Codex 3050.

40. Cf. Lecouteux, *Tradition of Household Spirits,* 58–66.

41. Florence, Biblioteca Medica Laurenziana, ms. Plut. 89 Sup. 38. Citation from Psalm 12:1, and 12:5: "How long, Lord, will you forget me?"

42. Ibid., Psalm 56, "Be merciful to me, O God, be merciful to me!" The use of the psalm is justified here because one declaims it when they find themselves in a sticky situation.

43. Ibid., Psalm 38, "I have said: I will guard the ways."

44. Cf. Lecouteux, *Au-delà du merveilleux,* 87–117.

45. Habets, "Middeleeuwse klokken en klokinschriften," 313.

46. *Malleus Maleficarum,* 506–7.

47. Cf. Lecouteux, *Charmes, Conjurations et Bénédictions,* 46.

48. Cambridge, Pembroke College, ms. 87.

49. The conjuration is in the oldest treatise on falconry in the medieval West, which dates from the tenth century; see Bischoff, *Anecdota novissima,* 171–82.

CHAPTER EIGHT.
MAGIC RINGS

1. Del Sotto, *Le Lapidaire du quatorzième siècle,* 118–26.

2. Philostratus, *Life of Appolonius of Tyana,* III, 41.

3. Albertus Magnus, *De mineralibus,* II, iii, 3.

4. The six rings of the planets are interpolated in the Hamburg Manuscript (Staats- und Universitätsbibliothek, ms. Fol. 188) cited by Pingree, *Picatrix,* 239–40.

5. Cambridge, Pembroke College ms. 87.

6. *Picatrix latinus,* IV, 9. In the Arab text closest to the Latin rendition, it is necessary to take a ring of Chinese iron and a carnelian.

7. London, British Library, ms. Sloane 29/332, fol. 81 r°–v°.

8. Florence, Biblioteca Medica Laurenziana, ms. Plut. 89 Sup. 38. Magic rings are attributed to the four principal planets. See also the Ghent ms. 1021 A, in which the illustrations are less complete and more crude. The rings have a square section, represented within the two squares of the illustration, and magical words are carved upon them. With the setting, represented here by a circle, a seal was imprinted on virgin wax and this had the value of an amulet.

9. King, "Talismans and Amulets," 229.

10. Cf. the dossier assembled in Harmening, "Zur Morphologie magischer Inschriften."

11. Cf. Ohrt, *Danmarks trylleformler,* vol. 2, 128.

CHAPTER NINE.
MAGIC OPERATIONS

1. The circles are reproduced based on the Florence manuscript: Biblioteca Medica Laurenziana, ms. Plut. 89 Sup. 38.

2. Ghent, University Library, ms. 1021 A, fol. 112 v°, 117 v°.

3. A translation of one of these benedictions can be found in Lecouteux, *Charmes, Conjurations et Bénédictions,* 108.

4. "O God, come quickly to my aid!" Psalm 69.

5. "Lord, pour hyssop in this place, you shall wash it with it and it shall be purified," a distortion of verse 9 from Psalm 50: *"Asperges me, Domine, hyssopo et mundabor, lavabis me."*

6. [Paracelsus], *Philippi Theophrasti Bombast von Hohenheim Paracelsi genannt: Geheimnüß aller seiner Geheimnüsse*; [pseudo-]Paracelsus, *Liber secondus Archidoxis magicae: De sigillis duodecim signorum et secretis illorum,* 1560, bk. IV.

7. Staricius, *Geheimnisvoller Heldenschatz.*

8. *Picatrix latinus,* IV, 7.

9. Cf. Agrippa, *Occult Philosophy,* III, 24.

10. Florence, Biblioteca Medica Laurenziana, ms. Plut. 89 Sup. 38, Psalm 9.

11. *Occult Philosophy,* IV. This fourth book has been added to the first three, but it is not by Henry Cornelius Agrippa.

12. Psalm 10, to be written up to the seventh verse.

13. Psalm 54.

14. Psalm 87.

15. Psalm 82.

16. Psalm 36.

17. Psalm 61.

18. Psalm 63.

19. Psalm 68.

20. Psalm 52.

21. Psalm 22.

22. Psalm 14.

23. Psalm 34.

24. Florence, Biblioteca Medica Laurenziana, ms. Plut. 89 Sup. 38, Psalm 5.

25. Ibid., the verse comes from Psalm 16.

26. Ibid., Psalm 84.

27. Ibid., Psalm 30.

28. Arnheim, Rijksarchief Fonds Gelderland, ms. Hof 4524, 1550, no. 6, six-teenth century.

29. Maastricht, Gemeentearchief, ms. 85.

30. Pembroke College, ms. 87, fol. 194 r°.

31. London, Wellcome Historical Medical Library, ms. 517, fol. 108 v°. The invocation means: "Come out! Come out! Come out and speak to me!"

32. Cf. Lecouteux, *The Return of the Dead.*

33. For two more complete rituals, see Lecouteux, *Au-delà du merveilleux,* 232–33.

34. Costus or costume is the name of an aromatic plant; some herbalists call it "couch grass."

35. Ghent, University Library, ms. 1021 A, fol. 145 r°.

36. Ghent, University Library, ms. 697, fol. 6 v°.

37. Cf. Lecouteux, *La Saga de Théodoric de Vérone,* 182.

38. Marburg, University Library, ms. B 20, fol. 113 v°.

39. Fifteenth-century manuscript, private collection.

40. Cf. pseudo-Agrippa, *Occult Philosophy,* IV.

41. Ghent, University Library, ms. 1021 B, fol. 71 r°–v°

42. For more on Ariel and Daniel (Dahariel), see the entries in Davidson, *A Dictionary of Angels.*

43. Ghent, University Library, ms. 1021 A, fol. 109 r°, 110 v°.

44. *Sachet accoucheur,* 346.

45. Florence, Biblioteca Medica Laurenziana, ms. Plut. 89 Sup. 38, Psalm 21.

46. *Sachet accoucheur,* 332.

47. Florence, Biblioteca Medica Laurenziana, ms. Plut. 89 Sup. 38, Psalm 19.

48. Ibid., Psalm 28.

49. Ibid., Psalm 81.

50. London, Wellcome Historical Medical Library, ms. 517.

51. Private collection, fifteenth-century manuscript.

52. London, British Library, ms. Royal MS 12 B XII.

53. London, Historical Medical Library, ms. 517; *Picatrix,* 111.

54. Florence, Biblioteca Medica Laurenziana, ms. Plut. 89 Sup. 38, Psalm 26.

55. Ibid., Psalm 85.

56. Steinmeyer, *Die kleineren althochdeutschen Sprachdenkmäler,* 396. This charm is in Latin but a more complete tenth-century version in Old High German also exists: "The Christ was born before wolves and thieves. Saint Martin was the shepherd of Christ. May the holy Christ and Saint

Martin deign to protect today these dogs so that no wolf cause them any hurt wherever they go, be it in the forest, on the road or on the moor. May the holy Christ and Saint Martin bring them back to me today in good health!"

57. Thiers, *Traité des superstitions,* 406.

CHAPTER TEN.
THE MAGIC OF IMAGES

1. Agrippa, *Occult Philosophy,* II, 35.
2. Albertus Magnus, *De mineralibus,* III, 5.
3. The planet images come from the *Picatrix latinus.*
4. Ghent, University Library, ms. 1021 A. This manuscript has been greatly damaged by moisture, which has made some of the seals barely legible.
5. In this entire subsection, the texts are taken from the *Speculum lapidum clarissimi artium et medicine doctoris Camilli Leonardi Pisaurensis: Impressus Venetiis per Ioannem Baptistam Sessa anno Domini MDII die primo decembris.*
6. Stars: Algomeisa (Procyon), Alhabor (Sirius), Aldebaran (Eye of Taurus), Tail of Capricorn, the Botercadent (Falling Vulture), Alchoraya, the Pleiades, Algol (Beta Persei), Alchimech (Heart of the Lion), Alramech (Regulus), Benenays (Ackaïr), Wing of the Raven, Alhaioth (Epsilon Ursae Majoris), Calbalazeda (Heart of the Scorpion), Alchimech Alaazel (Spica), Alfecca (Corona Borealis). Plants: Sunflower and primrose, savine, euphorbia, marjoram, savory, fennel, black hellebore, celandine, plantain, chicory, sorrel, black horehound, sage, rosemary. Cf. Delatte, *Textes latins et vieux français relatifs aux Cyranides,* 241–88.

CHAPTER ELEVEN.
ORISONS

1. Cf. Saintyves, *Les Grimoires à oraisons magiques.*
2. Cited by Thiers, *Traité des superstitions,* 93.
3. *Sachet accoucheur,* 327. "Jothe" is a distortion of *o theos.*
4. Cited by Thiers, *Traité des superstitions,* 402.
5. Thiers, *Traité des superstitions,* 93–94.
6. Ibid., 402.
7. *Picatrix latinus,* IV, 9.

CHAPTER TWELVE.
MAGIC ALPHABETS

1. Trithemius, *Polygraphiae libri sex Joannis Trithemi abbatis peapolitani, quondam spanheimensis, ad maximilianum caeserem.*
2. I have borrowed the alphabets and notes from Matton, *La Magie arabe traditionnelle,* 166–67.
3. Waçîf-Châh, *L'Abrégé des merveilles.*
4. Most famous for his treatise *Conciliator differentiarum, quae inter philosophos et medicos versantur,* published in Mantova in 1472.
5. Cf. Reusch, *Der Index der verbotenen Bücher,* vol. 1, 34–35.

CHAPTER THIRTEEN.
THE *ROMANUS-BÜCHLEIN*

1. Spamer, *Romanusbüchlein.*

CHAPTER FOURTEEN.
THE DOCTOR OF THE POOR

1. Cf. Andries, *Le Grand Livre des secrets,* 112–13. This author was unaware of the edition I have reproduced here, which was printed in Troyes by Baudot, but undated.
2. For a good conjuration of fevers, see Ohrt, *Danmarks trylleformler,* vol. 1, 203 and following (no. 268 and no. 271).
3. For more on the Latin prayers, see also Ohrt, *Danmarks trylleformler,* vol. 1, 220–26 (nos. 327–32).

CHAPTER FIFTEEN.
EXTRACTS FROM VARIOUS GRIMOIRES

1. Pope Leo, *Enchiridion Leonis papae.*
2. *Magia de furto,* fol. 13 r°.
3. Reproduced in Peuckert, *Gabalia,* figure, 526; and text, 523.
4. Birlinger, *Volksthümliches aus Schwaben,* vol. 1, 462.
5. *Petit Albert,* Lyon, 1602. The final names are those of the three children in the furnace.
6. Ibid.
7. *Magia de furto,* fol. 16 r°. Other accounts, Ohrt, *Danmarks trylleformler,* vol. 1, nos. 966–67. In the second, help is requested of Astaert, Belail, and Ællebus.

8. *Magia de furto,* fol. 17 r°. The beginning means "Take quicksilver."

9. Collected in the Côte d'Or region by J. Durandeau in 1880.

10. Pseudo-Paracelsus, *Archidoxis magicae.*

11. *Grimoire du pape Honorius,* in Ribadeau-Dumas, *Grimoires et rituels magiques,* 31–44.

12. *Le Véritable Dragon noir,* in Ribadeau-Dumas, *Grimoires et rituels magiques,* 133–66.

13. *Enchiridion of Pope Leo.*

14. Mathers, ed., *The Key of Solomon,* 117–18.

15. [Pseudo-]Agrippa, *Occult Philosophy,* Liber IV, in Heinrich Cornelius Agrippa von Nettesheim, *Opera,* 549–51.

BIBLIOGRAPHY

MANUSCRIPTS CONSULTED

Arnheim, Rijksarchief Fonds Gelderland: Ms. Hof 4524, 1550, no. 6, sixteenth century.

Berlin, Preußische Staatsbibliothek: Ms. Germ. Folio 751, Part 6, fourteenth century; Codex Germ. 244, second half of the fifteenth century.

Brussels, City Archives: Vieux fonds, liasse 829 (3), seventeenth century.

Cambridge, University of Cambridge: Pembroke College. ms. 87, thirteenth century; Trinity College, 0.1.20, thirteenth century.

Copenhagen, Royal Library: GKS 1657, fifteenth century; GKS fol. 234, early seventeenth century.

Florence, Biblioteca Medicina Laurenziana: Ms. Plut. 89 Sup. 38, fifteenth century.

Florence, National Library: Ms. II iii 214, fifteenth century.

Ghent, University Library: Ms. 697, fifteenth century; ms. 1272, fifteenth century; ms. 1021 B, sixteenth century; ms. 1021 A, sixteenth century.

Halle, Landesbibliothek: Ms. 14 B 36.

The Hague, Royal Library: Ms. 133 M 27, sixteenth century.

London, British Library: Add. 15236, circa 1300; Harley 3, fourteenth century; Harley 273, fourteenth century; Harley 585, tenth/eleventh century; Royal 12 B XII, thirteenth century; Royal 12 D.XVII, tenth century; Royal 12 G IV, fourteenth century; Sloane 146, late thirteenth century; Sloane 962, fifteenth century; Sloane 3160, fifteenth century; Sloane 3550, circa 1300.

London, Wellcome Historical Medical Library: Ms. 577, late fifteenth century.

Maastricht, Gemeentearchief: Ms. 85, fifteenth century.

Magia de furto, das ist Unterschiedene Geheimnüße, Seine Sachen Vor Dieben zu Verwahren. Leipzig: Municipal Library, ms. C.M. 66.

Marburg, University Library: B20, sixteenth century.

Oxford, Bodleian Library: e Musaeo 146, fifteenth century.

Paris, Arsenal Library: French ms. 2872, fourteenth century.

Paris, National Library: Greek Codex 2419; German ms. 196, fifteenth century; ms. New Latin Acquisition 7743.

Vienna, National Library: Codex 3050; Codex 3317.

TEXTS AND STUDIES

Agrippa, Henry Cornelius. *De occulta philosophia libri tres.* Cologne: 1533.

———. *La Philosophie occulte de Henri Corneille Agrippa.* The Hague, 1722.

———. *Opera.* Lugduni: Per Beringos fratres, 1600.

Andries, Lise. *Le Grand Livre des secrets. Le colportage en France aux XVIIe and XVIIIe siècles.* Paris: Imago, 1994.

Arnold, Klaus. *Johannes Trithemius (1462–1516).* Wurzburg: Königshausen & Neumann, 1971.

Aymar, Alphonse. *Le Sachet accoucheur et ses mystères. Contribution à l'étude du folklore de la Haute-Auvergne de XIIIe au XVIIIe siècle.* Toulouse: Privately published, 1926.

Bader, Richard-Ernst. "Sator arepo. Magie in der Volksmedizin." *Medizinhistorisches Journal* 22 (1987): 115–34.

Balletto, Laura. *Medici e farmaci, scongiuri ed incantesimi, dieta e gatronomia nel medioevo Genovese,* Genoa: University of Genoa, 1986.

Bang, Anton Christian. *Norske Hexeformularer og Magiske Opskrifter.* Oslo: A. W. Breggers 1901–1902.

Bartsch, Elmar. *Die Sachbeschwörungen der römischen Kirche.* Andernach: Maria Laach, 1967.

Baudry, Robert. "Magie noire, magie blanche et merveilleux." In *Le Merveilleux et la Magie dans la literature,* edited by Gerard Chandès. Amsterdam and Atlanta: Rodopi, 1992.

Berthouin-Mathieu. Anne. *Prescriptions magiques anglaises de X^e au XIIe siècle. Étude structurale.* 2 vols. Paris: AMAES, 1996.

Best, Michael R., and Frank H. Brightman. *The Book of Secrets of Albertus Magnus.* Oxford: Oxford University Press, 1973.

Biedermann, Hans. *Handlexikon der magischen Künste von der Spätanike bis zum 19. Jahrhundert.* Graz: Akademische Druck- und Verlagsanstalt, 1968.

———. *Medicina magica. Metaphysische Heilmedizin in spätantiken und mittelalterlichen Handschriften.* Graz: Akademische Druck- und Verlagsanstalt, 1978.

Birlinger, Anton. *Volksthümliches aus Schwaben.* 2 vols. Freiburg-im-Breisgau: Herder, 1862.

Bischoff, Bernhard. *Anecdota novissima: Texte des vierten bis sechzehnten Jahrhunderts.* Stuttgart: Hirsemann, 1984.

———. "Übersicht über die nichtdiplomatischen Geheimschriften des Mittelaters." *Mitteilungen des Instituts für österreichische Geschichtsforsung* 62 (1954): 1–27.

Bodin, Jean. *De la démonomanie des sorciers.* Paris: Jaques du Puys, 1580.

Boutet, Frédéric. *Dictionnaire des sciences occultes.* Paris: Librairie des Champs-Elysee, 1937.

Braekman, Willy L. *Middeleeuwse witte en zwarte magie in het nederlands tallgebied. Gecommentarieerd compendium van incantamenta tot einde 16de eeuw.* Ghent, Royal Academy: 1997.

Brillet-Dubois, Pascale, and Alain Moreau. *La magie, bibliographie générale.* Montpellier: Université de Montpellier III, 2000.

Brunel, Clovis. *Recettes médicales, alchimiques et astrologiques du XVᵉ en langue vulgaire des Pyrénées.* Toulouse: Bibliothèque méridionale, 1956.

Bulk, Wilhelm. *St. Apollonia, Patronin der Zahnkranken. Ihr Kult und Bild im Wandel der Zeit.* Munich and Bielefeld: Zahn-Haus Wilhelm Bulk, 1967.

Camus, Dominique. *Paroles magiques, Secrets de guérison: les leveurs de maux aujourd'hui.* Paris: Imago, 1990.

———. *Voyage au pays du magique. Enquête sur les voyants, guérisseurs, sorciers.* Paris: Dervy, 2002.

Cardano, Gerolamo. *Hieronymi Cardani Mediolanensis medici de Rerum varietate libri XVII.* Basel: Henri Petri, 1557.

Carmody, Francis J. *The Astronomical Work of Thabit ibn Qurra.* Berkeley: University of California Press, 1960.

Comes, Didier. *Silence.* Paris: Casterman, 1980.

———. *La Belette.* Paris: Casterman, 1983.

Conybeare, F. G., ed. and trans. "The Testament of Solomon." *Jewish Quarterly Review II* (1898): 1–45.

Coulon, H. "Curiosités de l'histoire des remèdes comprenant des recettes employés ay Moyen Âge dans le Cambrésis." *Mémoires de la Société d'Émulation au de Cambrai* 47 (1892): 1–153.

Davidson, Gustav. *A Dictionary of Angels including the Fallen Angels.* New York and London: Free Press, 1967.

Daxelmüller, Christoph. *Zauberpraktiken, Eine Ideegeschichte der Magie.* Zurich: Artemis & Winckler, 1993.

De Fontenelle, Julia. *Manuel complet des sorciers ou la Magie blanche.* Paris: Roret, 1831.

Delatte, Louis, ed. *Textes latins et vieux français relatifs aux Cyranides: La traduction latine du XIIᵉ siècle, le Compendium aureum, le De XV stellis d'Hermès, le Livre des secrez de nature.* Liège and Paris: Faculté de Philosophie et Lettres, 1942.

———. "Le traité des plantes planétaires d'un manuscript de Léningrad." *Annuaire de l'Institut de philologie et d'histoire orientale et slave* 9 (1949): 145–77.

Del Sotto, Isaac. *Le Lapidaire de quatorzième siècle.* Vienna: Imprimerie impériale et royale de la cour et de l'état, 1862.

Deonna, Waldemar. "Abra, Abraca La croix talisman de Lausanne." *Geneva* 22 (1944): 114–37.

Descombes, René. *Les Carrés magiques. Histoire et technique du carré magique de l'Antiquité aux recherches actuelles.* Paris: Vuibert, 2000.

Dornseiff, Franz. *Das Alphabet in Mystik und Magie.* Leipzig: Teubner, 1925.

Fahd, Toufy. "Anges, démons et djinns en islam." *Sources orientales* 8 (1971): 155–214.

Flint, Valerie. *The Rise of Magic in Early Medieval Europe.* Princeton: Princeton University Press, 1991.

Franz, Adolph. *Die kirchlichen Benediktionen im Mittelalter.* 2 vols. Graz: Akademische Druck- und Verlagsanstalt, 1909.

Gaerte, Wilhelm. "Beschriftete Thau-Amulette aus dem Mittelalter." *Rheinisches Jahrbuch für Volkskunde* 6 (1955): 225–34.

Gauthier, J. "Grimoire d'un sorcier du XVᵉ siècle." *Revue des Sociétés savantes, 7ᵉ série,* VI (1882): 200–9.

Giles, J. A., ed. *The Miscellaneous Works of Venerable Bede.* London: Whittaker, 1843. 6 vols.

Gombert, Ludwig. "Der Zachariassegen Gegen die Pest." *Hessische Blätter für Volkskunde* 17 (1918): 37–52.

Grabner, Elfriede. "Ein Arzt hat dreierlei Gesicht. Zur Entstehung, Darstellung und Verbreitung des Bildgedankens Christus coelestis medicus." *Materia Medica Nordmark* 24 (1972): 297–317.

Grässe, Johann Georg Theodor. *Bibliotheca magica et pneumatica*. Leipzig: Engelmann, 1843.

Grambo, Ronald. *Norske trolleformler og magiske ritualer*. Oslo, Bergen, Tromsø: Universitetsforlaget, 1984.

———. "A Catalog of Nordic Charms. Some Reflections." *NIF Newsletter* 2 (1977): 12–16.

———. "Norske Kjærestevarsler." *Maal og Minne* (1966): 122–34.

Gregory of Tours. *Glory of the Martyr*. Translated by Raymond van Dam. Liverpool: University Press, 1988.

Guaita, Stanislas De. *La Clé de la magie noire*. Paris: Carré, 1897.

Guibert de Nogent. *Autobiographie*. Edited and translated by Edmond-René Labande. Paris: Société d'édition "Les Belles Lettres", 1981.

Habets, Jos. "Middeleeuwse klokken en klokinschriften." *Publications de la Société historique et d'Archéologie dans le Limbourg* 5 (1868): 313–46.

Harmening, Dieter. "Das magische Wort." *Perspektiven der Philosophie, Neues Jahrbuch* 23 (1997): 365–85.

———. *Hexen heute, magische Traditionen und neue Zutaten*. Wurzburg: Königshausen & Neumann, 1991.

———. *Zauberei im Abendland. Vom Anteil der Gelehrten am Wahn der Leute*. Wurzburg: Königshausen & Neumann, 1991.

———. "Zur Morphologie magischer Inschriften. Der Donauwörther Zauberring und Formkriterien für seine Interpretation." *Jahrbuch für Volkskunde,* new series 1 (1978): 67–81.

Hartlieb, Johannes. *Das Buch aller verbotenen Künste, des Aberglaubens und der Zauberei*. Edited and translated by Falk Eisermann and Eckhard Graf. Ahlerstedt: Param, 1989.

Haver, Jozef Van. *Nederlandse incantatieliteratur: Een gecommentarieed compendium van Nederlandse Bezweringsformule*. Ghent: Royal Academy, 1964.

Hieronymi Cordani Mediolensis medici de Rerum varietate libri XVII. Basel: Henri Petri, 1557.

Hunt, Tony. *Popular Medicine in the Thirteenth Century*. Cambridge: Brewer, 1990.

Isidore of Seville. *Isidori Hispalensis Episcopi Etymologiae*, VII, 2. Oxford: 1911.

Jacoby, Adolf. "Heilige Längenmasse. Eine untersuchung zur Geschichte der Amulette." *Schweizerisches Archiv für Volkskunde* 29 (1929): 181–216.

Jacquart, Danielle. "Médicine et astrologie à Paris dans la première moitié du IVe siècle." In *Filosofia, scienza e astrologia nel Trecento,* edited by G. Federici Vescovini and F. Barocelli. Padua: Poligrafo, 1992.

Joly, V. *Les Ardennes*. Brussels: Van Buggenhund, 1854.

Kaindl, Raimund Friedrich. "Ein deutsches Beschwörungsbuch aus der Handschrift herausgegeben." *Zeitschrift für Ethnologie* 25 (1893): 24–47.

Kieckhefer, Richard. *Magic in the Middle Ages*. Cambridge: Cambridge University Press, 1989.

King, C. W. "Talismans and Amulets." *Archaeological Journal* 26 (1869): 225–35.

Kropatscheck, Gerhard. *De amuletorum apud Antiquos usu capita duo*. Gryphiae: Typis I. Abel, 1907.

Labouvie, Eva. *Verbotene Künste: Volksmagie und ländlicher Aberglaube in den Dorfgemeinden des Saarraumes (16.–19. Jahrhundert)*. Sankt Ingbert: Röhrig, 1992.

Le Braz, Anatole. *La Légende de la mort chez les Bretons armoricains*. Paris: Lafitte, 1980.

Lecouteux, Claude. *The Tradition of Household Spirits: Ancestral Lore and Practices*. Translated by Jon E. Graham. Rochester, Vt.: Inner Traditions, 2013.

———. *The Return of the Dead: Ghosts, Ancestors, and the Transparent Veil of the Pagan Mind*. Translated by Jon E. Graham. Rochester, Vt.: Inner Traditions, 2009.

———. *La Saga de Théodoric de Vérone*. Paris: Honore Champion, 2001.

———. "Agla, Sator. Quelques remarques sur les charmes médicaux du Moyen Age." *Revue d'Études mythologiques et symboliques, Nouvelle Plume 2* (Nagoya: 2001): 19–34.

———. "Les pierres talismaniques au Moyen Âge." *Nouvelle Plume: Revue d'Études mythologiques et symboliques* 1 (Nagoya: 2000): 2–19.

———. *Au-délà du merveilleux. Essai sur les mentalités delà Moyen Âge*. Paris: P.U.P.S., 1998.

———. *Les Nains et les Elfes au Moyen Âge*. Paris: Imago, 1997.

———. "Trois hypothèses sur nos voisins invisibles." In *Hugur: Mélanges d'histoire, de littérature et de mythologie offerts à Régis Boyer pour son 65e anniversaire*, edited by Claude Lecouteux and O. Gouchet. Paris: P.U.P.S., 1997.

———. *Charmes, Conjurations et Bénédictions, Lexiques et formules*. Paris: Champion, 1996.

———. *Mondes parallèles: l'univers des croyances du Moyen Âge*. Paris: Champion, 1994.

Leonardi, Camille. *Les Pierres talismaniques (Speculum lapidum III)*. Edited, translated, and annotated by Claude Lecouteux and Anne Monfort. Paris: P.U.P.S., 2003.

Ludvik, Dušan. *Untersuchungen zur spätmittelalterlichen deutschen Fachprosa.* Ljubliana: Izdala in zalozila Filozofska fakulteta Univerze v Ljubljani, 1959.

Maalouf, Amin. *Le Périple de Baldassare.* Paris: Grasset, 2000.

Malleus Maleficarum of Heinrich Kramer and James Sprenger. Translated by Montague Summers. New York: Dover, 1971.

Manassé, Benjamin. *Rituel de magie blanche, IV, Le Livre des Secrets.* Paris: Bussiére, 1988.

Mathers, S. L. MacGregor, ed. and trans. *The Key of Solomon the King (Clavicula Salomonis), now first translated and edited from ancient Mss. in the British Museum.* 4th ed. London: Kegan Paul, 1974 [1889].

Matton, Sylvain. *La Magie arabe traditionelle.* Ibn Khaldûn: *la Magie et la Science des talismans;* Al-Kindi: *Des Rayons ou Théorie des arts magiques;* Ibn Wahshiya: *La Connaisance des alphabets occultes dévoilée; Picatrix, Le but des sages dans la magie.* Paris: Retz, 1977.

McCown, Chester C. *The Testament of Solomon.* Leipzig: Hinrichs, 1922.

Meyer, Paul. "Recettes médicales en français." *Romania* 37 (1908), 358–77.

Migne, J. P. *Patrologia graeca.* 161 vols. Paris: Imprimerie Catholique, 1857–1866.

Montaigne. *Essais.* 2 vols. Lausanne: Rencontre Lausanne, 1968.

Morin, Alfred. *Catalogue descriptif de la Bibliothèque bleue de Troyes.* Geneva: Droz, 1974.

Moscherosch, Hans Michael. *Wunderliche und Wahrhafftige Satyrische Gesichte Philanders vom Sittewald.* Frankfurt: Schönworth, 1645.

Müller, Gottfried. *Aus mittelenglischen Medizintexten.* Leipzig: Tauchnitz, 1929.

Niedermann, Maximilian. *Marcelli de Medicamentis Liber.* Berlin: Teubner, 1916.

Nux, H. "Sainte Apolline, patronne de ceux qui souffrent des dents." *Revue d'Odontologie et de Stomatologie* 3 (1947): 113–53.

Ohrt, Ferdinand. "Zu den Jordansegen." *Zeitschrift für Volkskunde,* new series 1 (1930): 269–74.

———. *Danmarks trylleformler.* 2 vols. Copenhagen and Oslo: Gyldendal, 1917–1921.

Önnerfors, Alf. "Zaubersprüche in Texten der römischen und frühmittelalterlichen Medizin." In *Études de médecine romaine,* edited by G. Sabbah. Saint-Étienne: University of Saint-Étienne, 1989.

Paniagua, Juan A. *Studia Arnaldiana: Tarabajos en torno a la obra médica de Arnau de Villanova, c. 1240–1311.* Barcelona: Fundacion Uriach 1848, 1994.

[Paracelsus]. *Philippi Theophrasti Bombast von Hohenheim Paracelsi genannt: Geheimnüß aller seiner Geheimnüsse.* Leipzig: Joh. Friedrich Fleischer, 1750.

Pseudo-Paracelsus. *Liber secundus Archidoxis magicae, De sigillis duodecim signorum et secretis illorum.* Basel: N.p., 1570.

———. *Philosophia sagax.* In *Paracelsus Werke,* edited by Will-Erich Peuckert, vol. 3. Stuttgart: Schwabe, 1967.

Peebles, R. J. *The Legend of Longinus in Ecclesiastical Tradition and in English Literature.* Baltimore: J. H. Furst, 1911.

Petzold, Leander, ed. *Magie et Religion.* Darmstadt: Wissenschaftliche Buchgesellschaft, 1978.

Peuckert, Will-Erich. "Das 6. und 7. Buch Mosis." *Zeitschrift für deutsche Philologie* 76 (1957): 163–87.

———. *Gabalia. Ein Versuch zur Geschichte der magia naturalis im 16. bis 18. Jahrhundert.* Berlin: Schmidt, 1967.

———. *Pansophie: Ein Versuch zur Geschichte der weißen und der schwarzen Magie.* Berlin: Schmidt, 1956.

Philostratus. *Life of Apollonius of Tyana.* Translated by F. C. Conybeare. 2 vols. Cambridge, Mass.: Harvard University Press, 1912.

Pingree, David. *Picatrix, the Latin Version of the Ghayat Al-Hakim.* London: Warburg Institute, 1936.

Pope Leo. *Enchiridion Leonis papae.* Rome: 1740.

Reusch, Franz Heinrich. *Der Index der verbotenen Bücher: ein Beitrag zur Kirchen- und Literaturgeschichte.* 2 vols. Bonn: Cohen, 1883.

Ribadeu-Dumas, François, ed. *Grimoires et rituels magicques.* Paris: Belfond, 1972.

Saintyves, Pierre. *Les Grimoires à oraisons magiques.* Paris: Nourry, 1926.

Schneider, Wolfgang. *Lexikon alchemistisch-pharmazeutischer Symbole.* Weinheim: Verlag Chemie, 1962.

Schönbach, Anton E. *Studien zur Geschichte der altdeutschen Predigt: Zeugnisse Bertholds von Regensburg zur Volkskunde.* Sitzungsberichte der phil.-hist. Klasse der kaiserl. Akademie der Wissenschaften 142. Vienna: Carl Gerold's Sohn, 1900.

Schultz, Monika. *Magie oder die Wiederherstellung der Ordnung.* Frankfurt: Lang, 2000.

Seligman, Kurt. *The History of Magic.* New York: Pantheon, 1948.

———. *Der böse Blick und Verwandtes: Ein Beitrag zur Geschichte des Aberglaubens aller Zeiten und Völker.* Berlin: Barsdorf, 1910.

———. "Ananisapta und Sator." *Hessische Blätter für Volkskunde* 20 (1921): 1–25.

Servais, J. C. *La Tchalette et autre contes de magie et de sorcellerie.* Brussels: Du Lombard, 1982.

Spamer, Adolf. *Romanusbüchlein: Historisch-philologischer Kommentar zu einem deutschen Zauberbuch.* Berlin: Akademie Verlag, 1958.

Staricius, Johannes. *Geheimnisvoller Heldenschatz.* Aschaffenburg: N.p., 1615.

Steinmeyer, Emil Elias von. *Die kleineren althochdeutschen Sprachdenkmäler.* Berlin: Weidmann, 1916.

Storms, Godfrid. *Anglo-Saxon Magic.* The Hague: Nijhoff, 1948.

Svartbok frå Gudbrandsdalen. Edited by Velle Espeland. Oslo, Bergen and Tromsø: Universitetsforlaget, 1974.

Svenberg, Emanuel. *Lunaria et zodiologia latina.* Gothenburg: Elanders Boktryckeri, 1963.

Thiers, Jean-Baptiste. *Traité des superstitions.* Paris: Dezallier, 1679.

Thorndike, Lynn. *The History of Magic and Experimental Science during the First Thirteen Centuries of Our Era.* 8 vols. New York: Columbia University Press, 1923–1934.

———. "Traditional Medieval Tracts Concerning Engraved Astronomical Images." In *Mélanges August Pelzer.* Louvain: Bibliothèque de l'Université, 1947.

Trithemius, Johannes. *Polygraphiae libri sex Joannis Trithemi abbatis peapolitani, quondam spanheimensis, ad maximilianum caeserem.* Basel: Adam Petri, 1518.

———. *Steganographia, hoc est Ars per occultam scripturam animi sui voluntatem.* Darmstadt: Ioannis Berneri Bibliopolae, 1621.

Trümpy, Hans. "Similia similibus." *Schweizerisches Archiv für Volkskunde* 62 (1966): 1–6.

Vigoroux, Fulcran. *Dictionnaire de la Bible.* Paris: Letouzey et Ané, 1895–1912.

Waçîf-Châh, Ibrâhim Ibn. *L'Abrégé des merveilles.* Translated by Carra de Vaux Paris: Klincksieck, 1898. Reprinted Paris: Sinbad, 1984.

Weber, Edgar. *Petit Dictionnaire de mythologie arabe et des croyances musulmanes.* Paris: Entente, 1996.

Weill-Parot, Nicolas. "Causalité astrale et science des images au Moyen Âge: éléments de réflexion." *Revue de l'Histoire des Sciences* 52 (1999): 207–40.

———. *Les images astrologiques au Moyen Âge et à la renaissance. Spéculations intellectuelles et pratiques magiques.* Paris: Champion, 2002.

INDEX

Page numbers in *italics* refer to illustrations.

abscesses, 76–77

Agobard, Bishop, 21

Agrippa, Henry Cornelius, 14, 17, 27, 28, *29*, *30*, 128, 165

Agrippa, The, 14, 22

Albertus Magnus, 4, 5, 128, 165

Alchamar, 148

Allah, 36–37

alphabets. *See* magic alphabets

amulets, 21–22, 30–31, 217

angels, 16–17, 26–27, 42–45, 148

animals, 125

anthrax, 214

Apolline, Saint, 76

Aries, Seal of, 222–23, *222*

Astaroth, 224, *224*

Bacon, Roger, 4–5, 6

bad dreams, 125

bad moods, 78

bad weather, 125–26

barking, 155

Bartsch, Elmar, 18

battle amulets, 154

Beard of God, 178

bees, 162–63

Belial, 183–84, *183–84*

bewitchment, 195

binding, 208

birds, 155

birth, 87–90

bites, 69, 92

black magic, 20

bleeding, 71–73, 211

blood loss, 71

Bodin, Jean, 22–24

body parts, 95–97

boils, 70

Book of the Kyranides, The, 6–7, 9–10, *10*

Book of Wings, The, 173–74

Brief of Pope Leo, 110–13

bullets, 205, 208

burns, 212, 215

canker sores, 76–77, 86–87

Cardano, Gerolamo, 53

Charlemagne, King, 112
children, 74
Christianity, 16, 25
Christian names, 38–40
cleaver seeds, 118–19
colic, 212
Colphoterios, *184*
Consecration of the Grimoire, 225
corn cockle seeds, 118–19
cows, 197
cramps, 135
crosses, 17, 32
cudweed, 118–19
Cyprien, Saint, 6

danger, 115, 196
days of week, 107–9, 171, *171*
dead people, 154–55
Demonic Circle, 139, *139*
demons, 16–17, 25, 26–27, 57–62,
    121–22, 148
devil, 117–18
Doctor of the Poor, The, 11–12, 209–16
dog bites, 69, 92
dogs, 155
dwarves, 57, 119

eagles, 126
earwax, 96
eggs, 85
eloquence, 164, *164*
elves, 57, 113–14
enchantments, 120
Enchiridion, 37–38
enemies, 102, 132, 150–52, *150–52,*
    203–4
epilepsy, 79–81, 178

Epiphany Mass, 141
Essays (II,37), 23
evil eye, 122
evil spells, 121–22
evil spirits, 120, 133, 205–6
eye problems, 86, 213–14

falling sickness, 79–81, 178
fear, 160
fennel seeds, 118–19
fevers, 82–85, 92–93, 115–16, 156,
    197–98, 211–12
fire, 193–94, 200–201
fistulas, 70, 76–77
flies, 163
Franz, Adolph, 18
freedom, 218
frenzy, 68
friendship, 103

Gabriel, 58
games, 200
garlic plants, 118–19
Garnier, Jacques-Antoine, 12
Geber of Seville, 9
God, 36–37, 39
good fortune, 153
good magic, 2
gout, 75, 76–77, 86
grace, 162
Grand Albert, 12
Gregory the Great, Pope, 21
grimoires, 1, 3–17. *See also specific*
    grimoires

Hartleib, Jean, 7
headaches, 67

head pains, 66

healing. *See* magical healing

hemorrhages, 72, 85, 202

henbane, 118–19

Hermes Trismegistus, 4, 5, 9, 172, 183–84, 185

Holy Mary, 178–79

homophony, 20

Honorius, 11, 186, *186*

hops, 118–19

horses, 91–92, 214

Hotarid, 148

human body, remedies taken from, 95–97

Hygromancy, 42–45, 53

illness, demons and, 57–62

images

  magic of, 30–31

  Mars, 166, *166*

  Mercury, 169–70, *169*

  Moon, 170, *170*

  Seals of the Days of the Week, 171, *171*

  Stones, 172–76

  Sun, 166–67, *167*

  Venus, 167–69, *168–69*

  See also magic images

impotence, 98, 121

incarceration, 153

invisibility, 132

invisible swords, 146–47

Isidore of Seville, 21

Isolde, 99

Jesus Christ, 25–26, 37, 38, 192, 205

John, Gospel of, 16

Joly, Victor, 13–14

Jupiter, 46, *55*, 179

Jupiter, Ring of, 129, *129*

justice, 201–2

Kabbalah, 15–16, 28

Key to Solomon, The, 24

Kramer, Heinrich, 16

labor, 89–90

Laodicea, 21

leek, 118–19

Leo, Pope, 11, 37–38, 110–13

leprosy, 96

lightning, 93

"like cures like," 25–26

Lion, Jacques, 11

Little Albert Grimoire, 12, 56

Little Book of Roman, The, 14, *190,* 191–208

liver complaints, 68

livestock, 200

loans, 153

locks, 153–54

Lovecraft, H. P., 11

love magic, 99–106, 218

Lucifer, 223–24

Luna, *55*

lunatics, 68–69

lupin, 118–19

lust, 118

LXXII sacred names, 38

Maalouf, Amin, 36

Macrobius, 36

magic

  of images, 30–31

supernatural forces and, 16–17

types of, 2–3

magical healing

Against Animal Bites, 69

Birth, 87–90

Bleeding, 70–71, 72–73

Against Canker Sores, 86–87

Charm for Fistulas, Boils, and
    Wounds, 70

Charms of Saint Apolline, 76

For Children, 74

Against Dog Bites, 92

Against Eye Problems, 86

Against Falling Sickness, 79–81

Fevers, 82–85, 92–93

Against Gout, 75, 86

Against Headaches, 67

Head Pains, 66

Healing the Sick, 78

Hemorrhages, 72, 85

Horses, 91–92

Know If a Patient Will be Cured,
    63–65, *63–65*

Against Lightning, 93

Liver Complaints, 68

Long Illnesses, 69

Lunatics, 68–69

Menstruation, 73

Phylactery, 69

Against the Plague, 67–68

Pregnancy, 90

Repelling Bad Moods, 78

Saint Susanna's Charm, 76–77

Sleep, 73–74

Teeth, 76

Against a violent death, 93–94, *94*

Worms, 74–75

magic alphabets, 181–87

Colphoterios, 184, *184*

D'Abano, 185–87, *186–87*

Hermes, 183–84, *184*, 185

Trithemius, 181–83, *182–83*

magic bells, 144–46

Magic Circles, 137–41, *138–41*

magicians, 20–24

magic images, 165–76

magic mirrors, 147–49, *148*

magic operations, 137–64

Battle Amulet, 154

To Be Eloquent, 164, *164*

Be Freed From Want, 152

To Be Well Received, 161

Conjuration of Bees, 162–63

Conjuration of Satan, 156–57

Conjure Belial, 183–84, *183–84*

Destroy the House of Your Enemy,
    150, *150*

Develop Your Memory, 162

Discover a Treasure, 141–44, *142*

Drive Flies Away, 163

Against and Enemy, 150–52,
    150–52

Enjoy Good Fortune, 153

Enter a City or Prince's Home, 152

For a Fearful Man or Woman, 160

Give Someone a Fever, 156

If Someone Has Fallen From Grace
    with His Lord, 160–61

If You Want Someone Who Hates
    You to Fear You, 154

For Incarcerated Individuals, 153

Introduce Yourself to a King or
    Prince, 149

Invoke a Spirit, 158–60

For a Loan, 153

Magic Circles, 137–41, *138–41*

Magic Mirror, 147–49, *148*

Magic Rings, 152, *152*

Make a Magic Bell, 144–46

Make an Invisible Sword, 146–47

Not Get Lost While Traveling, 152

Open All Locks, 153–54

In Order Not To Lose the Grace of
    One's Lords, 162

Planting the Vine, 163

Prevent Dogs From Barking, 155

Remove Fear of Evil Folk, 160

To Retain the Good Will of One's
    Lord, 161

Speak With the Spirit of a Dead
    Person, 154–55

Understanding the Song of Birds,
    155

Weapon Spell, 164

Wolf Spell, 163

Magic Rectangle, 140, *140*

Magic Rings, 134–35, *135*

magic rings, 127–36

Magnus, Albertus, 6

magus, 2

Malachim Script, 186, *186*

mallow, 118–19

Marrech, 148

Mars, 46, 55, 166, *166*, 179

Mars, Ring of, 130

Mass of the Dead, 141

Matthew, Book of, 25–26

memory, 162

menstrual blood, 96

menstruation, 73

Mercurius, *55*

Mercury, 169–70, *169*, 180

Mercury, Ring of, 130–31

Messala, 6

Michael, 142

Michaelmas, 141

Middle Ages, 20–21, 36–52. *See also*
    Part 1

misfortune, 196

months, 108–9

Moon, 170, *170*, 180

murderers, 203–4

Musteri, 148

myrtle, 118–19

names, 26–30
    Christian, 38–40
    demons and spirits, 40–46
    in the Middle Ages, 36–52
    on the use of, 52

nomen, 32

nosebleeds, 70–71

numerology, 28

obedience, 133

operations. *See* magic operations

opium, 96

orisons, 177–80, 211–15

Oudot, Nicolas, 11

palindromes, 20

Paracelsus, 2–3, 27–28, 31

paranatellonta, 127

parchments, *54*

Paschalis, Archdeacon, 21

pentacles, 104–5

phylactery, 69, 109–10, 113–14, 196,
    203

Picatrix, 6–8, 31, 41, 46
plague, 67–68
planets, 9, 53–56, *54–56,*148, 179–80
Poimandres (XVI, 12), 25
poisons, 131
poppy, 96–97
prayers, 192–93
Prayer to Ares, 46
Prayer to Cronos, 46
Prayer to Zeus, 46
protection, 194–95, 203
protection of humans, livestock, and
    property, 107–26
  Auspicious and Harmful Days,
    108–9
  Against Bad Dreams, 125
  Against Bad Weather, 125–26
  Balm Against Elves, Spirits Who
    Roam the Night, and Those With
    Whom the Demon Copulates,
    114–15
  To Be Spared From All Kinds of
    Danger, 115
  Brief of Pope Leo, 110–13
  Conjuration of the Eagle, 126
  Cursed Days, 107–8
  Against Demons and Evil Spells,
    121–22
  Against the Devil, 117–18
  Dismiss Enchantments, 120
  Dispel Evil Spirits, 120
  Against a Dwarf, 119
  Against the Evil Eye, 122
  Excellent Amulet, 113
  Excellent Phylactery, 113
  Against Fever, 115–16
  Against Lust, 118

  For One Who Is Unable To Know
    His Wife Carnally, 121
  Against Perils and Evils, 112–13
  Phylactery, 109–10
  Against Poisons and Potions, 116–17
  To Preserve Your Health, 116–17
  Remove Fear of Animals, 125
  Against the Storm, 125
  Against Theft and Thieves, 122–24
  Against a Wicked Witch, 120
  Against Your Enemies, 114
provincial council of Rouen, 21–22
pustules, 76–77

Quadripartitus, 172–73

Rabelais, 7
Ragiel, 173–74
Raziel, 4
Renaissance, 21
rheumatisms, 211
Ring of Saturn, 128–29, *129*
rings
  Become Invisible, 132
  characters of planets for, *54*
  To Earn the Good Will of Enemies,
    132
  Find Treasure, Gain Victory, 133
  Magic Rings, 131–32, 134–35, *135*
  Obtain Obedience, 133
  Protect Against Cramps and Spasms,
    135
  Ring of Jupiter, 129
  Ring of Mars, 130
  Ring of Mercury, 130–31
  Ring of Saturn, 128–29, *129*
  Ring of Venus, 130

Against Spells and Poisons, 131
Summon Evil Spirits, 133
Win Partiality, 133
ringworm, 211
Romanus-Büchlein. *See Little Book of Roman, The*
Rupert, 6

Sachet accoucheur, 37
Satan, 156–57
Saturn, 46, 179
Saturn, Ring of, 128–29, *129*
Saturnus, *55*
scabies, 96
scandal, 153
Seal of Taurus, 54
seals, characters of planets for, *54*
seduction, 103, 218, *218*
Sergius, Pope, 21
Seventy-Two Names, 225
signatures, 26–30
of spirits, 41, 47–51
signs, 26–30
Similia Similibus curantur, 25–26
sleep, 73–74
Sol, *55*
Solomon, 31, 41–45, 57–62,
174–76
sorcerers, 20–24
spasms, 135
spells, magic, 131
spirits, 158–60, *159*
Sprenger, Jacob, 16
Staricius, 28, 30
stones, 172–76
storms, 125
Sun, 166–67, *167*, 179

Susanna, Saint, 76–77
swarms, 214–15
swords, 146–47
symbols, 16

talismans, 30–31
teeth, 76
Testament of Solomon, The, 57–62
Tetragrammaton, 37, 143
Thiers, Jean-Baptiste, 22–23
thieves, 122–24, 198–200, 203–4,
208, 217, 220–21, *220–21*
thorns, 212
Thousand and One Nights, The, 31
Three Marys, 222
toothaches, 209
traveling, 152
treasure, 133, 141–44, *142*
trench fever, 84
Tristan, 99
Trithemius, Johannes, 6–7, *7*, 181–83,
182–83

umbilical cords, 96
Uriel, 142

Variety of Things, The, 53
Venus, *55*, 167–70, 179
Venus, Ring of, 130
verbena, 118–19
victory, 133
Villeneuve, Arnaud de, 9
vines, 163
Viper's Bugloss, 118–19
Virgin Mary, 37
virgin parchment, 24
voyages, 207

weapons, 204–5, 206–7

weapon spell, 164

white magic, 20

White Magic Circle, 138–39, *139*,
      140–41, *141*

white paternoster, 177–78

William of Paris, 4–5

Wings, Book of, 173–74

witches, 120

wolf bites, 69

wolf spell, 163

worms, 74–75, 76–77

wormwood, 118–19

wounds, 70, 201

Xemz, 148

XXIII Patriarchs, 40

Yahweh, 68

Zahel, 6

Zeherit the Chaldean, 6

Zohal, 148

Zohara, 148